# GINA L. MAXWELL

*Madison—
Get Hot for the
Fireman!
Gina Maxwell*

This book is a work of fiction. Names, characters, places, and incidents are the product of the author's imagination or are used fictitiously. Any resemblance to actual events, locales, or persons, living or dead, is coincidental.

Copyright © 2017 by Gina L. Maxwell. All rights reserved, including the right to reproduce, distribute, or transmit in any form or by any means. For information regarding subsidiary rights, please contact the Publisher.

Entangled Publishing, LLC
2614 South Timberline Road
Suite 109
Fort Collins, CO 80525
Visit our website at www.entangledpublishing.com.

Select Contemporary is an imprint of Entangled Publishing, LLC.

Edited by Liz Pelletier
Cover design by Letitia Hasser
Cover art from Hot Damn Stock

Manufactured in the United States of America

First Edition March 2017

# Hot FOR THE
# FIREMAN

*For all the brave men and women in the fire service.*

# Chapter One

"Jesus, Wolf, it's a nightclub, not a funeral. Lighten up, will ya? No one wants to screw a fuckin' grave digger."

Erik "Wolf" Grady cut a look over at his best friend of seventeen years, Gavin "Dozer" Greer, and shot him a silent *Fuck you very much, asshole* as they sat at their table in the back of their regular hangout, Phoenix Club. "This whole situation is bullshit, and you know it," he ground out.

Dozer shrugged a massive shoulder, letting him know the big man was no more concerned about Erik's ire than hearing a call come through at the fire station for a "frequent flyer"—a civilian who was paranoid, lonely, or usually both, and repeatedly required the presence of first responders in non-emergency situations. "Nothin' you can do about it now, man. Chief said his piece. The faster you get it over with, the faster you're back at the house."

Erik held back the dozen or so responses firing in his brain. His current predicament had nothing to do with Dozer. Built like a Sherman tank with rugged good looks, Dozer was like the poster child for the army's all-American hero—albeit with a thick Boston accent. He was also a cocky, take-it-or-leave-it kind of bastard, but when the shit hit the fan, there wasn't another man Erik would rather have on his six.

Trying to distract himself, Erik did a visual sweep of the scene. Pretty typical for a Friday night. The bass from the house music beat down on him from all angles and vibrated through his chest like a second heartbeat. Colored lasers shot through the darkness in rapid-fire succession from the ceiling over the dance floor, making it an epileptic's worst nightmare.

If Erik had his choice, he'd rather sit in a local pub like Charley's with the old townies, drinking tap beer and eating stale pretzels while watching a game or shooting pool with friends. At thirty-five, he felt too old for the dance club scene, which was part of the reason he rarely went out anymore. But the other four guys on his team—his brothers, for all intents and purposes—still liked the rave atmosphere that let them forget about everything else and just *be* for a few hours.

Erik tried to shake off the chip on his shoulder, but it was no use.

As a career soldier turned rescue firefighter, obeying his CO had been a part of his mental DNA for the last fifteen-plus years. Sure, there'd been times he pushed back and argued contrary points to his superiors—being a soldier didn't mean he was a mindless sheep—but when it came down to it, he followed his orders and expected the same from every man under his command, whether it was back in the army or now as a lieutenant in the BFD.

But this...*fuck!* He'd never wanted to balk at an order so badly in his entire life.

He shook off the memory and tried to appear chill despite the turbulent rage crashing through his solid six-four frame like a rodeo bull in a cramped chute. Releasing a resigned sigh, Erik forced himself to relax—a physical oxymoron if he'd ever heard one—and sit back in his chair. He'd been sleeping like shit ever since he and his team had been on scene when a power plant exploded a few months ago. The deafening boom, the flash of light and curling flames, people shouting in distress as they ran for cover… It had taken him back to a time and place that haunted the darkest shadows in his mind and dragged the nightmare out into the light of day. Since then, it'd been a living, breathing thing he'd had to fight against. He knew he looked like he could use at least a week's worth of rack time, but that didn't mean he couldn't still do his job.

Dozer took a pull of his Sam Adams and made a disgusted face at Erik's drink choice. "Maybe if you weren't sucking on a bottle of water like a pussy, you wouldn't look like you're already in the shrink's office and ready to jump out of your skin."

Erik had decided to drive his truck tonight instead of cabbing it. He knew that without the responsibility of driving home, inebriation and bad choices were a lot more likely given his current state of mind. So water it was.

"Thanks for the reminder, asshole," Erik answered, shaking his head. "Last thing I need is a goddamn shrink to tell me I can do my job."

"Apparently, our last psych eval begs to differ. And not for nothin', Wolf, but don't think I haven't noticed the panic attacks at working fires lately."

Erik scoffed and said, "You don't know what the fuck you're talking about. If I have problems catching my breath, it's because half the time we don't wear our SCBA and it's finally getting to me. I'm not the first jake to come out of BFD with leather lungs, and I certainly won't be the last."

"You're right about that." Dozer took a swig of his Sam Adams and narrowed his gaze at Erik. "But *you're* the jake whose eval came back with PTSD stamped all over it in big, bold letters."

Erik flipped him off while glancing around the bar again, not really seeing anything. Every day he seemed to lose more control over what went on in his head. Experiencing that power plant blast had caused breaches in the mental hull he'd buried his shit behind years ago. The tiny fissures had grown into full cracks over the weeks, letting his demons seep through to wreak a fuck-ton of havoc in his life.

But it's not like he'd gone bat-shit crazy. Not yet, anyway. He still decided when, where, and how much of the darkness was released at a time. It was his method, and it worked. His control might be a little more strained than usual recently, but the added stress wasn't anything he couldn't handle.

No fucking way was he letting himself get axed just because his new shrink might not agree. He loved his job, and that went double for the men and women he served with in the BFD. He'd rather die than abandon them, and it would take permanent paralysis before he chained himself to a desk to push papers and play politics.

He'd known as much when he stood in front of the chief earlier. Erik took a long pull of his water as his mind replayed the earlier conversation. He'd looked his chief square in the eyes and asked, "Where do I need to go?"

Bill had let out a rush of air, like he'd been holding it, waiting for Erik's answer, then grabbed a file off his desk and handed it over. Erik had opened it to find forms filled out on his behalf, along with information on a shrink whose name sounded like a cross between a breakfast drink and a character in *Raiders of the Lost Ark*. And because he didn't know what else to say, Erik went with something totally inane. "Is that name a joke?"

"Pretty sure shrinks aren't allowed to have a sense of humor," Bill deadpanned. "You report at zero-eight on Monday. Don't be fucking late, and don't fuck this up. It's your ass on the line."

Erik had repressed the few choice words running through his head. "Yes, sir."

"All right, get outta here, son. I'm sure you have plans with your crew. Go blow off some steam, and I'll check in with you next week."

He'd answered the chief with a curt nod and left to head home and get ready before meeting the guys at Phoenix. *Home.* Erik scoffed at the reference to the scant apartment that held all his worldly possessions. The Roxbury firehouse on Columbus Ave was his home.

Erik had lived for his job as a firefighter from day one. It gave him the chance to help people in his adopted community, and best of all, it kept him too damn busy to dwell on the past.

Or at least it *had*. "Fuck," he muttered to himself as the noise of the club drowned out the memory. "I'm gonna need a damn hobby."

"Listen," Dozer said, "why don't you grab yourself a baddie from that bachelorette party over there and get your mind off things. Just don't open your mouth or you're liable to kill the mood."

True to the call sign he'd earned early on in the army, Dozer didn't bother mincing words. The phrase "tread lightly" didn't exist in his vocab, whether he was dealing with people's emotions or delivering an ass-whooping to the enemy. No matter the situation, Gavin bulldozed his way through life and never bothered to glance back at the trail of carnage he left behind. Not because he was an insensitive prick—mostly— but he figured if something he said or did laid you out, there was a damn good reason for it. Only two people existed in the world who the man turned into a sentimental sap for, and that was his mom and younger sister, Gabrielle.

"Last I checked, Doze, I didn't need any tips from you on how to get laid. And forgive me if I'm not in the best of moods after losing my fucking job."

"Hey, what did I tell you?" Dozer demanded. "This is nothin' more than some extended R and R until you can pull your shit together."

"And I told *you* that my shit doesn't need pulling together." *Much.*

"Look, man, I get it. I do—"

Yeah, his friend did get it. As did the three other men on their team. They'd all done tours in Iraq and Afghanistan for the army before joining BFD. They'd all seen more than their fair share of nightmares during the war.

"—but you know they're not going to budge on this. Go to your sessions, get the shrink guy to sign off, and get your ass back where it belongs."

Erik grabbed his water up again and took another long pull.

"And make it snappy, will ya? Cap made me acting LT, and I'm not happy about the promotion. Too much paperwork and responsibility. You can keep that shit."

Erik shook his head. "I'll never understand that, man. You were a damn good ranger. Hell, you could've been a damn good regimental commander if you hadn't kept turning down promotions to stay with the platoon. Now you're content as my second again when you could easily make lieutenant yourself."

"Then who'd be there to save your ass all the time? You're lucky I like you enough to stick with you."

Erik arched a single eyebrow. "Or maybe you just like being my bitch."

"Yeah, okay, tough guy. Why don't we get together at the courts for a friendly pickup game tomorrow night? Then we'll see who the bitch is."

"You're on. And don't forget about your tampon. You'll have to remove that if you want a shot at beating me." Dozer flipped him off, and Erik felt the first sign of a smile on his face since getting called into Bill's office. Nodding at the three empty chairs at their table, Erik asked, "Where'd the kids get off to?"

The other three members of their unit—Ashton "Smoke" Donovan, Sean "Bowie" Evans, and Tyler "Preacher" Connelly—had a habit of squabbling and wrestling like actual brothers. Dozer and Erik had taken to calling them "the kids" as a joke. Then they kept doing it because the other three hated it.

Dozer pointed to a corner booth. "That's Smoke over there with a pretty redhead sitting on his lap and sucking on his face like a goddamn Hoover." Smoke was the token lady-killer of the group. The guys joked that if he notched his bedpost for every woman he fucked, it'd look like a termite playground. "Bowie and Preacher are somewhere in that mob on the dance floor, getting their freak on."

Erik almost shot water through his nose. "I don't think that's an expression people still use. You might want to take a stroll through the Urban Dictionary, old man."

Dozer made a face that clearly said *as if I care*. "So how 'bout that bachelorette party?"

Inwardly sighing, Erik contemplated whether he shouldn't just take Dozer's advice and find a willing woman to lose himself in. He used to be a skirt chaser like the other guys, but lately he'd been less than enthusiastic about hooking up with random women. There wasn't any one thing he could pin it on, but somewhere along the line, the one-night stands had lost their appeal. The women all ran together in his mind with nothing distinctive or unique to set them apart from one another.

When he realized he didn't even remember their names for the duration of their time together, he took a long look in the proverbial mirror and didn't care for the man staring back at him. After that, he tended to burn off any extra adrenaline from the job with grueling workouts and training exercises.

But there were times when the workouts weren't enough. They exhausted his body but never his mind. On the days Rescue 2 dealt with really bad calls—the kind that threatened to coax the ugliness from the depths of his soul—he turned to the only thing that could shut down his mental side long enough for him to push his reset button. Sex. The kind that's quick and rough and dirty with the type of women who enjoyed it when the darker parts of him rose to the surface. But he did his best to keep those instances few and far between.

Erik made a decision and downed the rest of his water, then crushed the plastic bottle and dropped it on the wooden table. "You go ahead," he said. "I'm not in the mood."

That got Dozer's attention like a five-alarmer. "The fuck, Wolf? You get the herp or something?"

Erik cracked a smile and shook his head. "Anyone ever tell you you're a real prick, D?"

"Every day and twice on Sundays, my friend."

"Sounds about right."

"I'm heading out." Erik rose and tossed a few bills on the table. "Get a round for you and the guys on me. Give me a call tomorrow if you want to put a game together."

"Roger that. Later, brother."

Pushing through the throng of bodies, he did his best to be civil and patient instead of barreling a path straight to the door, casualties be damned.

As soon as he reached the outside, he dragged the fresh air of the warm April night deep into his lungs and released it slowly. Grabbing his keys out of his pocket, he made his way to where he parked his truck. All he wanted to do was get to his apartment and end this shit show of a day with a bottle of Jameson and highlights on SportsCenter. First, he needed to make a quick stop for the essentials.

Twenty minutes later, he pulled up to a liquor store and

parked his Dodge Ram 2500 behind a powder blue Mini Cooper. Climbing out of his truck, he chuffed at the difference in size. His truck looked like it could eat the tiny car in front of it. It was a wonder those things were even street legal. Erik would bet money it was owned by some bubbly college co-ed gathering supplies for a house party. It'd be nice if his biggest problem right now was as easy as which flavor of wine cooler to go with.

The bell above the door tinkled as he walked through. The older lady behind the counter glanced up from her magazine over the reading glasses perched on the edge of her nose and smiled in greeting. Erik answered in kind and started his search for the bottle of whiskey that would keep him company tonight.

The clicking of high heels on linoleum echoed from somewhere in the store, a staccato rhythm that contradicted the smooth jazz being piped in softly from the radio. Out of habit, he did a quick mental check of the place, determining any and all exits and using the large, round mirrors hanging in the corners to get a body count. He saw a flash of a blonde woman in a red dress as she clipped her way along the back wall, but she appeared to be the only person there besides the clerk.

He turned down the correct aisle and found the bottles of Jameson easily enough. The clicking got louder as the woman perused the wine selection in the next aisle over, eventually coming to a stop directly on the other side of the shelves he was facing.

"I don't get it," she mumbled. "It shouldn't be this damn hard to find."

If he wasn't in such a sour mood, he'd offer his assistance. Instead, he plucked a bottle of whiskey from the shelf and turned to head back to the front. He'd send the clerk back to help her.

"I'm officially done with the dating scene. I should just have a hot one-night stand. Find some guy to screw my brains out and be done with it."

He hadn't gone farther than two steps when the woman's words halted his hasty retreat. Feeling like a dog perking up at the sound of a command whistle, he waited in anticipation to hear what came next.

"I'm being serious, Angie. I'm so sick of all these failed dates." She must be on the phone. He shouldn't listen in, he knew that, yet he couldn't bring himself to move, either. "I want a man who knows how to make me feel like a real woman. Is that so much to ask?"

The tone of her voice held dejection and disappointment that reminded him of when his sister's boyfriend dumped her in high school. He didn't know this woman, but part of him sympathized with her all the same. The other part of him—the one currently waking up behind his zipper—was still stuck on the hot one-night stand.

"I don't know; it's not like I have a list of qualities with checkboxes." Her friend—Angie—must have asked for clarification. "Someone who doesn't awkwardly fumble through a kiss or treat me with kid gloves like I'm a damn China doll would be a step in the right direction." Glass clinked together as she finally pulled a bottle from the shelf. "A man who can make the past disappear and render the future immaterial. A man who makes it impossible to focus on anything but him and the wicked hot things he's doing to me."

Erik dragged a hand over his mouth and tipped his head back to look up at the water-stained drop ceiling. Fucking hell, the images her words conjured had his blood running hot. When was the last time he'd been with a woman? Two months? Three? It suddenly felt like years.

"Yeah, I'll just proposition the next guy I see," she said.

Erik could almost see her accompanying eye-roll. "Okay, I'm going to let you go, chica. I need to buy my wine and get home to my pity party, party of one. I'll call you tomorrow."

Her heels striking the floor again as she moved toward the front of the store snapped him out of his daydreaming. Shit, she had to pass his aisle to get to the register. She'd know he heard her entire conversation and think he was some kind of creeper. *You* were *being a creeper, dumbass.* Countering his position to hers, he moved in the opposite direction and slid around to the next aisle just as she vacated it. He should wait until she was gone, but the desire to get a better look at her had his feet moving before he could think better of it.

Rounding the front of the aisle, he let his gaze rove over her body in profile as he made his way to the counter. Her sleeveless red dress scooped low over the swells of her large breasts and molded itself to her curves, hitting her at mid-thigh. He wondered if she wore matching red panties underneath, then noticed the absence of panty lines and wondered if she wore any at all. *Christ.* Images flashed in Erik's head of twisting her long, wavy hair around one of his hands and pulling it back so he could devour her mouth, her neck— *Shit.* If he kept up those thoughts, he'd have a permanent zipper imprinted on his dick.

"Shit," she swore, dropping her head back on her shoulders. "I think I left my purse at the bar."

"I'll buy your wine," Erik said, stopping next to her and already retrieving his wallet.

The Lady in Red turned to face him, effectively trapping the air in his lungs. Her body might be a knockout, but her face was nothing short of stunning. Delicate features inside of a heart shape with creamy skin, high cheekbones, and hazel eyes. Her bold makeup—heavily lined eyes and candy apple lips—contradicted the vulnerability and hint of innocence in her expression.

"Thank you, but I can't let you do that," she said, her cheeks infusing with color. "I don't really need the wine."

"With the night it sounds like you're having, I think you do." Her eyes grew big and he realized too late she must think he meant her phone conversation, so he added, "Because you left your purse at the bar."

Relief flowed out of her on an exhaled, "Oh, right. Still though—"

He held up his hand as he smiled. "Listen, if we were at that bar, I would've offered to buy you a drink anyway." She hesitated, biting on the corner of her lower lip, which tightened his gut into a knot. "Tell you what," he said, handing his credit card to the older lady behind the counter who'd been watching the exchange like it was a scene from one of her soap operas. "I'm going to buy the whiskey and the wine. But I'm only leaving with the whiskey. You can either take the wine with you, or gift it to…"

He arched a brow in question to the clerk. "Betty," she responded with a smoker's rasp and a yellowed, toothy grin.

"To Betty. Up to you." Erik nodded to Betty who then rang up the two bottles of alcohol and placed them in separate brown paper bags. Red glanced awkwardly between him, Betty, and the bottle of wine.

"Don't look at me," Betty said with a wink at the woman. "Wine gives me a massive headache."

Erik grabbed the Jameson and stepped into her space. Looking down at her, he spoke low, his mouth hitching up in one corner. "Enjoy your wine." Then he strode past her and pushed out through the door, the jangle of the bell announcing his exit.

He only made it a few feet when he heard the bell again. "Thank you," she called out to him.

Erik turned around to see her standing in the middle of the sidewalk, her phone and the bottle of wine clutched in her hands. It was an opening, an invitation to continue talking. She'd had the opportunity to wait until he drove away before leaving the store, but she'd rushed out after him instead.

On any normal night, he probably would have walked back to her and tried flirting. But she'd had a shitty night and he'd had an even shittier day. He honestly didn't have it in him to pull out the full charm. Besides, he doubted she'd been even half serious about a one-night stand and he wasn't looking to fix her bad dating streak. So instead, he gave her a nod and a farewell grin, then turned and headed for his truck, trying to ignore the odd feeling of regret prickling in his chest.

# Chapter Two

Olivia Jones's gaze locked onto the ass of possibly the sexiest man she'd ever met as he walked toward the gigantic black truck parked behind her Mini. In the liquor store, she'd heard his voice first. *I'll buy your wine.* All low and rumbly, it caused her belly to flip over before even setting sight on the man attached to it. And a second later, when her head turned and she saw him for the first time… *Dayum.*

Her breath had caught in her chest and every thought in her head melted. He was a giant of a man, several inches over six feet, wearing an untucked black dress shirt that fit him like a tailor had designed it around his incredible body. He was gorgeous, but not in a perfect male model sort of way. More like he grew up in the wild and had fought tooth and nail for everything he had, and he wouldn't hesitate to do that and more to keep it. Jet-black hair, buzzed close to his head, matched the shadow of a beard that seemed to exist as if to tell society that he might act civilized, but he refused to pander to their whims and fully conform.

Why couldn't any of the guys she went on dates with be

like *this* one?

Her date earlier had been a disaster, a feeling she'd had before ever stepping foot outside her door. On her drive over to the bar—he was within walking distance and couldn't be bothered to pick her up—the voice in her head had told her to turn her happy ass around, go home, and curl up with a book and her cats. But that's what she'd done almost every other night for the last two years, and she didn't want to be that person anymore. It was the whole reason she'd started dating again. Though, if she'd known it was going to be this hard to connect with anyone, she would've stuck with her cats.

As the man cut between their vehicles, she decided she couldn't be too upset about her bad date anymore. After all, it had led her to this store and the few minutes of interaction with that sexy eye candy would be enough to fuel her fantasies for a while. *Worth it.*

Blowing out a breath, Olivia stepped into the street and walked around to her driver's side door, keeping her eyes firmly trained on the ground so she wouldn't be tempted to sneak more peeks at Hottie McBulgypants. *Oh my God, I did* not *just call him that. I didn't even notice his bulge. I mean, I didn't notice if he even* had *one.* She mentally winced. *Shit! Stop thinking about it!* Still averting her gaze, she heard him climb into his truck and pull the door closed. When the engine roared to life, some of the tension in her shoulders eased.

Until she tried getting into her own vehicle...and couldn't.

Olivia's stomach dropped as she saw the two things she *should* be holding right now laying on her passenger seat. "Shit, shit, *shit!*" she muttered, dropping her forehead to the window. When her best friend, Angelina de la Vega, had called on the drive over, Olivia had been so caught up in rehashing her disastrous date that she'd gotten out of her car with her phone...and nothing else.

She supposed she should be grateful she at least had her

phone so she could call a locksm—

"Something wrong?"

The deep timbre of *his* voice startled her. She'd been so caught up in her blunder that she hadn't heard the truck's engine cut off, or its door opening and closing or the approach of the sexy stranger until he stood behind her and spoke. If her father knew how unaware of her surroundings she'd been, she'd get the lecture of a lifetime.

Before turning to address him, Olivia discreetly tugged the hem of her red dress down and the low scoop neck up. It felt two sizes too small, but a few months ago, when they went shopping for Olivia's "dating wardrobe," Angie insisted it was the perfect amount of sexy without flashing the goods. After experiencing the current local bar scene, Olivia understood what Angie had meant. A lot of girls went out more naked than not, and that alone was a stark reminder of how long it'd been since she'd ventured into a place where the single and horny reigned supreme. Hell, it'd taken her forever just to admit she was once again a part of the single crowd, but she doubted she'd ever feel totally comfortable in clothes this small.

Hoping her poker face was more believable than it felt, she turned around…and promptly forgot how to speak. He was so damn *big*. She stood at five foot seven flat-footed and had on three-inch heels, but he still had a good half a foot on her, making him something akin to the Jolly Green Giant or— "Paul Bunyan."

He arched a brow and the corner of his mouth twitched. "Did you just call me Paul Bunyan?"

Of course it was too much to ask that her internal monologue actually stay *internal*. She mentally smacked her forehead. Taking a deep breath, she shrugged and said, "You have that man-of-the-wild look about you. Considering your height makes you part giant, I'd say you're at least a distant relative."

Paul Bunyan's smile revealed a hidden dimple in his right cheek that melted her insides, and if he kept it up, she didn't hold out much hope for her brain. And his eyes…dear God, his eyes…they were the color of amber, like the whiskey he'd bought, and absolutely breathtaking. Add in his thick, dark lashes she'd give her eyeteeth for, and she might as well just hand over her vagina. *Here you go. I'm fairly certain it'll never work for anyone else now anyway, so you might as well keep it.*

Nodding to the car behind her, he said, "So what seems to be the trouble?"

She glanced back and then met his assessing gaze. "Well, the good news is, I didn't forget my purse at the bar after all because it's on my passenger seat. The bad news is, so are my keys, and my car is locked."

"You really aren't having the best night, are you?"

"You have no idea," she said on a sigh.

He knelt down on one knee and looked up at her as he untied the lace on his black motorcycle boot and started pulling it from the holes. "Bad date?"

"Try a nightmare," she said, cocking her head to the side as she tried to figure out what the hell he was doing.

After freeing that lace, he switched out feet and started on the other. "What were his crimes, if you don't mind my asking? You know," he said with a crooked grin, "so I don't make the same mistakes the next time I take a lady out."

There's no way she would believe that this man could be rude to a date. In the few minutes she'd been with him, she knew he was attentive and thoughtful. She'd bet any date of his would feel like the only girl in the room. Just thinking about it sent a tiny shiver through her. *Stop it, Livvie. You're through with dating, remember?*

Banishing the lust that had been creeping in from the moment she laid eyes on Paul Bunyan, she played along and spoke with a professorial tone. "In the interest of sparing women in the greater Boston area the kind of pain I experienced tonight, I'm happy to share. Let's see. He answered three calls during dinner—one of which was another woman with whom he set up a date for tomorrow night, incorporated the Yankees into every topic of what little discussion we managed, and then had the audacity to look shocked when he learned I wasn't going home with him, which, by the way, is an apartment over his parents' garage."

A final tug and the second lace was completely extracted from his boot. Standing, he gave her an incredulous look. "He was a Yankees fan? You're right, that *is* a nightmare."

She rolled her eyes. "Yes, that was definitely the most tragic part of the entire evening." He smiled to himself as he tied the laces together and then made a quarter-sized loop in the middle with a weird knot. "What are you doing?"

"Rescuing you, m'lady." Grasping the black laces with both hands, he tucked the loop behind the upper corner of her door, then worked it back and forth while simultaneously dragging it down. "So," he said casually, keeping his eyes trained on what he was doing, "what fictional character are you?"

Her eyes widened in fascination as she watched the loop he'd made get lower and lower inside her window until it settled around the lock pin. He pulled both ends in opposite directions, making the loop tighten around the pin like a noose. "I'm sorry, what?"

He paused and flashed her a smile. Good Lord, that dimple was lethal. "If I'm Paul Bunyan, what does that make you?"

She peered down at her hooker dress in consideration. It reminded her of Julia Roberts's character in *Pretty Woman*. "I think it's a toss-up between Vivian Ward and Dance Club Barbie." With a simple upward yank, the laces pulled on the pin and unlocked her car. Holy shit, that was cool. He was like a real-life MacGyver. Oddly, it was a total turn-on.

Opening the door, he pocketed his laces and turned to face her, draping one arm over the top of the door. "There you go."

"That was amazing, thank you so much," she said with equal parts wonder and relief. "Where'd you learn to do that?"

He shrugged. "Just one of the life-hacks I've picked up over the years. You're way off, by the way."

"Way off?" Her brows drew together in confusion.

"About your fictional character."

"I wasn't aware there was a correct answer."

"Maybe not," he said, "but comparing yourself to a prostitute or club bunny is asinine."

Something flipped in Olivia's stomach. Something she was certain had no business tipping, much less flipping, and her mouth suddenly felt like she'd been sucking on cotton. Trying to keep her outer appearance from matching the hot mess going on behind the scenes, she shifted the bottle of wine from one cradled arm to the other.

"I suppose you have a better comparison?"

He took the wine and phone from her and bent to set them on her passenger seat, grabbing her keys in the process. Straightening, he closed her door, placed her keys in her palm, and curled her fingers around them. The warm, callused feel of his hand wrapped on hers sparked a flare of arousal between her legs. But then he took a step in, leaving only inches between their bodies, and she felt her nipples harden into tight buds against her dress like they were straining to reach his hard chest. And hell if she could blame them.

She tilted her head up to meet his gaze and swallowed to banish her dry throat. *Ruggedly beautiful.* That was the only way to describe him. The man was a solid ten on his looks alone, but add in his innate alpha magnetism, and his rating flew off the charts.

His gaze lowered to her lips briefly before capturing hers again. "You're a siren."

Olivia blinked a few times. "I'm...an ear-piercing warning signal?"

One side of his sexy mouth twitched like he was fighting a smile. "The mythological creature whose beauty and sweet songs lure men to crash upon the rocky shores as they try to reach her."

*Whoa.* She was sooooo out of her league with this guy. Her freshman year in college, she'd entered a serious relationship with Brett that eventually led to marriage, so it'd been nearly a decade since she'd dated. Is this what pickup lines had evolved into? Lines that actually *worked*? How did one even respond to that sort of thing? "I can't sing. I'm extremely tone deaf."

Her inner self slapped her palm to her forehead—again—and groaned. *That is* not *how you respond to that sort of thing. Way to go, genius.* But despite her lamenting, he rewarded her with a full smile and hearty chuckle. *Lord have mercy.*

"No karaoke bars, then. I'll keep that in mind for future reference."

"Future reference?" she asked with an arch of her brow. "Don't you think you're getting a little ahead of yourself?"

"Possibly," he said. "Or maybe I'm just hoping my timely rescue and power of suggestion will get me a date with my damsel in distress."

His voice sent a frisson of electricity dancing down her spine. She almost told him the odds were high that it would, but at the last second, she remembered her minutes-old decision. "Sorry, but I'm no longer in the market for a date. Been there, done that, burning the T-shirt when I get home."

"Fair enough." He gave her a half grin before pinning his full lower lip with his teeth. His gaze dipped to her mouth.

Not long, but enough for her to feel its weight as her knees threatened to buckle. Meeting her eyes again, he asked, "What's your position on something more casual?"

"What's more casual than dating?"

"One night."

She swore her heart skipped a beat. Had he overheard her conversation with Angie in the store? It was entirely possible; she hadn't exactly been paying attention to her surroundings. She waited for mortification to set in, but it didn't come. The things this man made her feel with his intensity and close proximity left no room for anything else.

"One night of what, exactly?"

Keeping his eyes locked with hers, he reached up and grazed her cheek with the back of his knuckles. "Whatever you need."

. . .

Erik had no idea what the fuck had come over him. Wasn't he just thinking about how he wasn't down with the empty one-night stands anymore? Apparently his dick hadn't gotten the memo. Then again, one night or not, something told him that a night with this woman would feel anything but empty.

A cab rushed by them, the burst of wind lifting the ends of her hair and reminding him they were still standing next to her tiny car on the edge of traffic, intermittent though it may be. "Come on, let's get out of the street," he said, leading her around the Mini and onto the sidewalk in front of the liquor store. Out of habit, he positioned her with her back to the brick facade and his to the street so that he stood between her and any possible harm. "What d'you say, gorgeous, want to get to know each other better?"

She shook her head. "Getting-to-know-you stuff is for dates."

"My version doesn't involve dinner or talking. At least not the clean kind," he amended with a crooked grin.

"So, what then, drinks and dirty talk?" she asked in a husky voice.

Erik barely bit back his groan. Damn, she smelled incredible. Like rose petals bathed in sunlight, subtle and natural. Completely opposite of the harsh perfumes most women doused themselves in. Erik wanted to bury his face in her neck and fill his lungs with her scent. "Sweetheart, I'm offering whatever you want. Name it."

She arched a dubious brow that added to her sarcastic tone. "And I suppose I should just assume you're not some kind of serial killer, is that it?"

Offering a reassuring grin, he said, "I can promise you I'm not a serial killer."

He'd almost said he wasn't "a killer," but that would be a lie. He *was* a killer. He'd killed more times than he could count. The fact that it'd all been in combat didn't absolve him. At least not for all of it. Hindsight was a motherfucker.

She chewed on the corner of her lip and studied him, her wheels turning. "How about a knight in shining armor? After all, you did rescue me in my hour of need."

He huffed out a cynical sound before he could bite it back. "Don't think I qualify. My armor hasn't been shiny for a long fucking time."

"Okay then, what are you?" she asked, canting her head to the side.

Her eyes told him she wasn't asking about what he did for a living or what his astrological sign was. She was digging for something deeper, something to help her understand him. But there was only one thing he wanted her to understand right now: that he was exactly what she needed in this moment. If he had to play a little dirty to drive his point home, then so be it.

Erik stepped into her so her sex brushed teasingly against the hard muscle of his thigh. He placed one hand on her hip as the other threaded into the thick hair at the nape of her neck, then he spoke low into her ear. "I'm a man who can make you feel like a real woman. A man who will make it impossible to focus on anything but me and the wicked hot things I'm doing to you."

Her eyes widened and her lips parted slightly with a sharp inhale as a blush bloomed on her cheeks. And then she did the most unexpected thing.

She fucking smiled.

The full kind that lit up her eyes and stopped a man's heart, and he was no exception. Something about her—beyond her incredible sex appeal—intrigued the hell out of him. She definitely wasn't the one-night stand kind of woman, and yet a string of bad dates had left her jaded enough to consider it. Her comment on the phone had been flippant and most definitely a joke. But that smile told him he might have crossed her path at just the right time. The universe had created the perfect storm—a series of shitty events that led them to this moment, and he'd be damned if he didn't try everything he could to make this night memorable for both of them.

"What's your name, sweetheart?"

She shook her head. "No names."

"You don't have to worry about me looking you up or showing up at your place of business, if that's what you're thinking. I'm not looking to make anything more out of this than you are."

"I believe you."

"Then what's the harm with exchanging names?"

She lifted a slim shoulder in a halfhearted shrug. "In my profession, I can't take that risk."

He could understand that. "We can use fake names."

She didn't answer immediately, seeming to give his idea some thought, but then she shook her head slightly. "I don't know…"

Erik cupped her jaw and stroked the corner of her mouth with his thumb, imagining how it would feel to press his lips there. "I can turn this night around for the both of us. I only have three conditions. One: since your place is out of the question, and you no doubt won't feel comfortable coming to mine, we'll go to a hotel—and nothing seedy or questionable, I mean a nice fucking hotel—and you'll text the information to a friend so someone knows where you are. Two: you *will* give me a fake name because not having something to call you, even in my own head, is frustrating as hell."

He could see the wheels turning in her head as she weighed her options of giving in or arguing. Softening his tone, he tipped her chin up and said, "Come on, gorgeous. I'd rather you give me a name, but I'll call you Goldilocks if I have to."

She sighed and he knew she'd given in. "Livvie. You can call me Livvie."

"I like that. Thank you, Livvie." He brought her hand up and placed a kiss on her knuckles. "You can call me Wolf. That's what my friends call me."

"Wolf." She said it softly, as though trying it out on her lips, and it stirred something primal deep in his gut.

"That's right, baby." Erik bowed his head and spoke low into her ear. "I'll make you come harder than you ever thought possible, and when I do, I want it to be *my* name that you scream and no one else's." He nipped her earlobe, making her gasp. "Not even God's."

Her shaky exhale bathed his cheek, making his cock twitch in anticipation. He pulled back just enough to watch the play of arousal over her features. Fuck, he wanted her more than he could remember wanting a woman in a long damn time. Her ample chest heaved with her quick breaths and her pupils swallowed her hazel irises. He hadn't held out much hope, but his lady in red was turned on as all hell, and it made him wonder what would really get her going in the bedroom.

When it came to sex, Erik loved it all, but his true tastes had always leaned a little on the rougher side. Scratching, biting, hair pulling, it was all fair game for his partners. The pain reminded him he was alive, and some days he needed it more than others—days like today. Which was why he was surprised to realize he didn't care how things went tonight, so long as it happened with *this* woman. He wasn't imagining the chemistry between them. He'd bet his beloved truck that if he dipped his fingers beneath her panties, he'd find her slick and hot for him.

"H-how did you get the name Wolf?"

Peering up at her through his lashes, he raised an eyebrow in challenge. "That's a get-to-know-you question, sweetheart. I'm happy to answer, but…"

She shook her head like she was trying to rattle things into place. "No, you're right, don't answer that. Wolf it is. If I agree to this, what's your third condition?"

"Number three is…" He paused for a beat. "Trust me."

Her brows drew together. "With?"

His gaze lowered to her succulent mouth, a hundred images of what he could do it flashing through his mind. "Your pleasure," he said gruffly. "I'm going to set your body on fire with sex so carnal and electric it makes you feel alive. I'll use my mouth, my hands, and my cock to fuck your tight little body just as my words will fuck your mind."

"Jesus," she whispered, her head dropping back to the wall as her lids lowered to half-mast.

"Not even close." Leaning in, he kept his mouth only a breath away from hers as he spoke. "I'm a man who knows how to read your body and the signals it's giving me. I can give you what you want—what you *need*—but you have to trust me."

Unable to stop himself, he grazed his lips over hers. It couldn't even be considered a kiss. Just a ghostly brush, a brief interruption of what little was left in the space of propriety between them—the space he desperately wanted to obliterate for at least the next twelve hours.

"So what do you say, gorgeous…do we get our night together?"

She touched her tongue to her bottom lip as though she could taste him there, then dragged it between her teeth. Goddamn, she tested his will like no woman ever had. His dick stood at full attention and strained against the fly of his jeans as it throbbed in time with his racing heartbeat.

Finally, a sweet smile curved her lush mouth and she answered with a confident, "Yes."

# Chapter Three

Olivia stood in the lobby of the upscale hotel while Wolf—she was still curious how he acquired the nickname—rented them a room for their agreed upon single night of anonymous sexual abandon. She hadn't stood a chance the second Wolf spoke to her. How the hell was a girl supposed to keep her wits about her under the attention of so much *maleness*?

After uncharacteristically agreeing to this arrangement, they decided on a hotel and she followed him in her car. On the way, she called her best friend again, but it went to voicemail. Olivia had left a message with a quick rundown of the situation and the hotel info, then promised to call her in the morning to let her know she was okay, which would inevitably turn into an interrogation for details.

Picturing the look on Angie's face when she finally listened to the message made Olivia chuckle to herself. The two women were opposite in almost every way, yet somehow complemented each other perfectly. She'd loved Angie from the first, when Olivia was enjoying her lunch in the commons at Boston College and saw the fiery Latina lay into a guy twice her size for making a lewd comment about her curvy ass. The guy's arrogance had shriveled faster than his nuts dipped in ice water, and after he apologized to her for being "a misogynistic pig" (apology script supplied by none other than Angie herself), he walked away in silence and gave her a wide berth from then on.

Olivia had been so impressed, she'd started a slow clap to a standing O, to which Angie responded with a deep curtsy and an introduction. They'd been best friends ever since, and Olivia never stopped admiring Angie for her strong sense of self and the fearless way she handled life.

Angie was going to have conniptions when she heard that her straight-laced, overly cautious friend agreed to a one-night stand with a handsome stranger on a whim. It certainly wasn't anything she'd ever do under normal circumstances, much less the one she'd been in for the past two years.

It had taken her a long time to move on from the marriage she no longer had—from the *life* she no longer had without Brett—but she'd finally started to actively date a few months ago. Lord knows she'd been on plenty since. Some, like tonight, were total busts, and some were decent with a handful going on to second and third dates. Unfortunately, they never made it further than that. Even the ones that made it *that* far were only because she was trying to give them the benefit of the doubt. It certainly wasn't from any sort of mutual connection or spark, and after so many failed attempts, Olivia couldn't help wonder if she wasn't the problem, not the men.

She hadn't realized how utterly exhausting the dating game would be. For the last couple of weeks, her heart hadn't been in it, and tonight's earlier disaster had been the last straw. She needed a good, long break from it all, and with the way she felt, it might be a permanent one. If she didn't already have a job she loved, looking into joining a convent wouldn't be a bad idea. That's how much she didn't want to go on any more dates right now.

*But that's not what* this *is*, she thought as her gaze landed on Wolf and drank in the subtle rippling of the muscles in his back. No, this is something entirely different. Erotic and carnal with a hint of wrongness that spread through her and sizzled beneath her skin. It was exciting and thrilling and nerve-racking all at once, and she loved it.

Tonight, she'd reconnect with the young, vivacious woman she used to be. Tonight, in a hotel room, Olivia and a stranger would engage in no-name sex with no possible future. And tomorrow morning, she would have her proof that it was possible to move on after nursing a broken heart for so long, and that she could in fact connect with another man, even if only sexually. *Or maybe* especially *sexually*.

Wolf turned from the front desk and suddenly she felt like her geeky high school self, watching in nervous anticipation as the captain of the football team steadily approached her. Only this man was ten times more intimidating with his predatory gait and the raw hunger she saw swirling in his whiskey-colored eyes.

Coming to a stop in front of her, he held up a plastic key card. "Shall we?" he asked, his voice deep and hypnotic.

Squaring her shoulders to inject more confidence into her spine than she currently felt, she smiled and answered, "Absolutely."

They walked to the elevators, waited in silence, then boarded the car and leaned against opposite walls as the doors slid closed. As they began to ascend, he studied her as though she were one of life's great mysteries.

Why did she feel like he could see right through her? And why the hell couldn't she read him? It was her damn *job*. After a few minutes of conversation with people, she could classify them and write a fairly accurate report on who they were and likely why. But for the life of her, she couldn't get a bead on this man. He was…enigmatic. A mystery. A puzzle. Fun and flirtatious, but with an edge, like he wouldn't shy away from danger, he'd *welcome* it.

So completely different from Brett in every way. Wolf was dark and massive with tanned skin and amber eyes, whereas Brett's physique had been more streamlined—less muscular and more toned, like a runner—with a blond hair/brown eyes combo. Brett had always been the life of the party and center of attention wherever they went, and more often than not, she wouldn't even see him until the end of the night at get-togethers with friends or family. He was like a politician, making the rounds and over-selling his excitement to see them. Though she couldn't be sure, something told her that if Wolf had a woman, she'd never leave his sight, even if he was on the other side of the room. He had that intensity about him.

"What are you thinking about?" he asked.

*Busted.* This wasn't exactly the time for deep thoughts, but she didn't see a reason not to be honest. "About how opposite you are from my ex."

Wolf crossed the elevator and crowded her in the most wonderful way. She stared at the glorious triangle of bare skin where his top button had been relieved of its duty. If she stared into his eyes right now, she'd end up as a puddle on the marble floor.

"How opposite?" he rasped, tempting her to lick a path over his sexy Adam's apple.

"Polar," she whispered.

He placed one hand on the wall high above her head and the other on the side of her face. Olivia couldn't move, couldn't breathe, his touch jamming the signals to her brain. "Is that a good thing?"

God, she wished she knew. "I honestly don't know."

Slipping his wide thumb from her cheek, he hooked it

under her chin and lifted until her eyes met his. Seriously, it should be illegal for a man—especially one so rugged and wild and huge—to have eyes as beautiful as his. If she took a picture of him and erased everything but his eyes, she'd bet ten to one that people would guess they belonged to a woman. And yet when seen with the rest of him, they didn't look the least bit feminine. Explanation? Paul Bunyan had miracle eyes.

"You trying to get over this ex of yours?"

"You could say that."

"That's why you've been going on all these dates."

Olivia swallowed thickly. "I don't want to think about the past anymore."

She didn't know if she meant her marriage with Brett or her recent dating mishaps, but the statement applied either way. Olivia only wanted to focus on the present, with this man; to live in this moment and all the ones after it until their one night came to an end. That's what she needed from Wolf.

"Then I'm going to help you forget." His thumb trailed over her chin, under the edge of her lower lip, the slow caress entrancing her. She swore he was about to kiss her, but then the chime signaled their floor and he pulled away.

He ushered her out and down the hall, his large hand always at her lower back. She didn't know if he did it as a way of steering her or for reassurance, or maybe he did it with all women who walked next to him. Whatever the reason, the presence of his hand quieted her nerves a little, and at this point, she'd take what comfort she could get.

He stopped in front of room 1610 and held her gaze, tense and still like a predator waiting to pounce or back down to hunt another day. "If you want to back out, tell me now, Livvie."

Chills of anticipation broke out over her skin. "I don't want to back out."

His nostrils flared the slightest bit as he pushed out a breath and gave her a slight nod of acceptance. Eyes still locked on hers, his hand ran the key card through the slot in the handle and then he held the door open for her.

Olivia stepped into a short hallway that led to the bathroom on the left and a closet on the right. In front of her, she saw the end of the bed on the left side of the room and an expanse of floor-to-ceiling windows.

That was all she had time to notice.

She heard the lock click over just before he grabbed her around the waist and pushed her back against the wall. His large hands came up to frame her face as he crushed his mouth onto hers, his tongue sweeping inside to demand its due.

Olivia clutched at the sides of his shirt as she met every ounce of his intensity with her own. He angled her head more and she reveled in his heady taste of mint and pure virility, stronger than anything she'd experienced before.

They wrenched apart, taking in greedy gasps of air. "Turn around," he said. She faced the wall, then he stretched her arms above her head. "Keep your hands there," he rasped next to her ear.

She nodded, unable to make her voice work, which was fine because he didn't seem to care one way or another. He slid his hands down her bare arms. Calluses scraped her skin and left goose bumps in their wake. With her forehead on the wall, she kept her eyes closed and a corner of her lower lip pinned between her teeth.

His hands took a detour to the front and hefted each of her breasts, a barely audible groan vibrating into her back. "I can't wait to see your breasts. I bet they're amazing."

"They're nothing special."

She winced as soon as she said it. Sure, she was nervous since a man hadn't seen her naked in forever, but insecurity wasn't sexy. Jesus, she was actually managing to screw up sex with a stranger. That had to be a first.

"You let me be the judge of that, gorgeous."

He pulled down the dress's stretchy scoop neck with both cups of her bra, pinched her nipples, and twisted. She gasped at the spear of pain that sliced through her and held her breath, not wanting to move even to empty her lungs. A taut cord of electric pleasure stretched from the tips of her breasts to the deepest recess of her sex. The raw carnality of the way his body pinned hers in place and his rock-hard erection pressed into the small of her back lit a slow burn deep in her belly, heating her from the inside out.

His big hands kneaded her heavy mounds, the sensations created by his calluses tingling through her sex. "They're fucking perfect," he said. "I plan on exploring those more later, but first things first. I want to know how wet you are for me."

*Embarrassingly so.*

He hooked his fingers under the tight hem of her dress and pulled it up over her hips, exposing her lacey red thong. In one swift motion, he lifted her dress up and over her head. The next to go was her matching bra, tossed somewhere off to the side. Thankfully, he didn't rip it off. She had a small addiction to expensive bra and panty sets. Her everyday wardrobe erred on the conservative side, but underneath she enjoyed wearing provocative lingerie. It made her feel sexy and gave her a little thrill knowing it was her secret. That Victoria had the right idea.

"Christ." His curse was quiet and sounded strained, but when he spoke again, the strength in his commands had returned. "Step out of your heels."

She complied, pushing each one back with her toes. Though she still faced away from him, Olivia sensed herself become even smaller than the giant standing behind her. If she had to guess, she'd say the top of her head might reach the top of his chest, if she was lucky.

One large hand made its way between her body and the wall, gliding up her stomach, through her cleavage, and over her collarbones. His touch set off sparks in her skin and fanned the flames growing wilder within. She tried to regulate her breathing as proof to herself that he wasn't affecting her to the point she had no control over her body, and she almost succeeded…until his hand slid up to loosely wrap around her throat, just enough to remind her of his strength, his power.

It should have freaked her out, should have yanked her back to her senses.

Instead, she released a shuddering sigh and tipped her head back to rest against the hard muscles of his shoulder.

"That's it, baby. Give over to me." He gave her throat a light squeeze before his hand retreated down her body. "Tonight you're all mine. Aren't you?"

"Yes," she breathed.

"That's good. Because I take care of what's mine, and I'm going to show you what it's like when a man puts your pleasure first."

*Dear. God.*

Without any instructions or commentary, Wolf dragged her thong down and off, then presumably tossed it over with the rest of her clothes. She bent her head to peer down her body and caught glimpses of his hands as he touched her. He remained crouched behind her and ran his hands up her calves, over the sensitive skin at the backs of her knees, and straight up her thighs to knead the globes of her ass.

His touch wasn't gentle. His fingers dug into her flesh, his hands squeezed, his mouth tasted. She felt his hot breath bathe her skin as he dragged his face over her. A myriad of sensations made her head spin as it tried to sort them all out. Soft lips, wet tongue, scratchy beard, blunt scrapes of teeth…

Finally, Wolf turned her by her hips so that she faced him. Still crouched as he was, his face now lined up directly with her sex. She plastered herself against the wall to put as much distance between it and him, but there wasn't any point. Going through the wall wasn't an option, and he only moved closer.

"You're turned on as fuck, Livvie." His deep voice sent vibrations through her sensitive body. She squeezed her thighs together in hopes of easing the ache it left. "The proof is right here in this sweet little pussy of yours." He swiped a thick finger through her slick folds, adding pressure as it passed over her clit, causing her hips to chase his touch and a whimper to escape her lips.

She needed him, badly—more than she could ever remember needing another man.

Wolf unfolded to his full height, banding his arms around her waist on the way up to lift her off the floor as he strode farther into the hotel room. "Let's get more comfortable," he said, setting her down in front of the posh microfiber couch that faced the foot of the bed. "Have a seat, gorgeous."

She lowered herself on the center cushion, staring up at him as he unbuttoned his shirt in slow motion. Little by little, he exposed peeks of tan skin as the edges of the shirt moved back and forth with his motion. As he reached the very last button, she held her breath. She felt his eyes burning into her, but her gaze was locked onto his chest and wouldn't let go.

Finally, he peeled the sides back and shrugged it off his large shoulders, revealing muscular perfection adorned by a set of dog tags hanging between his pecs. Damn, those were so sexy. A military boy, which meant that Wolf wasn't just a nickname. It was his call sign, as much his name as the one given to him by his parents. The man intrigued her more and more every minute.

Despite several raised scars, Wolf had one of the finest bodies she'd ever come across, whether in movies, magazines, or other mass media. Certainly the finest she'd ever seen personally by…was saying "a million" hyperbole? She didn't think so. A million seemed pretty accurate to her.

He had more muscles than she knew existed in the human torso. Rounded shoulders, cut pecs with dusky nipples, blocks of abs, and deep slashes over his hips angled in a *V* that disappeared beneath his low-slung dark jeans. And the sexy icing on the man cake was the smattering of dark hair on his chest that picked up again below his navel to form one hell of a goody trail.

The clinking of metal on metal drew her attention to his fingers undoing his belt buckle, then the button and zipper. Seemingly content to just give himself some breathing room, he let the two sides hang open and blatantly palmed his erection over his underwear, moving it up and down like he was priming a pump. Holy shit, who knew watching a man touch himself could be so hot?

"Open your legs," he said in a gruff voice.

As she separated her legs, she pictured him loaded with gear and commanding others just as he did with her. Orders tripped off his lips naturally, and the look in his eyes said he was used to being obeyed, in the bedroom and out. The image sent another rush of wet heat between her legs.

He lightly kicked her ankles farther out, then sank to his knees and hauled her butt to the edge of the couch so her head and shoulders were braced against the back of it. When he held her open with his hands pressing out on her inner thighs, his pupils completely engulfed the bright amber of his eyes.

"Fucking amazing," he rasped, working her folds open. He swiped his thumbs through her own lubrication and spread it over every part of her exposed sex. Sensations of rough against smooth flooded her until it was a struggle not to squirm under his touch. "Your cunt is dripping, begging me to use my tongue to lap up every drop it spills. And there's nothing else I'd rather do right now than make you come all over my mouth."

Holy hell. Every time he talked dirty, his words strummed over her clit, playing her as effectively as his fingers. She'd never been spoken to like that, much less had a man refer to her dripping "cunt." She'd always thought it a vile word, but Wolf said it with a kind of reverence in his voice, and it made her impossibly wetter.

When she realized he meant to make good on his last statement and started lowering his head, she panicked. Her hands shot out from under her and pushed on the top of his head to stop him. "Don't do that."

"Why not?" Wolf sat back on his heels, turning his steady gaze on her. His voice deepened and sounded gruff, barely controlled. Every bit the epitome of the wild man she imagined him to be.

She struggled with the words. Angie had always told her it was the most asinine thing a female could say, but she couldn't help it. "I've never been comfortable with…that."

"Have you ever let anyone try to change your opinion?"

She bit her lip and shook her head.

A wicked grin curved his mouth. "Then you can thank me later."

# Chapter Four

Erik couldn't stop himself from placing a gentle kiss to the side of her neck. He heard her take in a sharp breath and felt her tense as though waiting to see if he was changing the tone of their evening together to something softer, more tender. A small part of him wondered what it would be like to truly make love to a woman as innocently passionate as Livvie. To take his time discovering her body's secrets and exploit them to give her hours upon hours of pleasure.

But that wasn't what either of them were there for, so he buried the thought and regrouped to be present for Livvie.

Channeling the man she needed, he licked a slow and wide path up the length of her neck. Her shiver vibrated through his tongue and his mouth twisted into a wicked grin of satisfaction. He fucking loved that her body reacted to him so easily. His only goal at this point was to make her come all over his tongue until she was lost to pure orgasmic euphoria.

"Hold still, baby. I'm going to make you feel good."

She sat frozen in place, her chest rising and falling and distracting the hell out of him. Her breasts were absolute perfection. If someone asked him to pick his favorite set of tits out of a catalog, he'd pick hers every time. They were only a little bigger than a handful, but then, he could palm a basketball like an NBA player. He molded her breasts to his palms, tested their weight. Damn, they were phenomenal. Nice and heavy with light pink nipples that turned bright red with the right kind of attention.

He latched onto one and then the other, sucking and drawing them deep into his mouth, flicking the tip of his tongue over the taut buds, then lightly pulling on them with his teeth. Livvie's hands held the back of his head, gently at first and then with more force. Her nerves had settled and she was beginning to let herself go.

Taking that as his cue, he again pushed her thighs open and moved quickly, sweeping his tongue through her slick cleft. Her hips jerked in time with her gasp, and Erik groaned as his cock strained in anticipation. Fuck, she tasted like sweet ambrosia, an elixir of the gods that he'd never get enough of.

Sensing her approaching orgasm from the way she writhed against his mouth, he licked and tongued her swollen clit, never letting up the assault despite the fact she'd taken to pushing on his shoulders and head.

Erik had never seen anyone so fucking beautiful in his life. Sweat slicked her skin, and the wispy curls surrounding her face had dampened and now clung to her cheeks and neck. Her back bowed and her nails scored his upper back. The pleasure-pain zinged down his spine, wrapping around his balls like an electric cock ring to hold him primed and ready to explode the moment he allowed himself to let go. But that wouldn't be for a while yet—not until she'd gotten hers. And then some.

She pushed at his head again and squirmed even more than before, this time calling out objections. "Omigod, it's too much. Wolf, I can't."

"Yes, you can." Using his wide shoulders to hold her legs apart, he slipped his arms under her knees, grabbed her hands, and pinned them to the back of the couch before diving back in.

She shook her head from side to side with her eyes squeezed shut. "No, please, I-I can't!"

Erik growled against her swollen flesh and doubled his efforts. In seconds, Livvie's legs trembled and she came, the walls of her pussy fluttering around his tongue as her screams bounced off the walls of their room.

*Fuck* me, *that was hot.* But he was far from done with this incredible woman. Standing, Erik picked her up and settled her onto the edge of the bed before quickly removing the rest of his clothes. He retrieved a condom from his wallet, kicked the pile of discarded clothing to the side, and rose to his full height at the foot of the mattress.

He fisted his thick cock and hissed out a breath as he squeezed, a futile attempt at tempering the lust threatening to erupt before he even got near her. Livvie's bright hazel eyes zeroed in on his end game, and she actually gasped as she scrambled back onto the bed, out of his reach. Her shock at his size was a nice ego boost, but he didn't like the underlying uncertainty that seemed to come with it.

"Something wrong, baby?"

She shook her head slowly. "Wolf, that… I mean, you won't…"

"Fit?" he finished for her. When she nodded, he let out an amused chuckle. Stroking his stiff length from root to ruddy tip, he said, "Oh, I'll fit, baby. I'll make sure of it."

Livvie bit the barest corner of her lip as he ripped the condom package open with his teeth and guided the condom onto his erection. Her gaze locked on his movements, and he watched with satisfaction as her pupils dilated until only a slim ring of color remained. The pulse in her neck fluttered wildly and her breaths were growing erratic. She licked her lips, drawing his attention to that glorious mouth he ached to see wrapped around his dick. Something he didn't have the patience for right now because the need to sink into the wet heat of her pussy all but consumed him.

"Get your cute ass back over here," he said.

A sly grin spread across her face, then she slowly shook her head. "You come over *here*," she challenged.

Instinct lit up his insides like a synaptic brushfire, the predator in him thrilling at the game she played. *Chase. Catch. Conquer.* He'd do it all and then revel in his victory as she begged him for more.

Stretching over, Erik snatched both her ankles and yanked her down the bed. A surprise yelp escaped her with a quick bark of laughter, but he cut it off with a demanding kiss, one that didn't bother to ask for permission or even participation. His tongue shoved inside and fucked her mouth, licking and sucking and biting, his only goal to devour her. The tentative woman from earlier had completely vanished, replaced by one who matched his every move and clawed at his back as she pulled him in, mashing the erect nipples of her full tits between them.

Enough. He couldn't wait another second. He untangled her arms from him and shoved them onto the mattress above her head. Holding her wrists there with one hand, he used the other to prepare her tight sheath with his fingers, curling them along her G-spot so she flooded with more slick heat.

Livvie writhed and whimpered and pleaded for more, but Erik held her at the edge of another orgasm, letting the intensity build and build. Finally, he lined himself up at her entrance. Time to put them both out of their misery.

In one smooth thrust, he slid home, burying himself completely inside the tightest, hottest woman he'd ever known. She cried out with her head thrown back and a look of rapture on her face that made him feel like a fucking king.

"Jesus Christ," he choked out when she canted her hips up. "Don't move a goddamn muscle or this'll be over before it starts."

Trying again, she said, "But—"

Growling at her disobedience, he ducked his head and snagged a taut nipple between his teeth and gave her a sharp nip before suckling it deep into his mouth. A keening cry escaped her lips as her back arched up to offer her heavy tits like a decadent dessert. He eagerly indulged himself, feasting on the flesh of her breasts. As soon as he knew he wouldn't blow his load on the first stroke, he braced up on his arms so he could watch her as he started to move.

He withdrew almost completely, then drove back in to the hilt with a force that rocked her forward on the mattress. Then he did it again. And again. And *again*. Their pace quickened, growing feverish and uncontrolled. She drew her knees toward her chest, opening herself up more and allowing him to go deeper than he thought possible. She felt made for him, a perfect fucking fit that stroked and pulsed around every last millimeter of his cock.

Gritting his teeth in concentration, he pistoned harder inside her scorching sex. Her body kept inching farther up the bed, causing him to follow on his knees or risk unseating himself, and if *that* happened, he might totally lose his shit.

Hooking his arms under her legs, he lifted and shoved her up the bed. When the half dozen or more pillows became little more than speed bumps, she hastily pushed them off each side. One of them took out a lamp on its way to the floor, but the sound of it clattering on the nightstand didn't so much as garner a glance from either of them. It could catch fire and Erik doubted they'd even slow down, much less stop. This burning need for each other was fast approaching the melting point, and the only thing to do was ride it out until there was nothing left.

At last he had them as far as they could go with her upper back pressed against the fancy padded headboard. He sat with his bent knees spread so his pelvis lined up perfectly with hers and his balls rubbed on the silky comforter, torching his pleasure sensors with every blessed stroke.

Erik continued to pound into her body, reveling in the sounds she made, the way she bit her lower lip and furrowed her brow, the way she bravely fixed her gaze on him and didn't look away with shyness or embarrassment.

He wanted to tell her how beautifully stunning she was, that she was a goddess who deserved to be treated as such. But that sort of thing wasn't what she wanted. Not tonight, at least. So he'd voice every dirty thought running through his head. They were no less true than their tender counterparts.

"I love the way you look with your legs pinned back, your big tits bouncing, your pretty nipples hard and begging for me." Every drop of moisture in his body now covered his skin, making his insides parched and his voice scratchy. "You're so goddamn tight. Fuck me, you feel *so fucking good*."

"So, so good," she panted. "So big and...*full*. You... *uhn*..."

Incoherent sentences meant she was getting close, but not close enough for his peace of mind. If she didn't come soon, he'd lose the last thread he had on his control, not to mention his Man Card for finishing before he made the woman he was with come again before he took his own.

"I can't decide where I like your sweet cunt more," he said. "Grinding on my tongue or riding my dick." Leaning back, he looked down to where their bodies connected. "Damn, baby, I really like seeing your body swallow my cock."

He grabbed her right hip with one hand for leverage, his fingers digging in hard enough they'd probably leave marks, making his inner caveman grunt with satisfaction. The palm of his other hand lay over the mound of her sex. Perfect placement for his thumb to stimulate her clit while his fingers pushed on her abdomen just above her pubic bone, causing more friction from his cock against her G-spot on the inside.

The double assault had the desired effect. A moan turned into a squeak, and her body jolted like he'd hooked her up to jumper cables. But when he expected her climax to follow shortly after, her brow furrowed and her moans turned to whimpers that sounded more distressed than the little mews of rapture he wanted to hear. Whether she knew it or not, she was fighting her orgasm.

"Come for me, baby. I want to feel your cunt squeezing me like a fist, bathing me in your sweet cum." He watched her ride that fine edge as her two sides fought for control—one refusing to give in and the other begging for release. Leaning in, he whispered against her ear. "Let go, Livvie, baby. I'm right here to catch you. Let yourself fall."

"Oh my— *Wolf!*"

Male pride swept through him to hear his name—or one of them, at least—ripped from her throat as she finally erupted beneath him and he roared through his own scorching release. Erik tunneled his arms under her and held her to him as he continued to slowly pump in and out, offering sweet encouragements as they rode out the last waves of their pleasure.

"Good girl, Livvie," he said with a kiss to her temple.

"That was..." She sighed and finished with, "Perfect."

Her body glistened with sweat and not an ounce of tension remained. The woman who just rocked every corner of his world peered up at him with a shy smile and hooded eyes that sparked something deep in his gut; he'd call it his gut for now, despite the location being decidedly higher. That was a revelation for later, if ever.

Erik turned down the bed, then slid her legs under the

cool sheet and comforter before pulling them up around her shoulders. He set the lamp to rights and headed into the bathroom where he took care of the condom and cleaned up. On his way back, he adjusted the thermostat up a couple degrees, redressed, and neatly arranged her clothes and shoes on the couch before returning to her.

She was already fast asleep, her breaths deep and even. He climbed onto the bed next to her, staying above the covers to avoid the temptation of her body and coaxing her from sleep for a repeat performance. As it was, it took ten times of mentally field stripping his M16 before his dick stopped hoarding his blood supply, the selfish prick.

As he lay on his side, he tried committing the finer details of her features to memory. She looked like an angel, resting peacefully, and it tugged on something in his chest he thought had died long ago. He knew nothing about her, and yet that something urged him to not let her go after only one night.

Maybe she'd let him take her out to breakfast. Then, after some friendly conversation, he'd ask for her number so he could see her again. It'd probably be pushing his luck, considering how against it she'd been from the beginning, but maybe she'd reconsider. It wasn't entirely outside the realm of possibilities.

Erik decided he'd stay awake in case Livvie woke up in the middle of the night. Unfortunately, his satiated body had other plans, and when he woke up from the sun piercing through his eyelids, the angel known as Livvie had vanished without a trace.

"Fuck," he muttered, scrubbing his hands over his face to get the blood flowing.

She was obviously fine. If she'd wanted him to contact her, she would have left a note or business card or her number drawn in lipstick on the dresser mirror. But she didn't. Their one-night stand would stay just that. One night.

Convincing himself that what he felt were pangs of hunger and *not* disappointment, he dressed and made his way to the elevators. According to the time on his phone, it was past checkout time, which meant the hotel most likely already billed him for a second night. Maybe he could talk his way out of the extra charge. The place wasn't exactly cheap. It wasn't like he didn't have the funds, but he'd rather add that money to his yearly donations to the Wounded Warrior Project and Fallen Firefighters Foundation than waste it on another night's stay he wouldn't even be using.

Sliding his phone into his pocket, his fingers brushed over a scrap of lace. *Her red thong.* He forgot he'd stuck it in his pocket last night instead of tossing it with her bra and dress. Hopefully she hadn't been too distraught when she couldn't find it this morning. Either way, he wasn't sorry he had it. The thong was the only thing he had as proof that she wasn't merely a figment of his imagination, conjured up by his damaged psyche. He wasn't at *that* level of crazy yet. His soon-to-be shrink would be thrilled to hear it.

Erik approached the front desk in the lobby and asked the girl behind the counter to check the computer to see if he'd been charged for a second night.

"Oh, you're with Dr. Jones," she said, her face brightening. "No, it's okay. She came down and requested a late check-out time for you, so you're all good."

Dr. Jones… Was she talking about Livvie? "Great. Hey, I'm curious how you know her name, since I was the one who rented the room."

The girl, probably in her early twenties if that, blushed a little then pushed a business card forward. "When she came down I was just starting my shift after having a huge fight with my boyfriend. She saw me trying not to cry and when she asked if I was okay, I kinda broke down into a blubbering mess. Anyway, she offered me her card and told me that if I needed to talk, she'd do it pro bono. She was so sweet. Please thank her again for me."

Erik picked up the card and stared hard at the name, wondering why it sounded so familiar... Dr. O.J. Jones, PsyD... Then it dawned on him. *A cross between a breakfast drink and a character in* Raiders of the Lost Ark.

Holy shit. He'd just fucked his therapist.

# Chapter Five

"*Shit*, that's hot." Olivia set her steaming latte on her desk and gingerly touched her scalded upper lip.

"Uh, yeah," Cindi said in her *duh* tone. "That's how it is when I hand you a fresh cup. You know"—her pregnant pause birthed droll sarcasm—"like I do every morning."

Olivia adored her assistant, but at only twenty-two, Cindi rarely censored her sass, despite working in a professional environment at Boston Behavioral Health. Luckily, in front of the clients, she was the picture of professionalism and discretion.

Dr. Edward Marion—owner of the clinic, lead psychologist, and all-around old-school Marine—wasn't exactly a fan of the pink highlights streaking through Cindi's white-blond shoulder-length hair, or her colorful and bold attire (the girl had a high-heels collection that rivaled the Kardashians'). However, he recognized that although she might be a little unorthodox for her chosen career path as an assistant to a psychologist, Cindi was damn good at her job and great with their clients.

And Olivia also appreciated the young woman as a friend

and a breath of fresh air in a practice dominated by stuffy old men.

"Very funny," Olivia mumbled. "Can you grab me a piece of ice? That's all I need to start my craptastic Monday—a swollen lip."

"Sure thing, boss. But while I'm gone, you might want to think about why you're so damn distracted in the first place."

Olivia opened her mouth to argue, but Cindi was already out the door.

Which was probably good. She *had* been distracted, from the moment she'd snuck out of the hotel room and left behind the stunning man who'd made the earth move beneath her. She never imagined it could be like that. So passionate and raw. He'd torn down her walls, ripped away her defenses, and laid her bare with his crude words and rough handling.

And yet, not once had she ever felt unsafe. She'd known the second she laid eyes on him that, at his core, he was one of the good guys. A good guy nicknamed Wolf who was former or current military and quite possibly psychic and/or empathic.

Olivia huffed a sound of disgust as her forehead plunked into her open hands. Psychic or empathic? Really? She didn't work her ass off in college to come up with cockamamie answers like that. But how else did she explain how he seemed to know exactly what she needed?

He'd been so in-tune with her, like he had a window into her mind. He knew when she questioned her sanity or something made her uncomfortable. A lesser man might not have sensed that at all, and even if he did, he might have taken her discomfort at face value and stopped everything.

But he'd seen past that and somehow knew exactly when and how far he needed to push her to prevent her from getting in her own way. And he'd given her the beautiful gift of permission.

Permission to submit.

Not to him, but to her own hidden desires without the weight of her past and her guilt. He'd narrowed her world down to the several inches where their bodies merged. And then he'd blown her whole world apart in the most explosive and all-consuming orgasms of her entire life.

"Okay, I wrapped it in a paper towel so—"

Cindi stopped in the middle of Olivia's office and stared at her. Again, Olivia touched her lip. "Shit, is it that bad?"

"No, not at all." Snapping out of it, Cindi walked the rest of the way and handed her the wrapped ice cube. "It's a little red, but I doubt anyone will be staring at your lips close enough to notice."

"Then what was that look for?"

"Because the rest of you is red, too. Your face and neck are flushed like you've just been…" Cindi gasped. Dramatically. "Oh. My. *God*. Did you have—?"

"Shhh! Jesus, Cin, keep your voice down."

Perching on the edge of a guest chair, Cindi winced by way of apology then continued her interrogation in a much quieter voice. "Oh, you *so did*. Come on, give me all the deets."

Olivia pulled the ice away. Though it made her lip feel better while applied, she suspected there wasn't a need for it otherwise. Sighing, she unwrapped the cube and dropped it into her latte. She needed the caffeine pronto. "It's not a big deal, okay?"

"Not a big deal? You're kidding, right? Boss, you haven't even *dated* until very recently, and then you play hide the salami out of the blue? It's definitely a big deal. Have you been seeing a guy I don't know about?"

"No, no, it wasn't like that."

Olivia took a drink of her much cooler and slightly watered down latte to give her a moment to think. Her marriage to Brett was before she'd hired Cindi, but over time as her assistant became more of a friend, Olivia had confided in her, letting her into her personal life more than a typical employee.

She didn't want to share details about her time with Wolf, but swimming through hardening cement would be easier than avoiding telling her friend at least the basics. "You know that most of my dates have been disasters from the start, and the ones I'd hoped were promising failed as soon as anything physical came into play."

Cindi cringed, empathy lining her face. "Yeah, you haven't had the best luck." Then her face lit up. "But wait, you were going out with a new guy on Friday. The one who wanted you to drive out to the bar by his house—which frankly, I thought was kind of douchey, but he must've made up for it in the sack. Damn, I did *not* see that coming."

"Hell no, it wasn't with him. That guy *was* super douchey."

"Then *who*? I swear, if you don't spill in the next five seconds—"

"Okay, okay," she stage-whispered, holding her palms out to settle down her feisty assistant. Olivia cleared her throat and smoothed a hand over her hair, despite knowing not a hair was out of place. Totally opposite of what it looked like the morning after being with Wolf. It'd been mussed in that thoroughly sexed kind of way that announces your recent romp to the entire world. Thankfully, she'd managed to smooth it well enough on the elevator ride down. "It was…a guy I met at the liquor store."

Cindi's jaw unhinged and her eyes widened so much that the tips of her faux lashes touched her lids. Before she could hit her with a game of 20 Questions, Olivia rushed out, "I didn't plan it or anything. He helped me out when I realized I'd locked the keys in my car and we got to talking and one thing led to another which led to a hotel room. These things happen all the time, it wasn't a big deal. End of story."

"You—Olivia I-never-do-anything-not-scheduled-in-my-planner Jones—had a random, anonymous hookup?"

"I know, it was totally crazy, and I honestly can't believe I did it. But I did and now you know so let's just move on, okay?"

"Um, *no*. Not okay. You have to give me more than that. *What was he like?*" Cindi leaned forward and urged, "Come on, you have to tell me something."

"He was…" Squinting at the ceiling, she tried thinking of the right words to describe her experience with Wolf and found her extensive vocabulary lacking. "He was everything I needed, and yet nothing I expected."

"Don't give me that Confucius crap, Jones. Was he hot?"

"As the sun."

"Did he rock your world?"

Olivia bit the inside of her lip as a latent wave of the heat he'd infused in her crept into her cheeks. "Try, my universe."

"Ho-ly shit." Grinning like she'd just been given the key to a legendary secret stash of shoes, Cindi fanned herself with the notepad by the phone. "I'm so beyond proud of you, boss. This is amazing; I can't wait to meet this miracle worker. When are you going to see him again?"

Olivia's smile drained from her face. Putting herself back into work mode, she delicately cleared her throat as she needlessly straightened a stack of papers on her desk. "I'm not."

"What do you mean, you're not? Damn, did he skip out on you? What a prick. Figures, though. Men who rock entire universes never stick around long enough to appreciate the universes when they're no longer moving." Cindi huffed out a breath and slapped the notepad back to its rightful place in obvious disgust.

"Actually, I skipped out on him. I insisted it only be the one time and that neither of us exchange information. Not even our real names." Cindi looked like Olivia had spoken in Swahili. "I wasn't looking for someone to date, Cin. In fact, I'd sworn off dating minutes before meeting him. He was the perfect guy to jump-start my sexual battery, so to speak. But just like a dead car battery, once you jump it, you disconnect the cables from the power source and it'll continue running on its own. That's what he did for me—and it was great—but now it's over, and so is this conversation."

Olivia refused to acknowledge that small voice in her head (okay, it was way lower than that) begging to see Wolf again. But she'd gotten exactly what she wanted Friday night, and no matter how much she might want another universe-rocking night with him, she needed to give herself time to acclimate to this rediscovery of her sexual self before she even thought about seeing someone again, much less *Wolf*. Hence, her new commitment to remain uncommitted.

*No more dating for me for a* very *long time.*

The service bell that alerted Cindi to someone's presence in case she stepped away from her desk dinged in the reception area. Both women glanced at the clock on the wall. It was eight o'clock and time to start the day.

"Shit, that'll be your first client," Cindi whispered and bolted to her feet. "This convo is most certainly *not* over, missy. I'll get more out of you even if I have to spike your latté to loosen your tongue."

Olivia snorted and readjusted her glasses on the bridge of her nose. "Get thee to work, assistant."

Cindi passed through the doorway, but then stuck her head back in. "By the way, that battery thing was a horrible analogy."

Olivia stuck her tongue out at her and received the same in return before Cindi disappeared again, closing the door behind her. Olivia shook her head with a quiet chuckle as she prepared for her first appointment of the day.

She pulled up the file on her computer and scanned it

over as a quick refresh. Every Sunday she took the time to look over any new clients she had scheduled for that week. Before she met the client, she wanted to know as much as she could about him or her so she knew the best way to approach the session and whether the client had any violent tendencies she should be aware of.

> *Grady, Erik. Former army lieutenant. Served ten years with the 75th Ranger Regiment. Six tours of duty; Operation Iraqi Freedom. Awards and achievements include: Silver Star Medal for Valor 4th award, Bronze Star Medal 6th award, Purple Heart Medal 3rd award. Joint Service Commendation Medal, Army Commendation Medal, Joint Service Achievement Medal, Army Achievement Medal, Army Good Conduct Medal 3rd award. Honorably discharged after ten years of service. Currently a Boston firefighter and lieutenant of Rescue 2 company in District 9. Recent incident on the job triggered PTSD from his last tour in Iraq, and since has been showing signs of anxiety during calls and growing worse over time.*

Olivia both loved and hated these types of cases. Loved getting the chance to help veterans heal and find their way back to themselves, but hated that cases like this existed in the first place. She wished that when the men and women who served their country came home, all of the nightmares they endured stayed overseas and allowed them to find the peace they deserved.

"I promise I'll do everything I can for you, Lieutenant Grady," she said softly to the file on her laptop screen. She heard a few raps on her door, signaling Cindi was about to enter with the client. Olivia checked her desk and made some last-minute organizational adjustments…

More knocks sounded.

Drawing her brows together, she called out, "Yes, Cindi, you may come in."

*Again* with the knocking. What the hell? Olivia huffed a quick exhale. The day was not starting off well thus far. She hoped that changed soon because she simply wasn't up for the typical Monday Challenge this week. Pushing herself up, she strode to the door and pulled it open.

"Cindi, didn't you hear—" Olivia's heart stopped.

"Cindi's grabbing herself some coffee. Sweet kid," said the deep, rumbling voice that had haunted her for the last two days, "but I'm here for *you*."

Her voice barely registered as a whisper. *"Wolf?"*

She couldn't stop her traitorous gaze from inventorying the man in front of her. Thick-soled black work boots led to faded jeans topped by a threadbare Red Sox T-shirt that hugged his chest and stretched around his biceps. Leaning a shoulder against the doorway, thumbs hooked in his front pockets and one ankle crossed over the other, Olivia's worst nightmare and favorite fantasy leveled her with his penetrating stare and wicked grin.

"What's up, Doc?"

...

Jesus Christ. Erik was in trouble.

Until about sixty seconds ago, he'd convinced himself that he'd feel nothing more than he would for any acquaintance if he saw her again. That Livvie couldn't possibly be as sexy and beautiful as he remembered. That the way she pulled him in like the moon to the tide was something his mind conjured as a way of justifying the encounter. And pretty much the best sex of his life.

What a fucking idiot. She was even more stunning in her work getup than the sinful red dress from Friday. Golden hair sleeked back into a bun at the nape of her neck. Blue and black rectangular glasses framed her hazel eyes rimmed with thick black lashes. Crisp white button-down shirt opened at her throat and arrowed down to just shy of showing cleavage. And his favorite, a powder blue pencil skirt and mile-high heels highlighted her toned calves.

That didn't even consider what divine things she might be wearing underneath. *God, kill me now.* Death might be easier than trying to control his need to bunch that skirt around her waist and take her against the wall of windows across the room.

Erik let his eyes blatantly rove over her body as she'd just done to him. "Damn, you look good enough to eat." He paused and flicked his gaze up to meet hers. "Again."

Livvie shook her head slightly. "How did you find me?" She let out a soft curse. "You know what? It doesn't even matter. I told you I wanted my anonymity and privacy. I don't know how you got around it, but the fact that you didn't respect my wishes tells me all I need to know about you." Spinning on her heel, she dismissed him. "Don't let the door hit your ass on the way out. Or do, I don't care."

He watched her cross to her desk with graceful determination. Then she sat and pointedly ignored him. Erik grinned and stepped into the office, closing the door.

"I'd love to oblige you and leave"—*Not really*—"but I'm afraid I can't do that."

She pinned him with a glare and tight smile. "And *I'm* afraid I must insist or I'll be forced to call security to escort you from the building. I'm expecting a client at any moment."

"Correction, Doc. You're *speaking* to your client."

Her eyes opened wide. Pink lips parted to suck in a sharp breath. Creamy skin drained of color. Maybe it made him a sadistic son of a bitch, but shocking her was rather addictive. In the few minutes since she opened the door, his quick assessment from her reactions and her OCD orderly office showed him a different side of her from the other night. One that didn't appreciate her pristine feathers being ruffled. Which only made him want to ruffle them even more.

Friday night, he'd met her slightly insecure, innocent side. He'd be lying if he said he hadn't reveled in shocking her sexually. He'd never been with anyone like her, someone who he'd bet had only known the softer side of sex before that night, and he'd fed on making her wetter with every shock.

Holding her gaze, he ambled over to the chairs in front of her desk and took a seat. As he leaned back and got comfortable, he continued to study her like he would an enemy target. What made Dr. Olivia Jones tick? Her strengths, weaknesses? Habits and tendencies? Erik found himself wanting to learn everything about her. Past, present, and what she hoped for the future. He didn't want to settle for knowing about her. He wanted to know *her*, full stop.

That thought should have had him hauling ass out of the kill zone as he had in the past, but…

Saying that Livvie was different than any woman he'd been with was like saying Afghanistan was a little sandy and dry. She'd had him eating from her palm before they ever said a word to each other. She had no idea she held all the cards. Self-preservation demanded he make sure she never found out, either. Not to mention the guys. Erik would never live it down.

Screw the red flags. That couldn't have been more of a warning than if a grenade had landed at his feet. But instead of running for cover, he'd taken the chance that it might be faulty and stood his ground.

Wasn't the first time he'd been wrong.

*Least no one died this time.*

"If you are who you claim to be," she challenged, "then kindly tell me your name and reason for being here, *Wolf*."

Erik braced his elbows on his knees and leaned forward, his upper body nearly touching the edge of her desk. Livvie sat back in her chair and crossed her arms over her chest to hide her discomfort. Seemed she didn't like feeling out of control and unsure. *Not in the office, anyway.*

"Name's Lieutenant Erik Grady of BFD Rescue 2 and former lieutenant, Second Battalion Seventy-Fifth Ranger Regiment. I'm here because a computerized test said I can't go back to work until *you* say I can. Believe me yet?"

Her slender throat moved as she swallowed thickly, then she nodded. "Yes."

"The other night, I told you Wolf is my nickname. More accurately, it was my call sign. My entire team—Dozer, Smoke, Bowie, and Preacher—is retired army, so we communicate the same way we did in the service when we're out on calls and on the walkies."

"And you're Wolf, I'm assuming of the lone variety," she mused. "Did you pick your own call sign?"

"That's not how it works." Erik winked. "I'd be one arrogant sonofabitch, naming myself after a deadly predator."

A single pale eyebrow arched. "You may not have chosen that name, Lieutenant, but that has no bearing on whether you're an arrogant son of a bitch."

An easy laugh escaped his chest at her surprise dig. "Got me there, but something tells me you'd have no problems keeping me humble, Livvie."

For a split second, a smile broke across her face, and it was like stepping out into the sunlight after years in a cave. Then she composed herself, passing a huge cloud overhead, casting him back in the shadows. He didn't mind, though. He knew it couldn't stay there forever.

"Olivia," she rasped. "My friends call me Olivia." She cleared her throat and took a sip of her coffee, then carefully set it down with both hands before clasping them tightly on her desk. "And my *clients* call me Dr. Jones."

Dropping the tone of his voice, he imagined his words

rolling over her naked body. "The man who made you come so hard around him that he thought he'd died and found heaven, what does *he* call you?"

Erik heard the breath catch in her chest. He saw her pupils swallow the hazel of her irises. He blatantly let his gaze touch every inch of her he could see, reminding her of how his hands had done the same thing less than sixty hours ago.

Closing her eyes, she focused on regulating her breathing for a count of ten (he'd counted) and wondered if she taught her clients that technique. It seemed to work well enough for her. By the time she finished and regarded him again, she'd regained control over her body.

He'd be lying if he said that didn't both piss him off and turn him on at the same damn time.

"I don't care what *that man* chooses to call me," she said coolly. "It isn't my concern, because what I am to *him* is a woman in his past, and that's where I'll stay."

"Nice try, Doc. But even without the signed paperwork in my back pocket saying otherwise, I don't buy it."

Livvie's eyes narrowed. "Did you know who I was from the very beginning?" She laughed without a drop of humor and shook her head. "Of course you did. You're former military; you can find out whatever you want. Probably put a bug in my phone or whatever it's called and have a file with everything about me back to my preschool transcripts."

Erik hitched an eyebrow. *Someone's been watching too many spy movies.*

"I'm sorry to disappoint you, Lieutenant, but I don't accept bribes, no matter how good the currency."

Damn, he loved it when she got all formal with him. The more put together she was, the more he ached to mess her up and make her lose her ability to form coherent sentences, much less fancy-sounding ones.

Remembering how her ass moved under that skirt had

him half hard already. But now was not the time to cater to his dick. *Stand down, soldier.* Yeah, right. Like it'd ever listened to him before.

Ignoring his body's baser call, Erik studied the beautiful doctor. Her hackles were up for sure, but something else lingered in her eyes. Embarrassment? Hurt? This woman was such a mystery. Every time he started to think he understood her, she'd do or say something that kicked him back to square one. Fine by him. He loved a good challenge.

"What makes you say that I must have known who you were?"

She scoffed and rolled her eyes as though he'd asked the dumbest question ever. "Why the hell else would you have been so insistent we spend the night together? I was a hot mess who admitted to a slew of bad dates under my belt, which screams 'more trouble than I'm worth' to any guy just looking to score. But not you. You did everything but break out a damn PowerPoint to make your case."

"What are you saying, exactly?"

"You know damn well what I'm saying."

Erik wasn't sure if he should be pissed or amused at her insinuations, but he'd keep himself on an even keel until he figured it out. "Do me a favor and spell it out for me."

"Come on, give me a little credit. It's not like no one's tried convincing me to sign a completion form without going through the therapy before." She stood and walked to her wall of windows to pace in front of them. "Granted, they've always waited until our first visit before trying to seduce me with their so-called charms, but it never worked. Every one of them was met with the frigid psychologist who deflected their attempts, and before they knew it, they'd completely opened up because I'm damn good at my job.

"Oh, but not *you*, Lieutenant. No, *you* snuck in under the radar and used a lot more than just your charms to seduce me, and you used my vulnerability on a shitty night against me."

Erik clenched his jaw and gripped the arms of his chair so he didn't do something stupid, like grab her and spread her across her desk before showing her just how much trouble she was worth. The idea that she could ever think otherwise made him furious. Knowing a bunch of assholes had tried seducing her for their own benefit made him downright violent.

Not that he didn't understand their desperation to get out of talking about their personal hells and get back to their jobs. Erik understood that perfectly. But when someone is repeatedly valued for what she can do for others, rather than valued for who she is, eventually her self-worth is going to take a hit. And it sounded like she'd taken plenty.

With every step, Livvie became more agitated. Not how he wanted her feeling around him, now or ever. In her mind, though, he was the enemy. He could deny things until he was blue in the face, but she wouldn't hear a word of it. But maybe she'd listen to the man she was with in that hotel room.

Pitching his voice lower, he used the dominating tone he'd used that night with her. "Stop, Livvie."

She froze midturn in the corner, her back to him, slim shoulders rising and falling. Erik pushed himself out of the chair and moved to stand directly behind her while still keeping a single, torturous inch between their bodies. He wouldn't be the one to initiate contact. She'd need to surrender and obliterate what little space was left.

Her rose-petals-and-sunshine scent wreathed around his face and tested his control. If a woman's body emitted pheromones, hers were on some serious steroids. Like next-level shit, because it took every ounce of his control to not take her up against the glass until they both collapsed.

Then he remembered. If he didn't play this right, she'd shut down for good, and he would've failed them both. Denied them of what could potentially be the most memorable affair of their lives. *Or maybe something more.*

But even with his brain in the right place, his fingers itched to grab her hips, slide up her sides, and cup her breasts. To ensure they didn't, he braced his palms on the window, trapping her between his arms.

"I hate hearing you put yourself down, Livvie. I hate it, and I won't stand for it." His breath stirred the fine hairs at the nape of her neck. He swore he saw a shiver run through her, but it wasn't enough to melt the steel in her spine. "No one should be allowed to put you down. Not even you."

From his height advantage, Erik could see her nipples straining against the crisp cotton of her shirt. He wanted to suckle them through the material, leaving wet spots behind like an animal marking its territory. Biting back his wanton growl, he went on, knowing his deep voice would vibrate through her with every word.

"I was so insistent because from the moment our eyes locked in that liquor store, I wanted you more than my next breath. Then we started talking. You were clever and funny and this intoxicating mix of adorable and sexy, and suddenly wanting you wasn't enough. I needed to make you mine.

"Every sound you made that night drove me crazy. When you touched me, I felt like five times the man I am. My God, Livvie," he said, lightly tracing the soft shell of her ear with his nose. "The scent of your arousal literally brought me to my knees. The way you tasted on my tongue…*fuck*. I'd happily spend the rest of my days with my face between your legs.

"And restraining myself right now is proving impossible. You can take a look and see for yourself, the affect you have on me."

Slowly, she turned around in his arms, sticking close to the window, then dragged her eyes over his body until they landed on the bulge in his jeans. Her breath caught and she flicked her gaze up to his. A wolfish smile tugged at his lips.

"As much as I like to think I have control, truth is, he has a mind of his own. Can't fake that kind of reaction, Doc. It's all for you." He took a hand from the window and adjusted himself. "And it's damned uncomfortable."

Livvie tried unsuccessfully to stifle a chuckle behind her hands. It made him feel lighter. He wanted to bottle it and take it out any time the darkness threatened him. Mostly, though, he wanted to do whatever he could to keep that smile on her face and make her laugh as often as possible.

Clearing her throat, she composed herself, but the rigid tension from before was now missing. Small change, but he'd take it. "So what you're saying is that this was all just one incredibly insane coincidence?"

"I'm not saying that at all. I don't believe in coincidence, Livvie." Erik shook his head and pushed off the windows to take a step back. His control was slipping. "You can believe that if it makes you feel better, Doc. I prefer to think the universe is trying to tell us something."

Lifting her chin an inch, she crossed her arms over her chest and cocked a hip out to the side. Back on the defensive. "Odd. You don't strike me as the philosophically romantic type, Lieutenant."

Erik shrugged. "I'm not. But I've witnessed a lot of so-called 'coincidences.' Eventually, I realized it's nothing more than recognizing the signs for when things line up the way they're supposed to. A person can choose to ignore them, and a lot of the time they do. Given the opportunity, I choose to follow and see where they lead."

"Well, I follow rules and laws, which is why I can't treat you."

Erik had wondered how long it would take her to turn him away. He'd known she would. Treating a man who she'd had sex with was highly unethical and probably broke all sorts of rules.

"You'll have to see one of my colleagues," she continued. "Would you prefer to set up an appointment now or do it yourself later?"

"I'd prefer to stick with you, Doc."

That was a goddamn lie. The very idea of spilling his fucked-up mental guts to this woman made him want to violently spill his physical guts. He had no intention of keeping her as his shrink. He *did*, however, intend on trying to spend more time with her. As he suspected, after finding out her anonymity was blown, Livvie didn't want to give him the time of day, much less a date. If he wanted a chance at getting to know her better, he'd have to play just a tiny bit dirty.

"I told you, that's impossible."

"No," he said. "Ill-advised, maybe, but not impossible. The thing is, when the hotel clerk said your name the next morning and I realized you were my soon-to-be therapist, I checked out your colleagues over the weekend. The head honcho, Dr. Edward Marion, is pretty slick when it comes to his business. He has a standing contract with both Boston PD and FD, so any time a cop or firefighter gets messed up in the head, they get sent here. Right?"

"That's true, yes."

"And here at Boston Behavioral Health, there are five mental health doctors, all with different specialties: cognition, pediatric, forensic, substance abuse… And then there's your area of expertise and the reason I was assigned to you specifically: PTSD."

She bit down on her lower lip for a second. He could tell she hadn't expected him to know any of that. But her setback was fleeting. Squaring her shoulders, she said, "Also true, Lieutenant. But any of the doctors here—"

"I don't want any of the others, Livvie." He moved to invade her space, standing so close she had to tilt her head back. "I want you."

# Chapter Six

*This isn't happening, this isn't happening, this isn't happening...*

No matter how many times Olivia chanted the damn saying, the scene never changed. Nope, this was truly happening. Right here, right now.

The man who'd basically fucked her within an inch of her life was her new client.

The man she'd chosen to jump-start her sex drive stood no more than a few inches away, claiming he wanted her. (In what capacity wasn't as important as the fact he used the words "I want you." Pathetic, but there it was.)

Wolf—no, *Erik*—ghosted over her top lip with the tip of a blunt finger. "What happened here, gorgeous?"

Heat pooled in her belly at the use of the pet name he'd often used on her the other night. His gravelly voice made the innocent endearment sound downright lascivious. "I burned it on my latte." She hoped that didn't sound as lame as she suspected. It was almost as bad as the infamous "I carried a watermelon" line from *Dirty Dancing*.

"Need to be more careful with lips as priceless as these."

Erik's eyes lifted to hers with a grin. "But since the damage is done, it's only right that I kiss it and make it better."

She opened her mouth to tell him he could do no such thing, but as his face lowered to hers, the air caught in her chest and the words of protest refused to dislodge from her brain.

After what seemed an eternity, his lips touched down and hugged her top lip, enabling her to do the same to his full lower one. It was an embrace as much as it was a kiss. A statement of his confidence and a definite claiming, gentle though it was.

God, what was she doing? *Wrong, wrong, so very, very wrong.* Olivia placed her hands on his hard chest to push him away. But then the tip of his tongue traced the line of her burn, and she lost all her motor skills. He'd somehow weaponized his saliva with a paralyzing toxin. It was the only logical explanation for why she continued to let a client kiss her in her office. It didn't matter what message her brain sent to her limbs. Nothing moved.

Oh look, her fingers curled into his T-shirt. And her mouth opened so his tongue could sweep in and…yep, her tongue had no problems moving, either.

Well, good. The toxin theory was a bust. Yay for her. Except that meant she was participating in this…this…

Holy shit, the man kissed like she imagined he fought fires. Whether slow and methodical or fast and hungry, he never let up on the intensity. Like he wouldn't be satisfied until he knew, without a doubt, he'd won and made her completely his. And that couldn't happen. Not now, not later.

This time she *did* push him away and, though the brick wall of a man didn't have the decency to at least pretend that she could make him budge, she also managed to pull her head back enough to break the amazing, toe-curling, panty-melting kiss.

"Shit," she said, taking a healthy step back. "This can't—No. Just *no*. I will not go down this road with you."

Olivia marched back to her desk and plopped into her chair before grabbing a bottle of water from the bottom drawer of her desk. She needed a nice, stiff drink, but this would have to do for now. Cracking it open, she tipped it to her kiss-swollen lips and drank half of it in one shot. As she went through her mini organizing routine—something she did to help collect herself and bring her mind back to center—Erik sauntered over and reclaimed his seat in front of her desk.

"Lieutenant—"

"Erik."

How did he manage to make his name sound like a command? And why did her body react every damn time he used that voice? Sighing, she continued. "Erik. You're right; I do specialize in dealing with individuals struggling with PTSD. But fraternizing with a client is not only highly unethical, it's grounds for losing my practicing license. I read your file over the weekend, and please believe me when I say that I would be honored to help a hero such as yourself—"

"I'm no hero, babe."

Olivia blinked. Each of those words had been hurled at her like throwing knives that purposely missed her body by a hair, and only because it was meant as a warning. That wasn't the typical "I was just doing my job, ma'am" response that most soldiers gave. No, Erik had a real problem with anyone considering him a hero. It was an obvious wound and only made her want to help him that much more.

"Okay," she said, using her calm therapist voice. "I truly want to help you, Erik. I know how badly you want to get back to work with your brothers." Appreciation flickered in his eyes before he masked it. Yes, she understood that firefighters considered it a brotherhood just like any of the military branches. They respected all members whether they knew them or not, and the men and women they fought fires with were often bonded closer than blood siblings. She found the relationships beautiful in their unwavering loyalty. "But I can't be the one who helps you, that's all there is to it. I'm sorry."

He shifted in his chair again. "Let me ask you this. If I go to another shrink in the office, will you agree to see me?"

"See you?"

"Go out with me. You know, dates, dinners, dancing…"

"You dance?"

"Not even a little, but I had an alliteration thing going." He winked at her, and Olivia bit the inside of her cheek, trying to prevent the huge smile attempting to break free. Erik braced his elbows on his knees and leaned forward. "I'll always be 100 percent honest with you. After I tucked you in, I told myself that I had to do whatever it took to convince you to have breakfast with me the next morning and then do whatever it took to get you to agree to see me again. But we both know how that turned out."

A pang of guilt tightened Olivia's chest. She'd hated leaving like that, but she knew that if he so much as opened his eyes and looked at her, she'd throw all her rules out the window and do whatever he wanted. She'd thought of leaving a note, but what's the appropriate thing to say in a situation like that? Hallmark could probably make a killing if they started a "Morning After" line. *Thanks so much; you were great. I enjoyed not having to masturbate.* Okay, so maybe she wasn't the right woman for the job of "clever rhyme writer," but there was definitely an untapped market there.

Erik drilled her with a heated look. "Livvie, I haven't stopped thinking of you since I woke up in that bed alone. I'd like to think I wasn't all that easy to forget, either. Why not see where things go?"

"I can't," she rasped. "Even if you see another doctor, I

can't. It was only supposed to be one time and then we'd never see each other again. I'm not ready for..." *You*, she mentally tacked on, but she said a different word entirely. "More."

Erik leaned back in the chair and studied her through slightly narrowed eyes. It felt as though he had X-ray vision and could see inside her head. All he had to do was move things around with his mind, and he'd know exactly how she worked. Usually, *she* was the one doing that to people in this room. Now she knew why some of her clients fidgeted under her gaze.

Running a hand over his jaw, he said, "Okay, renegotiation."

She sighed. "Erik, you can't *re*negotiate when there was no negotiating to begin with."

"I'll agree to see another shrink if you can get Dr. Marion to see me. Out of everyone here, he's the only one I'll feel comfortable with. He's at least former military."

Olivia released a long, shuddering sigh. At last, the stubborn man had come to his senses, and Marion would take him on for her. She was relieved, of course. The twinges in her chest were likely a slight case of heartburn, because they certainly weren't ones of regret that she'd managed to convince him to back off. "That's perfectly understandable. I can take you over there now, if you like. Dr. Marion never sees clients before ten a.m., so I can make the introductions and hand you off to him."

"Not so fast," he said as she started to rise from her seat. Deflated, she dropped back down and waited for him to continue with his terms. "Since I'm agreeing to something for you, I think it's only fair that you give me at least a chance to get something I want in return."

"What do you mean 'a chance'?"

"If you won't agree to go on a date with me, then I'm willing to gamble for it. After the introductions, I'll ask Dr. Marion flat-out if he thinks you should see me in a dating capacity. If he does, you agree to no less than three dates of my choosing. I promise to keep them in public, and we'll start from a clean slate with no expectations. However, if he doesn't think you should, I promise to never bother you again."

"What in the world would make you think Dr. Marion would agree to something like that?" she asked, reaching for the bottle of water.

One muscled shoulder lifted in a noncommittal shrug. "I could say that I'm hoping he'll take my side out of sympathy as a fellow man. You know, Bro Code and whatnot."

Olivia almost choked on her sip of water. The idea of the sixty-four-year-old man doing anything for the sake of the "Bro Code" was laughable. But then, she knew Dr. Edward J. Marion better than almost anyone. Outside of the office, he was Uncle Eddie, her father's lifelong friend and Olivia's godfather. The man was as fiercely protective of her as he was with his own daughters.

"But if you want the truth," he continued, piercing her with his whiskey-colored eyes, "like I mentioned earlier, I'm betting this thing you call coincidence is bringing us together for a reason. And if that's true, then I also have to believe the good doctor will rule in my favor."

Olivia chewed on the corner of her bottom lip. She felt bad about dashing his romantic notions—especially since Erik's opinion of the cosmos playing matchmaker between *her* and a *man like him* made things flutter wildly in her belly—but her guilty conscience wouldn't change the outcome. There was no way Uncle Eddie would encourage her to date someone he didn't know and who was about to be treated for symptoms of PTSD.

She tapped a fingernail repeatedly on the wood surface of her desk as she studied him. He wore his brave front like a Kevlar vest that could protect him from anyone getting in. But body armor—whether literal or metaphorical—could only protect a man so much. It still left him with plenty of vulnerable areas. Areas she was trained to recognize and expose with slow and subtle guidance. To break him down so he could then build himself back up, stronger than before.

Olivia had been too preoccupied with her own series-of-unfortunate-events Friday night to notice his suffering. Even now, when she knew for a fact that he was haunted by his past, he did a damn good job disguising it behind his confidence and male bravado. Better than most. And like what was typical for first responders or those in the military, he kept his demons at bay by using his compulsions to help and protect others.

Though she didn't doubt it was desire and chemistry that initially drove Erik to pursue her, he'd been sincere when he told her he'd do whatever she wanted, give her whatever she needed. And not because it posed a challenge or inflated his ego, but because underneath the base and primal drive for sex…he cared.

The need to help others was simply a part of who Erik was. He saved people. For a few short hours, he'd saved her from herself. And now she had the opportunity to save him back.

If that meant turning him over to Eddie so his sessions wouldn't be clouded by the indomitable sexual tension radiating between her and Erik, then all the better. Because bottom line: she didn't trust herself around Lieutenant Erik Grady.

Decision made, she pushed up from her seat and walked around the desk. By the time she reached him, he'd stood as well. With her heels on, her eyes lined up with that delectable mouth of his, which was why she made sure to keep her gaze strictly on his whiskey eyes. Not that those tempted her any less. *Damn him.*

He arched a brow in question. "Doc?"

Right, yes. Saying things. Fabulous idea. Lifting her chin,

she cleared her throat and did just that. "I agree to your terms. I'll get Dr. Marion to see you as a client."

"And?"

"And," she added reluctantly, "if by some miracle he agrees to your ridiculous condition, I'll go on your requested three *public* dates." His lips curved into a smug grin, which irritated her just enough to add, "But *I'll* be the one to ask him the dating question, not you."

"I can live with that," he said with an arm sweeping toward the door. "After you."

Squaring her shoulders, she led Erik out of her office, past the desk of a very intrigued (read: salivating for details) Cindi, to the other side of the suite. "Good morning, Ruth," she said to the woman sitting at a large desk covered in framed photos of her kids and grandkids. Ruth had been Uncle Eddie's assistant for as long as Olivia could remember. He teasingly called her his office wife. Ruth was like a Boston version of a typical Southern grandma: the friendliest, warmest woman, who loved spoiling everyone in the office—and their diets— with her blue ribbon–worthy baking.

"Well, good morning to you, Dr. Jones." Ruth's gaze flitted quickly to Erik and back. Olivia could almost see the kernel of mischief blooming in the woman's eyes. Shit. "Why, don't you look especially beautiful today," she said with all the subtlety of a jackhammer.

"I told her that very thing, Ruth."

The rosy-cheeked woman held a hand against her heart and inhaled dramatically. "You did?"

Erik gave her a wink and a wide smile. "Technically, I said she looked good enou—"

"Ruth, is Dr. Marion available?" Olivia interrupted, ignoring the man chuckling next to her.

"Of course, dear. Go on in."

After rapping a few times on the door, Olivia let herself in and closed it after Erik joined her. Her uncle was seated at his massive desk, reviewing papers in front of him. She cleared her throat, and he raised his head. The indulgent smile and familiar greeting he always had for her stalled the second he noticed Erik at her side. Curiosity danced in his pale blue eyes as he removed his reading glasses.

"Ah, good morning, Dr. Jones. To what do I owe this early pleasure?"

"Good morning, Dr. Marion. I have a bit of an issue I need your help with. This is—"

"Lieutenant Erik Grady," her godfather said as he stood and they shook hands. "Good to see you, son. How are you?"

"Very well, sir, thank you."

Olivia closed her gawping mouth. "You two know each other?"

Uncle Eddie walked around to the front of his desk. "I've been good friends with Bill Marshall, his fire chief, for twenty years. I've met the lieutenant several times while visiting Bill at the station. Upstanding young man and a hell of a leader to his men."

"Thank you, sir."

She couldn't believe her ears. Erik had led her to believe she had the upper hand, and now she learned that he might as well be golfing buddies with her uncle.

"So what can I do for you, Lieutenant?" Eddie asks, sliding his hands into his pockets.

Olivia took back control over the conversation. "He's been placed on temporary leave due to symptoms of PTSD from past tours overseas and it's interfering with his performance on the job. His case has been assigned to me."

"I'm sorry to hear that," Uncle Eddie said to Erik solemnly. "I didn't know you were former military, son. What unit?"

"Second Ranger Bat., sir."

Eddie nodded. "I'm a Marine corps major myself. First Battalion, Third Marines. Served in Saudi Arabia and Kuwait for Desert Shield and Desert Storm. What you're going through is perfectly normal."

"Logically speaking, sir, I know that. It's the ranger in me that refuses to acknowledge that fact."

The man nodded. "I understand." Then he turned his attention back to Olivia. "What can I help you with?"

"I need you to take his case."

Eddie raised a brow in her direction, and since she'd known the man her entire life, Olivia knew exactly what that subtle arch said—*What in the hell are you doing discussing this in front of the client?*—and she deserved every bit of that scrutiny. Under normal circumstances, she would have waited to have a private discussion with her uncle about Erik's case, then followed up with Erik after they'd made a decision about his treatment. Not only was this approach highly unorthodox, it was completely unprofessional. But, desperate times and all that.

She pushed forward before he gave her his *wait till I tell your father* look. Not that she'd seen that one since she was a kid, but Olivia didn't doubt he still had it in his arsenal. "This past weekend, before either of us knew the other, we met in a social capacity. Professionalism dictates that I give him to someone with whom he has had no prior connections."

Olivia refused to look over at Erik, but she didn't need to. From the corner of her eye, she saw him standing with his feet braced apart and his muscular arms crossed over his chest, and she could *feel* his cocky half smile from way over here. Eddie's gaze bounced between them.

"Let me make sure I understand this," the older man said, rounding his desk to sit down again. "The two of you met each other over the weekend in a social setting of some kind, and now you're not comfortable treating him for his PTSD?"

"To be frank, sir," Erik said, "we hooked up."

Olivia gasped, her head whipping to the side to stare at him in utter shock. He didn't... He *wouldn't*...

Eddie sat in his worn leather chair and rocked back into a reclined position.

*"Lieutenant,"* she warned through a clenched jaw.

Erik acted like she wasn't even there. "We kept it anonymous, and it was only supposed to be a one-night thing—her rules, by the way, not mine—but now here we are, two days later, hooking up again."

"We are *not* hooking up again," she sputtered.

At last, Erik met her gaze, smug grin still in place. "Well, not in the same sense, but I told you my thoughts on the matter. Fate is trying to tell us something." Tossing her a quick wink, he turned his attention back to her uncle. "At any rate, Major, Dr. Jones has agreed to my condition of letting her pass me off onto someone else for therapy."

Olivia knew her face had to be ten shades of red from Erik's brazen comments, made worse by the fact that a sudden coughing fit attacked her godfather, no doubt to cover his barks of laughter.

"And what exactly is this condition," Eddie asked after he'd calmed down.

"Good question, sir, but I'm afraid *her* condition was that she be the one to discuss it with you." Erik looked at Olivia and gestured his upturned hand in Eddie's direction. "Floor's all yours, Doc."

She glared at him with what she hoped were missiles shooting from her eyes, then did her best to compose herself. His childish antics didn't matter, because this was where she pulled ahead and won this whole mess. As soon as she told Uncle Eddie Erik's ludicrous idea of her going on three dates with him, this nonsense would finally end.

Clearing her throat as delicately as possible, she faced the man she'd known her entire life. "For the record, Lieutenant Grady has *greatly* exaggerated what happened between us Friday night. That being said, now that our identities are no longer anonymous, the lieutenant wants to pursue things further. I turned him down, of course, because I'm not looking to date anyone."

"You're not?" her uncle asked in that way that said he disagreed and wanted you to rethink your statement. She *hated* it when he did that. And anyway, what the hell? She hadn't made her pathetic attempts at dating known to him yet. As far as he knew, she still wasn't ready to move on.

"No," she emphasized. "I'm not. Last weekend was a one-off, an experiment of sorts, and one in futility at that." Erik dramatically cleared his throat. Olivia sighed and rolled her eyes. "However, I've agreed to go on three dates with him if…" Damn it, she couldn't believe she was about to say this. "If you agree that I should. Now—"

"Absolutely."

Olivia froze. "Excuse me?"

"I said absolutely. I think it's a fantastic idea. Even if it's going to a Sox game or one of those music festivals you young people like going to. And even if nothing comes of the dates romantically, at least you'll have gone somewhere other than the office."

She tried to come back with something witty and disproving—without revealing the truth—but all that came out was, "I go other places. How do you think I get groceries?" *It's official. My life is pathetic and has been proven as such in front of the sexiest man on the planet who's already on* extremely *intimate terms with my vagina. Where's a good coma when you need one?*

"Don't worry, Dr. Jones," Eddie said. "You'll be in good hands with the lieutenant here. I'm sure he wouldn't act as anything less than the perfect gentleman, isn't that right, son?"

"Oh, yes, sir," Erik said with amusement tugging on just the one corner of his mouth. God, why did that hint of smugness have to be so damn sexy? "She's fond of rules and boundaries, and I promise not to cross a single one." His head swiveled to pin her with his golden gaze. "Not until she asks me to."

The phone buzzed and Ruth's voice came through, informing Uncle Eddie that his wife needed a minute of his time for an urgent question. He instructed Ruth to put the call through and excused himself. "This will only take a minute."

As soon as her uncle had the phone receiver to his ear, Olivia whispered to the huge man standing next to her, but she kept her eyes forward. "'Not until she asks me to'?" She scoffed. "I'd advise you not to hold your breath, Lieutenant."

"Wouldn't dream of it, Doc." He chuckled softly. Then he leaned over so his words tickled her ear as they slid inside and shot straight to her sex. "The only breath I'll be paying attention to is yours, Livvie. I'll be watching, waiting for it to get shallow and heave those beautiful breasts, telling me you want me. Just. Like. Now."

Cue sharp intake of breath. *Fuck, fuck, fuckity* fuck*!* She might as well hand over her body on a silver platter. What was wrong with her? It was like the man shorted out the power to her control center every time he got near. He was like the fricking Vagina Whisperer.

Aggravated with herself for not staying in control around him, and yet frustrated as hell because a big part of her that she'd rather not acknowledge wanted to do nothing but cede her control to him, Olivia spun on the balls of her shoes and strode out of Eddie's office.

"Hey, where're you going?"

She knew it was too much to ask that he stay behind. "To work," she said without breaking stride or giving him the satisfaction of making eye contact. "You got your answer, so there's no reason to loiter in Dr. Marion's office. You need to go back and schedule an appointment, though, so you should probably do that."

Cindi looked up from her desk as they approached at the speed of professional mall walkers. "Oh, you're back. I have a client on the line one who…" Olivia felt Cindi's eyes follow her as she kept right on going, heading for the women's restroom. He wouldn't be able to follow her in *there*. Then maybe he'd go away and stop tempting her to beg him to finally fuck her already.

With both hands, Olivia pushed open the swinging door and made her way to the long vanity of sinks. She didn't even get as far as turning a faucet on before Erik was at her side. "You can't be in here. It's the ladies' room, for shit's sake, Erik."

"I like it when you say my name, Livvie. My real name." He stepped into her space, dominating her little bubble in the world.

Seconds. That's how long she had left before her resolve to stay professional and unaffected crumbled into dust. "Please," she whispered, her eyes beseeching him for a reprieve she didn't entirely want. "I need some space. Some time to process and catch my brain up to the present, because I think it's still in shock from seeing you walk through my door." His eyes softened, the predatory glint no longer threatening her. Or exciting her. *Shit, make up your damn mind, Olivia!* "You may not know this, but you have a very…overwhelming way about you, and it's just a little much for me right now. Okay? So you win on all counts. Congratulations. Now will you *please* just go."

Olivia forced herself to shut up. There was only so much pleading she'd allow herself, even for him. Erik reached up to stroke the backs of his knuckles down her cheek as he studied her, a myriad of things he wasn't saying flashing in those amber pools.

"I'll dial back my more...*overwhelming*," he said, emphasizing her description of him, "traits for now. Don't mistake it for anything other than respecting your wishes. It won't mean that my interest in you has diminished. But after I walk out of here, I promise to back off the heavy stuff, as long as you promise that eventually you'll come around and honor your part. I want those dates, Livvie. I want a chance with you. Deal?"

She nodded, unblinking, for fear she'd miss a moment of the desire so plain on his face. Desire for *her*. His voice rumbled through her as he grasped her hand and lifted it to his lips to place a warm kiss on the inside of her palm.

"Until next time, Livvie."

She didn't move, didn't even breathe, as he gave her a smile that promised she'd be thinking about him later while giving her vibrator a workout. He had her so dazed that it wasn't until he left the bathroom that she realized he'd tucked something into her hand before walking away.

Turning it over, she opened her fingers and felt her cheeks flush bright red. The same color as her missing thong, now crumpled in her palm... *How inhaling your scent makes me instantly hard.* "You're in big trouble, missy," she informed her reflection. "Big, big trouble."

# Chapter Seven

It'd been all of five hours before Erik tried taking advantage of the deal Olivia had agreed to in her godfather's office. He'd called her work line, which always rang at her assistant's desk first unless Cindi was absent. The short beep on Olivia's phone preceded Cindi's voice coming through the intercom speaker.

"Hey, boss, there's a hot fireman on line one."

Olivia's hand stuttered on the legal pad where she'd been taking notes, making her scribble mid-word. She grimaced at the mark, hating how it ruined the neatness of the entire page. A fitting metaphor for the man now disrupting her orderly world.

She sighed and set her pen down. "Forward him to Ruth, Cindi. I told you he's Ed's client now."

"Yes, I know, but he wants to speak with *you*."

Olivia snorted. "I just bet he does," she mumbled.

Too bad *she* didn't want to speak with *him*. Not after the humiliation she had suffered at his blunt statements to Eddie about their recent history. Nope, she had no desire to talk to him today, and the near future wasn't looking too promising, either.

Her spine snapped straight as an idea came to her. Maybe if she kept putting him off, he'd give up. Not that she planned on reneging on her end of the deal, but if the man decided he had better fish to fry, Olivia couldn't be blamed for that.

Surely no "piece of ass" was worth so much effort for a sex god like Erik Grady. Even he had to know that his theory of fate giving them signs was flimsy at best and a total bullshit line at worst. Right now, she held his interest because she hadn't thrown herself at him upon their second meeting, but Olivia knew the challenge would thrill him for only so long. She wasn't the type of woman who inspired men to wage wars or even cross a room. Helen of Troy, she was not. She gave it a week before he moved on.

"Put him to my voicemail," she told Cindi. "And I mean every time he calls. He's not my client, and I don't accept personal calls at work."

"What? Since wh—"

*"Cindi."*

"Okay, got it." After a short pause, Cindi said, "I'm guessing you don't want me giving him your cell number, either."

"You guessed correctly."

Cindi's frustrated sigh came through loud and clear. "As your assistant, I say, 'Aye-aye, Captain.'"

Olivia lowered her eyes to the speaker as though Cindi lived in the base of her phone like a sassy genie in a speaker box. "But as my friend?" she asked ruefully.

Though the words were probably meant to be harsh, Cindi's tone was more gentle than the tough love she was going for. "As your friend, I say you're a complete idiot."

The beep signaled the end of the connection and about thirty seconds later, the voicemail indicator lit up. She forced herself to ignore it as she finished her paperwork for the day, but it hadn't been easy. The incessant blinking was about as nonintrusive as a glaucoma test at the optometrist.

When she was satisfied that everything was ready for the next day, she grabbed her things and strode across her office. Olivia made it all the way to the door before stopping, her hand on the knob as the memory of that damn blinking light taunted her from behind.

"Don't do it, Olivia. Don't fall down the rabbit hole," she warned herself.

She lasted all of five seconds before huffing in defeat and returning to listen to whatever it was Erik had to say. When the automated voice announced that she had three new messages, her stomach flipped. That couldn't be good, could it? Pressing the button, she braced herself to hear Erik's deep voice.

Beeeeep.

*"Hey, Doc. I was hoping to get your cell, but Cindi's not allowed to give it out, and you must be with a client. My number is 617-555-2469. Shoot me a text so I can save you in my contacts."*

Beeeeep.

*"Me again. I forgot to tell you how incredibly beautiful you looked today. I suddenly have a thing for glasses and pencil skirts. I didn't think it was possible for you to be any sexier than you were the night we met. I was wrong. Later, gorgeous."*

Beeeeep.

*"Fun fact. My senior year of high school I was voted Most Likely to Date a Woman Named Olivia, and I refuse to show up to the next reunion a failure. Have a good night, Doc. Be talkin' to you soon."*

Dear God, the man was a nuisance. *A sexy, dominant, giver-of-mind-blowing-orgasms* nuisance. "Shit, I'm so screwed."

Later that evening, as she sat curled up on her couch with her cats, Ben and Jerrys, enjoying a bowl of Chunky Monkey and a glass of wine (because she was classy like that) while binge-streaming *Arrow* on Netflix (because maybe his abs reminded her of a certain firefighter's), her phone chimed with an email notification. Most likely an office memo, but she had to make sure it wasn't one of her clients.

Keeping her eyes glued to a shirtless Stephen Amell on the salmon ladder, she absently swiped her phone screen to bring up her email app and then paused the show before glancing down at her inbox. "Oh crap," she grumbled. Now she *wished* it'd been a simple office memo. Instead, she stared at the name of a very persistent suitor with the subject line reading "Mistake."

What was a mistake? His attempt at keeping her as his therapist? The request for the dates? Her brows scrunched together as she bit down on her lip. *The night we spent together?*

That one word could mean so many different things, and not one of them gave her the warm fuzzies she told herself they should. Downing the last of her wine, she set the glass on the end table and thumbed the email open with all the enthusiasm of a bomb expert cutting one of several red wires.

*From: Grady, Erik*
*Subject: Mistake*

*Doc,*

*Your assistant seems to think you don't want to take my calls, but I'm sure what you said is that you can't wait to take my calls. Honest mistake, really. Please don't fire her on my account.*

*Talk to you tomorrow,*

*E*

Groaning in frustration, Olivia buried her face in a throw pillow and let her body fall to the side, displacing her sleeping cats from their spots on the couch.

The next two weeks passed with more of the same, with him leaving a few messages every day in varying forms: voicemail, email, and even leaving messages with Cindi to pass along. However, he'd stopped insisting that Olivia didn't mean to avoid him and instead talked about all things random. It was like giving her snippets of some imaginary conversation of inane topics going on between them.

Wednesday, he'd left a voicemail.

*"Hey, it's me. Did you catch the game? I'm originally from Georgia, so I grew up rooting for the Braves, but you can't live in this town for long without converting to the Mandatory Religious Order of the Red Sox. It was a great game until they got robbed in the eighth from that shit call by the blind-as-a-bat ump. Anyway, I hope your Hump Day is going well. No, scratch that. The only reason I want any humping going well for you is if I'm involved. With that in mind, the day's still young and I'm available for house calls. Later, Livvie."*

Monday morning she'd received an email.

*From: Grady, Erik*
*Subject: Crime Scene Spaghetti*

*Doc,*

*I'm writing to inform you of your involvement in a cooking catastrophe. Turns out I haven't been getting a lot of sleep lately due to the hours I spend staring helplessly at my cell, waiting for you to take pity on a desperate man and contact me about our pending dates.*

*Yesterday, it was my turn to host the game-day dinner, which means the guys expect me to make my mom's famous homemade spaghetti. It's not difficult, but the sauce needs to simmer with the Italian sausage for several hours, requiring a close watch and frequent stirring.*

*However, my recent bouts of insomnia—again, just a reminder that you are the reason for said bouts—caused me to fall asleep at the kitchen table. When I didn't wake up to their knocks, Dozer used his key, and I woke up to the guys shouting and shaking me like a CPR dummy.*

*Confused, I looked around to find myself and my kitchen covered in a red spray pattern that would give the BPD's CSI unit a serious hard-on. Unfortunately, the men of BFD's Rescue 2 company weren't nearly as amused. I got the feeling they were more upset about the ruined state of dinner than if I'd actually been the vic of a brutal crime. But don't worry, I took the blame, so you're in the clear.*

*Have a good day, gorgeous.*

*E*

She'd almost choked on her coffee from trying to hold in her laughter and had to break out the emergency outfit she kept in her office closet on the off chance (frequent occasion) she spilled something on herself during the day. She fully intended on sending him the dry-cleaning bill. Probably. Maybe.

But those instances were highly innocuous compared to the ones he saved for her assistant. Several days after the spaghetti email, Olivia walked into the office and stopped by her friend's desk like she did every morning. "Good morning, Cin. Anything for me?"

"Morning, boss, and yes," Cindi said, picking up the pink pad for taking messages. As she relayed each one, she tore off the note and handed it to Olivia. "Mr. Kramer's wife called and said he won't be making it to his appointment today due to a nasty case of the flu. Ms. Esperanza would like to know if you can authorize a refill on her scrip. And Lieutenant Grady wanted you to know that he liked the red but, for future reference, thinks pale blue would be even more stunning."

Olivia froze and gasped. "No. He. Did. Not," she whispered, emphasizing each syllable like rapid strikes of a hammer on a nail.

"Oh yes. He. Did." Olivia glared at Cindi for mimicking her with the addition of a wide smile and mischief shining in her eyes. The cool look didn't faze her assistant in the least as she propped her chin in her hands and asked, "What's he talking about? Is it underwear? It sounds like he's talking about underwear." Cindi clasped her hands together and gazed up at the ceiling. "*Please God*, let him be talking about her underwear."

Snatching the message away, Olivia tried to hide the smile at her friend's antics with a scowl. "You're completely off your rocker, you know that? Maybe you should make an appointment for yourself. Employees get a discount."

"Sweetheart, if seeing a shrink meant getting ordered to date one of the hottest men in New England, you can bet your ass I'd be having daily sessions. *Only you* seem to think it's a fate worse than death."

"Then I guess that makes *me* the smart one," she said before closing herself in her office.

Sitting at her desk, she clicked open her email and started a new message.

*To: Grady, Erik*
*Subject: My panties*
*Dear Lieutenant Grady…*

...

Erik rolled his shoulders and took a fortifying sip of the fire station coffee the men depended on to keep them running just as sure as The Animal—the name of Rescue 2's rig—ran on diesel. He'd finally finished the mound of paperwork that Dozer had let pile up and then suckered Erik into doing for him. At least that's what he let Dozer think. Truth was, Erik felt so useless without his job that he was grateful for the chance to sink into the tedious task.

Now that he was done, he planned on getting in a workout with the guys, and hopefully no calls would come in until after he left the station. Any time the tones sounded, it dumped a pound of salt into his suspension wound. Inactive wasn't a good look on him, and it threatened his sanity to watch his brothers suit up and ride out without him.

Just as he stood from his desk, his office phone rang, the caller ID showing his parents' number. Erik muttered a curse as he wondered if he should answer or check the voicemail later. He'd been avoiding calls from home, or making them as short and sweet as possible, to prevent his mother from sniffing out what she would consider problems that needed solving. Like him being suspended.

Norma Grady was like a bloodhound when it came to her children. No matter how hard he, his brother, and two sisters tried burying any issues they had growing up, their mother saw right through their bullshit and kept at them until she dug it all up.

Tom Grady, on the other hand, left the digging to his wife and then stepped in afterward to offer unsolicited advice on how to deal with things like a man—even when talking to Erik's sisters. Force of habit as a former ranger. The only saving grace he and his siblings had was that their mom wasn't as effective over the phone. Her talent was all in the eyes. They saw *everything*.

Sending up a silent prayer he could make this quick and painless, Erik punched the speaker button and braced his hands on the desk. "Hey, Mom, how's it going?"

"Don't you 'hey, Mom' me, Erik Nathanial," she scolded, her strong Georgian accent warming him despite the chill in her voice. "You should start out by apologizing for not speaking to your mother on a more regular basis. If I didn't know better, I'd say you were dodging me."

Erik winced. As the youngest, he'd always had a special bond with his mom, and though he hated doing it, he knew how to exploit it when it served him. Justifying his reasons by promising himself that he'd find a way to make it up to her, he let his now nonexistent native accent slip into his speech. "Come on now, Momma, you know you're the last person I'd ever wanna dodge." *Truth. But* wanting *didn't equate to* doing. "I'm sorry I've been so scarce lately; I've just been keeping real busy here, but I plan on coming down for a nice, long visit just as soon as I can get away. I miss you lots, and Pop, too."

"That's because you know what's good for you," she said, her smile evident in her voice. "Oh, speak of the devil, your father just walked in the door. Let me get him."

"Actually, I—"

Norma didn't hear his protest because she was too busy yelling across the house for her husband to pick up the phone in the kitchen. He sighed, knowing there was no way out of the parental tag team conversation about to happen. Raucous chatter echoed in the hall outside his office a few seconds before his crew barged in without so much as a knock.

"Come on, Wolf, let's go. Time to get in some PT before

we hit up the PC," Smoke said as he leaned against the back wall, then made a show of grabbing his junk, "'cause I got women wantin' my special gift of TLC."

"Sounds nice, Edgar Allen Smoke." Preacher dropped his tall and lanky frame into one of the guest chairs and propped his crossed ankles on the desk, despite the glare of disapproval from Erik. "But I think the acronym you're looking for is *STD*."

Bowie, who'd taken up residence in the other chair, fist-bumped Preacher, and the men laughed and jeered in easy camaraderie for a few seconds before Dozer flung the shit in Erik's direction. "How 'bout it, Grady? You coming to Phoenix Club tonight or is your dick still broken?"

Erik opened his mouth to retaliate, but his mother beat him to it. Too bad for Dozer, his gravel-rough voice was so distinctive. "Gavin! I'm not sure whether to blast you for your language or the inference that my son's equipment is faulty."

Four sets of wide eyes whipped to the phone's speaker box, and Erik couldn't keep his laugh at bay. Dozer leveled him with a *fuck you* glare and matching hand signal as he responded to the woman who'd treated him like one of her own for more than fifteen years. "My apologies, Mrs. Grady. Had I known you were on the line, I would have curbed my tongue."

"Damn straight, you would have," she said. "Are all the boys there? It's been forever since Tom and I've heard from y'all."

"Yes, ma'am, they are."

As Smoke, Bowie, and Preacher offered hellos to his mother and answered her questions, Erik noticed his cell's screen light up with an email notification. Seeing the name he'd given her pop up had his face splitting into a wide grin.

Tuning out the others, he quickly swiped into the message, unable to wait a second longer to see what she had to say.

*From: Sexy Livvie*
*Subject: My panties*

*Dear Lieutenant Grady,*

*The next time you leave a message with my assistant like the one this morning about my panties, I will "accidentally" dial the wrong extension and leave a voicemail on Chief Marshall's phone expressing my joy in discovering that you love wearing sexy lingerie every bit as much as I do. Then I'll sign off by confirming our weekend plans for the Victoria's Secret shopping spree you suggested.*

*Respectfully,*

*O*

*P.S. I'm reluctantly including my cell number so that I may reclaim my inbox for work purposes. Please use sparingly.*

Erik chuckled as he lowered himself into his chair again and opened a new text message. Remnants of the man he was only a few weeks ago tried suppressing the elation swelling in his chest, calling his strong reaction to a mere email from a woman unnatural and dangerous, but it didn't stop his fingers from flying across the keys as he responded.

*Does this mean you'll finally commit to our first date if it's a trip to VS? I'm very OK with this plan.*

"*Erik.*"

The booming voice of his father snapped Erik to attention like a drill sergeant to a private. "Yes, sir, I'm here. How are you, Pop?"

"How *am* I?" The old man grunted. "I get heartburn

if I even catch a whiff of acidic foods, my knees seize up at the smallest hint of rain, I can't shit for a week unless I force muffins that taste like sawdust down my gullet, and yesterday a proctologist got so intimate with my prostate I made him buy it dinner afterward."

A gasp came through the phone loud enough to hear over Erik and the guys as they practically doubled over in laughter. "Thomas Grady, that's more information than anyone outside this house needs to know," his mom scolded. "A simple 'I'm fine' would have sufficed."

"The boy asked a question, Norma, and I answered…"

Erik's phone vibrated in his hand. Keeping one ear on the conversation, he glanced down at her response.

*Your talent for selective "hearing" is astonishing. But yes, we can make that a date, on one condition.*

He smirked, anticipating an answer he'd no doubt hold issue with.

*Which is?*

*Anything I try on, so do you.*

The image of him wearing a skimpy teddy in a Victoria's Secret dressing room for the sheer pleasure of seeing Olivia's lithe body in the same thing made him laugh out loud at the exact moment the phone conversation experienced a brief lull. Four sets of shrewd eyes nailed him to his seat.

"What's so funny over there?" Erik's dad asked. "Did Preacher drop another one of Bowie's toys on his toe again?"

At that, the entire room howled with laughter, though Preacher was defending himself more than actually laughing. "I didn't *drop* it," he yelled over the others. "Damn thing ricocheted off the target and *speared* my foot like a fucking kebab."

Bowie leaned over and smacked the back of Preacher's head. "Language," he admonished as a reminder that Norma was still present. "And don't go blaming my throwing knife for your incompetence, jerkwad."

In all the commotion, Erik didn't notice Dozer adjust his position to stand behind his chair. "Sexy Livvie wants to know if you have a deal," the big man announced.

Erik glanced down just in time to see the text notification on his lock screen before it went dark. He pushed up to his feet and pocketed his phone, making a mental note to change the settings so the actual message didn't appear for anyone to see.

Norma gasped. "Sexy Livvie? Who is she and what sort of deal are you making? Erik Nathanial, do you have a girlfriend you haven't told us about?"

The interest and excitement in his mom's voice registered somewhere in the range of *When's the wedding?* and *I want more grandbabies.* He needed to nip this shit in the bud before she got carried away and posted something on Facebook about his pending engagement.

"Of course not," Erik said to the speaker box. "Dozer's just talking out of his a—er, rear. Mom, Pop, we gotta go. There's a call coming in, but I'll talk to you soon, all right? Love you guys."

The men called out their good-byes, but Erik punched the button to disconnect the call before either side got them out completely. He didn't want to risk one of these jokers suddenly saying it was a false alarm so the conversation could continue. In reality, the alarm didn't even exist, but it couldn't be considered an outright lie if it eventually came true. That was his rationalization anyway.

"What'd you do that for? I wanted to tell Norma the good news," Smoke complained.

Erik folded his arms across his chest and narrowed his gaze. "What good news?"

"That now she has three daughters, since her baby boy seems to have grown a vagina recently." Erik settled back against the wall while the guys did the usual shtick of obnoxious laughing, pointing, and high-fiving at the expense of one of their own. "Don't worry, Wolf—I mean, Wolfetta—we'll always be your brothers, no matter what. Besides, I always wanted a sister."

Bowie chimed in with, "They've probably shared Pinterest beauty tips and a crying jag to the movie *Beaches*. That right, LT?"

"All of this because I'm talking to a woman? Careful, boys, your skin's looking a little green."

"Talking," Dozer countered. "Your thumbs are showing signs of early arthritis for as much as you're on that phone 'talking' to her." He'd thrown air quotes around the word talking that time. "Do you force yourself to wait a whole minute before you text her back so you don't seem too eager? Or are you already at the stage where you're letting her glimpse 'the crazy' and hoping she finds it endearing and romantic?"

Try as he might, Erik couldn't keep a straight face. They might be assholes, but they were *his* assholes. Though he smiled—and *maybe* chuckled a little—at their antics, he balanced it out with a double-fisted middle-finger salute. "All right, all right," he said, "let's get the fuck outta here and head to the gym. I'll show you who the *real* pussies are in this outfit."

...

The third week after the awkward office visit, Erik went radio silent. It made Olivia even more anxious than when she'd counted on hearing from him several times a day. If she had a dollar for every time she dialed into her voicemailbox (regardless of if the light was blinking or not), checked her phone notifications, and refreshed her email, she'd have enough cash for a trip to Fiji.

The absence of his silly notes also made her realize how much she'd looked forward to them every day. They brightened her mood, made her smile, and she even laughed out loud in public a few times, causing her to slap a hand over her mouth and flush red with embarrassment.

She'd cursed his persistence at least a dozen times while fighting the urge to answer an email or return a call. In the beginning, all she'd turned down was one hell of an amazing sex partner because that's the only interaction she'd had with him. But with every message he sent, he revealed something new about himself, until what once was merely a crude drawing of a stick figure turned into a beautifully detailed sketch. And damn it all, she *liked* what she saw. A *lot*.

Olivia sighed, frustrated that this man had her so off balance and grateful it was Friday. Tonight she had plans to hang out with Angie, and she couldn't wait. She hadn't seen her best friend since before "the night that shall not be named" and desperately needed the girl time.

The train's brakes screeched and echoed in the tunnel as it pulled into the Park Street Station. Once the doors opened, the Red Line morning commuters spilled into the underground station like water from a dam. Commuters like Alvin the Elf, whose unnaturally pointy ears framed perpetually rosy cheeks that highlighted his ever-ready smile for everyone he passed. Frail and shy Madge the Mouse, who made drawing into oneself an art form and never made eye contact with anything other than the ground between her feet. And the always upbeat Dan the Drummer, who bobbed his head to whatever music pumped from his earbuds while drumming out the beat on his briefcase.

Of course, those weren't their real names but rather silly monikers she'd given them. Because, for as often as she saw the Red Line patrons—along with those on the Green Line that took her the rest of the way to her office at the Prudential Tower—she only knew as much as she'd observed of their habits while on the train. Still, if she thought of the people in her life as rings that encircled her, with her family in the nearest ring and moving out from there, the people who shared her daily commutes fell after her coworkers but definitely before random strangers.

"Good morning, Jeremiah," Olivia said to the man behind the counter of the *Herald & Globe* newsstand. She stopped there every morning on her way to work to grab her first coffee of the day from Old Jeremiah. He was a man of few words, and their quick exchanges never failed to amuse her. He was like a man bound by the laws of Twitter. Not a single thought expressed was longer than 140 characters.

"Miss Jones," he said with a grin and a dip of his head. "Sure hate to see how troubled those pretty eyes of yours are lately," he added, his gaze trained on the coffee filling the cardboard cup.

Olivia blinked at the odd statement. "Troubled?"

"Only three kinds of trouble I can think of that would be cause for them clouds." She opened her mouth to reassure him she was fine, but apparently the old man wasn't finished. "Family trouble, work trouble"—Jeremiah's gaze finally locked on Olivia—"or man trouble."

She laughed nervously and forced herself not to glance around at the herd of people milling in the area to see how many were suddenly curious about her emotional state. "I'm not even sure what to say to that."

He gave her a wink and set the cup of coffee and a newspaper in front of her. "One black coffee to go."

"What? I never take my coffee black."

"Nope." The man looked off to the right and squinted slightly. "But Trouble does."

Following his gaze, Olivia realized what the old shopkeeper had been trying to convey. *Trouble, indeed.*

A rather sizable man holding a to-go cup from Jeremiah's was heading straight for her, parting the sea of people with his broad shoulders and confident stride. Wearing black athletic shorts and a white army muscle shirt, he looked like a warrior on casual day mixing it up with the corporate folk to see how the boring half lived.

The closer he got, the more Olivia's body sparked to life, as though his proximity controlled the speed in which the blood flowed in her veins and the air filled her lungs. It reacted to him before he was even within reach, and knowing he had that kind of power over her was both unnerving and exhilarating—the latter being the cause of the former.

Erik stopped directly in front of her and pinned her in place with an imposing stare.

And just like that, twin pools of amber had set fire to the walls she'd so carefully erected between them, crumbling them like so much ash. His eyes spoke a truth. That he could have her anytime and anyplace he wanted, that the freedom he'd afforded her thus far was a kindness he didn't have to give. Because with nothing more than a look—*this* look—and a gruff command, Olivia would happily give herself over to him.

Her breath caught in her chest and the need to retreat battled with the need to jump his bones where they stood, public audience be damned. Fortunately, she was spared the embarrassment from either "need" winning when his lips curved into a slow smile and rendered her completely immobile. Then he hit her with his deep voice that made everything he said sound like wanton sex dipped in Godiva chocolate.

"Good to see you, Livvie. How've you been?" He only

waited a beat before turning to Jeremiah and grabbing the black coffee. "Thanks, man. I managed to get that lady's wallet back to her for you, but it was a close call. She was almost through the turnstiles by the time I caught up with her."

Finally, her tongue unfroze. "Erik, what are you doing here?"

He lobbed one of his sexy half grins at her. "Buying you coffee on your way in to work. Here, this one's yours. Cream, two sugars."

She accepted the cup he'd been holding and simply stared for a few moments, then pulled herself together. "My assistant sneaks you way too much intel, Lieutenant." Olivia stepped around him and made her way toward the flight of stairs that would take her up to the Green Line platform. Of course, Erik matched her step for step. "So now you're stalking me, is that it?"

"Not at all. If I were stalking you, you'd never know it. Perks of being former spec ops. Nope, this is a surprise visit for the purpose of extending an olive branch by way of buying you coffee."

"An olive branch," she repeated. "Is this your way of apologizing for your brazen behavior in my office, your inappropriate sharing in my boss's office, and then handing me my panties in the women's bathroom?"

"Negative. Watch your step, Doc," he said, guiding her around a puddle of spilled coffee she hadn't noticed.

She muttered a "thanks" on autopilot as she attempted to solve the complex puzzle that was Erik Grady. "Why?"

"Why, what?"

"Why aren't you apologizing? Don't you think that would be a step in the right direction if you're trying to date me or whatever?"

He spared her a glance and wicked grin before returning his rapt attention to their surroundings, like he was expecting danger to happen at any moment. "Oh, there'll be plenty of 'whatever,' and I think you've already had a good enough preview to know that I don't *try* anything. I *do*, and I take pride in knowing that I 'do' damn well."

Yes, he did, damn him. "You're changing the subject."

"I won't apologize for what I did, because I don't regret doing any of it."

She huffed and looked away. "Of course you don't."

"However…" Grasping her lightly at the elbow, Erik guided her onto the train and tucked her into his side between him and the pole he grabbed high above her head. Her irritation dissolved when his forefinger, extra warm from holding his coffee, lifted from his cup to tuck errant strands of hair behind her ear. "However," he started again, "I *am* sorry if my actions did more than get a little under your skin. Believe it or not, my intention wasn't to upset you."

*Don't go soft, Olivia. Don't you fall for his honeyed eyes and tender touch and sweet words and…shit.* "What about getting me fired?" That had sounded a lot more pissy in her head, but it came out sounding more like Marilyn Monroe inviting a lover into her bed. "I'm lucky I still have a job after you blabbed about my sex life to my *boss*."

"Your pseudo-uncle isn't about to fire you for getting laid. I thought he kind of looked impressed, actually."

She was sure her jaw hit the ground. "You knew he's my uncle?"

"Gotta admit, Livvie, your lack of faith in me is shooting holes in my ego. Keep it up and I'll be using it to strain my pasta." She ground her teeth, refusing to let him see the amusement tugging at the corners of her mouth. "Come on, sweetheart, give me a little credit. I wouldn't have said any of that if I thought you'd have any negative repercussions."

Olivia took a deep breath and turned her head to look at him. "At what point does this olive branch come into play,

Lieutenant?"

"First, you have to tell me you're not mad at me."

Finally, the train pulled into her stop and the crowd started shuffling, preparing to exit or to capitalize on a newly vacant seat. The commotion gave her the perfect excuse to keep her eyes forward and not on his mouthwatering features. "I'm not mad at you," she whisper-shouted, her tone incongruous with her statement. "I'm *irritated* with you. There's a difference."

"Then don't be irritated with me," he pressed as the doors opened.

She didn't say anything at first, choosing to let him stew while they made their way onto the platform, up the stairs to ground level, and through the station doors to the street. Finally, she said, "Give me a reason *not* to be irritated with you."

"You drive a hard bargain, Doc, but I like that you push back. Keeps things interesting, makes it all the more satisfying when—"

*"Erik."*

"Right, okay, olive branch. I'm no longer holding you to the three dates you reluctantly agreed on. Consider the nonexistent contract of our original deal shredded and burned."

*No! Wait,* yes. *Yes, Olivia, that's what you want. Stop panicking like you were secretly excited about those dates.*

"I see," she said, thankful they were now approaching the safety of the Pru. Surely he wouldn't follow her inside in his sweaty running clothes. "So what will you demand instead, then? I'd set you up with Cindi, but she has a giant of a fiancé who I wouldn't recommend any man tangle with, even you."

"What the hell are you talking about? Why would I want to be set up with Cindi?"

Olivia snorted. "Is this a rhetorical question? Gee, I don't know," she said with a sarcastic bite as she turned and followed the walkway leading to the tower. "Maybe because once you realized I wasn't worth the trouble, you figured you'd set your sights on the sexy, young blonde with an obvious wild streak."

Just as she reached for one of the large glass doors, Erik wrapped a hand around her wrist and tugged her toward the side of the building.

They rounded the corner, and he led her several feet into the landscaped courtyard that separated the tower and the Shoppes at Prudential Center. When they reached a larger shade tree, he turned to face her, blocking her path with his body and a decently pissed-off expression.

"I'm going to say some things, and I want you to hear me. Not let it in one ear and out the other because you assume it's a bunch of bullshit lines, but *really hear me*."

Erik took a step in to her as she retreated, then another until her back made contact with the tree's trunk and she had nowhere to go. He stood so close that her nipples would brush his chest if she took a big enough breath.

"Okay," she whispered, her breaths coming fast. "I'm listening."

"The fact that you'd ever think I want someone like Cindi is insulting. She seems like a great girl, but she's a fucking *kid* who's barely legal to drink. Why the hell would I want a girl of any kind when I can have a real woman like you?"

She nodded in understanding. "I'm sorry I insulted you, Erik. I didn't mean to insinuate you have a penchant for co-eds. I'm sure you keep your dating pool very age-appropriate." Oh, God, she sounded like they were in a session. Why couldn't she talk to him like a normal person?

"That's another thing," he growled. "You keep making these comments about the kind of women I supposedly want and yet blatantly ignore all the times I've told you that the woman I want right now is *you*."

Her heart almost skipped a beat, but his choice of words gave it pause. "Right now?"

"Yeah, Livvie, *right now*. I'm not going to feed you

bullshit about forever when we don't even know if we'll last a month. But I sure as fuck know what I want now, and honestly, I don't see that changing any time soon." Erik braced both hands on the tree on either side of her head, and the way his jaw muscles flexed when he wasn't talking told her he was keeping a tight leash on his control. "Christ, you're all I think about. It's making me crazy. I haven't even noticed another woman since the night we spent together."

He couldn't have shocked her more if he'd told her he was wearing women's underwear. "You're serious."

"Fuck yeah, I am," he rumbled. "I'm trying to get you to see that this isn't some game to me. I'm not looking for a challenge to earn bragging rights like some frat boy, and if all I wanted was pussy, I'd get it at Phoenix from the Hose Hunnies jockeying to get into a fireman's bed. Believe me, they're not in short supply."

Olivia clenched her fists at the image of different women sliding over him like their personal firehouse pole and reminded herself that she was not the type of person to claw someone's eyes out. "If you're dropping the deal we made, what is it you want from me?"

"A shot," he said, his eyes dropping to her mouth. And just like that, her rage melted into an aching need. Olivia bit down on her lower lip to stop herself from openly panting. "I want a shot with you in the form of three dates."

She frowned. "But you just said the deal is off."

"I said the original deal is off. We both know I had the advantage that morning, and I manipulated the situation to get my way. It wasn't a fair playing field, so I'm leveling it now." Erik cupped her face with one hand, then used his thumb to release her lip from the punishing grip of her teeth. "I want you to *want* to give me those three dates, Livvie. I want the chance to know you better and for you to get to know me so I can better state my case as to why we're so good together."

One side of his mouth hitched up in a small lopsided grin that hit her in the back of the knees. "I'm only asking for dates, sweetheart. Nothing more. Anything that happens beyond that will be entirely up to you."

Olivia thought carefully about everything he'd said. She had to admit, the fact that he essentially released her from their silly bet eased the underlying anxiety she'd had since the moment he strode into her office. Already, some of the tension drained from her shoulders. She didn't relish getting backed into a corner. At least not in a mental capacity. It's not like she could deny her arousal when he used his body to crowd or pin her. The proof was in the dampness between her legs.

"If I said no," she began pensively, "you'd accept my decision and move on?"

She held her breath, waiting to hear his answer before deciding anything. At least, that's what she told herself. Deep down, she knew she wasn't changing her decision from the one she made three weeks prior. But there were only two words he could say at this point, and her psychological curiosity was dying to hear which one he chose.

Erik's jaw muscles fluttered as he exhaled harshly through flared nostrils. With his face close enough to trade breaths, she watched his eyes bounce back and forth between hers as though searching for his answer in their hazel depths. Then something changed in him. His pupils grew and the air of authority once again filled him, making him much larger than he was a moment ago, even as she knew it to be physically impossible.

He sank his fingers into her hair, disregarding the destruction to her sleek ponytail style, and held her firm as he uttered a single word. "Don't."

Why did it not surprise her that he chose to break the rules and create a third option? This man refused to conform, to do anything simply because it was what was expected.

Unpredictable and wild. All traits that should frighten her away, not turn her on to the point of soaking her panties.

Swallowing hard, she whispered, "Don't what?"

"Don't say no."

"Okay," she answered. "I won't."

He held still for several beats, possibly trying to decide if he'd heard her correctly, then pushed out a heavy exhale and gave her a smile that lit up his whole face. She only had a moment to enjoy it before he crushed his lips to hers in a kiss so hot, she swore their lips melted together.

When they finally broke apart, he looked like a kid at Christmas, so handsome and happy. She hated that what she said next might ruin his little high, but it couldn't be helped. There was only one more concern to get out of the way before she committed to this completely.

"Erik, this is going to sound ridiculous considering we already…" Olivia dropped her gaze to the grass between them. "What I mean to say is that I'd like to take things slow. Physically speaking." God, this couldn't be more awkward. She continued on, her words now coming out in a rush. "It's not that I don't like it when we get physical, because believe me, I do. I really, *really* do. But—"

"Hey, stop." He lifted her chin, forcing her to meet his steady gaze. "You don't need to explain yourself. I'm not going to pressure you into anything. That doesn't mean I'm not going to kiss you or that I'll be able to ignore the air growing thick with enough sexual tension to suffocate us. There's no point pretending to be something I'm not, and you already know I'm a man who goes after what I want."

That was an understatement if she'd ever heard one. Memories of that hotel room and the things he did flooded her brain. And then her panties. At this rate, she'd have to ditch them and go without the rest of the day.

"But the minute you tell me to back off, Olivia, I will. I

swear, I'll listen. Got it?"

"Got it." She tried hiding her smile but wasn't very successful.

He quirked an eyebrow at her. "Why do you look so amused?"

"That was the first time you ever called me Olivia."

"Yeah, well, don't get used to it. You'll always be my Livvie." Erik placed a soft, sweet kiss on her lips. "I'll call you later." Then he walked away, leaving her in a daze as the words *my Livvie* echoed in her mind and warmed her blood.

"Oh, and Doc?" he said after spinning around to walk backward as he talked.

"Yes, Lieutenant?"

"You might want to fix your hair before heading into the office." A smug half grin hitched up the corner of his sexy mouth, and then he turned and disappeared into the small crowd along the street.

Letting her head fall back on her shoulders, she took in deep lungfuls of air to rid herself of Erik Grady's intoxicating scent so she could think clearly again. Her head was going to have one hell of a time trying to convince her libido to take things slow. She wasn't even sure it was possible where that man was concerned.

"Shit," she whispered to herself as she righted her hair and clothes. "Might as well let him tie me to his bed and tattoo 'sex slave' on my ass."

Making her way into the lobby of the Pru and onto an elevator, Olivia had the distinct feeling the next time she saw Erik, her pride would take a swift kick to the teeth. She watched the heavy door as it slid closed, and there on the reflective metal surface was the hint of a smile she couldn't contain.

# Chapter Eight

Erik wondered if Olivia would actually stand him up after all this time. The thought hadn't occurred to him until about fifteen minutes ago, and then with every passing minute, he'd grown less certain she'd show.

Standing next to the aquatic-themed Ben & Jerry's ice-cream cart in front of the New England Aquarium, he checked his watch for the hundredth time. Two minutes past their agreed-upon meeting time. No big deal. She said she was taking a cab, so there were several legitimate reasons why she might be late. But that didn't stop him from scanning the area like he was back on watch detail in a red zone, taking in and cataloguing every detail so he'd know the second she arrived.

The Harborwalk was alive with locals and tourists alike, meandering along the brick-paved wharf as they enjoyed the cloudless June afternoon. He adjusted his mirrored sunglasses and turned his face into the strong breeze coming in off the water, which was just as busy. The rectangular inlet between the aquarium and the weathered-looking Boston Marriott was the docking area for the Charlestown Ferry and other attractions, including the Boston Harbor Cruises, which he and Olivia would be going on later.

If she showed.

Erik clenched his fists, then just as quickly forced his hands to open and relax. What the hell was his problem? He told himself it was his ego bucking against the unprecedented feeling of rejection, nothing more. That's all it *should* be. But he knew it had nothing to do with ego and everything to do with disappointment. He might put a certain amount of stock in fate, but there came a time when a man had to know when to walk away. He'd have to let it go. Let *her* go.

Screw that. He could no more give up on this thing, whatever it was, between him and Livvie than he could on finding a trapped vic in a burning building. It'd be one thing if she truly had no interest in him, but if that were the case, he wouldn't have pursued her past that first night. No, there was more than enough interest, and he'd be damned if he let her continue to run.

Time check. Five minutes late.

*Fuck*. If his BFD brothers saw him right now, they'd be giving him shit about being pussy-whipped before he even got the pussy. Although that wouldn't entirely be true, would it? He'd had it, all right. Had it right up against his face and wrapped hot and tight around his stiff cock.

Perfect. Now he'd be sporting wood for their family-friendly date. Nothing screams "safe and unassuming" more than an unsightly bulge in the crotch area. She was sure to be impressed. Luckily, he'd taken that into consideration when choosing his clothes this afternoon. Dark jeans and a light blue button-up shirt, untucked with the sleeves rolled back on his forearms. Casual but not sloppy, with the benefit of hiding his dick's reactions. Something he'd had to deal with on a daily basis since meeting Dr. Olivia J. Jones.

"Hey, mister."

Erik glanced down to see a young boy squinting up at him. Curious, Erik repositioned his body to face the boy so that his much larger frame cast the kid in his shadow. "What's up, little man?"

With wide eyes, he asked, "Are you a under-the-covers cop?"

Erik's left brow arched in question as he tried to keep his amused grin at bay. "You mean an undercover cop?"

The kid nodded emphatically with a fair amount of hero worship shining in his dark brown eyes. He was cute, with shaggy blond hair and dimples that were evident even without a smile, but he couldn't be more than five or six years old. No way he should be wandering around by himself.

Keeping his head tilted down at the kid, Erik used the cover of his mirrored glasses to discreetly search for a frantic adult who might be missing a child. "What makes you think that?"

Canting his head to the side, he answered, "My Rose says you can always tell a undercovers cop"—well, that was closer than his original attempt at the title—"because they wear sunglasses you can see yourself in and they hold real still and look real scary."

Erik assumed Rose was a person who probably watched too many cop shows, but he stalled by pretending to misunderstand. "A talking flower said all that, huh?"

"No, not a talking *flower*." The kid giggled like it was the funniest thing he'd ever heard, then suddenly cut off and his ears perked up like a dog hearing a dog whistle. A second later, Erik heard it: a girl calling out a boy's name, over and over again in clear desperation.

"Your name wouldn't happen to be Drew, would it?"

The boy's eyes widened again, but for an entirely different reason. He was in deep shit and he knew it.

"Drewwwwwwww!" A girl in her mid-teens rounded the

side of the ice-cream cart and clutched her hands to her chest at the sight of the boy, safe and sound. "Oh thank God you're okay!" She dropped to her knees and hugged the rascal fiercely before shoving him out to arm's length and narrowing her gaze. "You almost gave me a heart attack, do you know that? Don't ever run off like that again or it'll be next summer before you even *see* another chocolate malt, understand?"

Drew actually rolled his eyes and hooked a thumb in her direction. "Don't worry, she always says that. This is my Rose."

Erik crossed one arm over his chest and rested the other elbow on it so he could hide his amusement behind a loosely fisted hand. He liked how the kid referred to her as his. Kind of like how Erik thought of Olivia as *his Livvie*. The little man was not more than three feet high, but was definitely a little alpha in the making. A man had to respect that.

"I'm his *babysitter*," Rose corrected in Drew's direction then said to Erik, "and his parents will kill me if they find out I lost him. Are you going to report me or something? I swear I won't let him leave my side, even if it means handcuffing him to me. Oh God, not that I have handcuffs or anything. What I mean is—"

Holding his hand up, Erik put the girl out of her flustered misery. "No harm, no foul." Then he crouched down and spoke so that only the boy could hear, or so he made it seem. "Listen up, little man. You can't take off on Rose like that. A real man never leaves a woman he cares about unprotected, even if she can take care of herself. You've got a good eye, you're observant, so you might notice something someday that keeps you and Rose out of danger. But you can't keep her safe if you don't stick with her. Got it?"

Drew puffed out his chest and gave Erik a stiff nod as well as any soldier he'd had under his command. "Got it."

Rose mouthed a thank-you as Erik stood up, and then he watched as the two walked away, arguing over the deservedness of chocolate malts. He hoped she caved and the kid got his ice cream.

Shit, how much time had passed? A cursory glance at his watch told him it was now fifteen minutes past. Gritting his teeth, Erik gave the area a wide sweep with his gaze, searching for a stunning blonde with the face of an angel and a body made for sin…and came up empty.

Goddamn it, he swore that if she wasn't here in the next—

"Looks like you've been waiting a while. Did she stand you up?"

The feminine voice came from behind and a little to the left and held a distinctly amused lilt. Relief flooded his system faster than a dose of adrenaline shot straight into the bloodstream. Erik cracked a smile, then did his best to school his features with the help of dragging a hand over his afternoon stubble. Without turning around or looking back at her, he said, "Yeah, it's starting to look that way. Probably just as well, though."

"Oh?" He felt her take a step toward him, stopping behind his left shoulder. "Why do you say that?"

"I think she was only using me for my body." She gasped dramatically, and he barely contained his laughter. "I know," he continued, "it shocked me, too. I thought she liked me for the important things."

He'd never seen her playful side—didn't even know she had one—and that she showed it to him now felt like a huge fucking win. Unable to resist any longer, he turned to face her and take her in.

"And what are the important things?"

Erik stepped in to her until she had to lift her face to maintain eye contact with him. Then he used a sex-roughened voice to say, "You know, like my collection of pre–Civil War coins and freakishly extensive knowledge of Sumatran orangutans."

Amusement danced in her eyes, and in order to prevent breaking character, she bit the center of her full lower lip. An act he very much wanted to do for her. "What a coincidence," she said, her tone a mix of seduction and innocence that had him harder than a fireman's Halligan. "Those are two of my favorite subjects. It's been such a long time since anyone's showered me with"—she peered up at him through thick lashes—"Sumatran orangutan facts."

Christ, even her playful side liked to kill him. "Sweetheart, I'll shower you with whatever facts you want," he said with a wink, "as long as I get to use my hands while I'm doing it." Erik watched as her pupils dilated in response, filling him with satisfaction. "You're late."

"I know, I'm sorry. It's such a beautiful day I decided to walk, but it's been so long since I've been down here, and I underestimated the time necessary to—"

"I don't care, Livvie. Long as you're here, I don't care what held you up." Grabbing her hips, he sank his fingers into her soft body, wishing like hell he had access to her skin. He lowered his head to take her mouth in a scorching kiss hello, but she braced her hands on his chest and leaned back to deny him.

"Not so fast, Lieutenant. This is only our first date, remember? You agreed to take things slow, and what you were about to do was *not* taking things slow. Now come on, I'm dying to see the new ocean tank since they redid it." With that, she skirted around him and sashayed her sweet ass toward the front doors, tossing him a come-hither look over her shoulder.

*Oh, fuck me.* Olivia had finally figured out who truly held the power in their relationship, and it appeared she planned to use the knowledge for evil and torture him with denied access to her body. Well, shit. There really was a first time for everything. Crazily enough, a wicked grin broke over his face as he followed after her. His Livvie was full of surprises, and the date was just getting started…

...

"It's surprising that something so long and hard can feel so smooth and soft, like velvet against my palm," Olivia whispered to Erik. She bit the inside of her cheek to keep from smiling when she heard him disguise a strangled groan with a sharp cough. Keeping her hand flat beneath the surface of the water in the Shark and Ray Touch Tank, Olivia gave him an innocent look over her shoulder. "Such an amazing contrast, don't you think?"

"I've witnessed a lot of amazing things today," he said, following the exhibit's rule of speaking quietly.

His amber eyes bore into her with the heat she'd purposely ignored all afternoon, difficult that it was. Unfortunately, when he looked at her like that, she had no control over her body's tendency to blush. Thankfully they'd kept their aquatic explorations light and casual since entering the building—well, that was until she hadn't been able to resist the stingray double entendre—or Olivia would have flushed herself into a dead faint by now.

Returning her attention to where her fingers skated over the graceful ray, she reflected on how much fun they'd had together. When he called her last night to set up the arrangements, she'd been at Angie's for a much-needed girls' night of wine, mud masks, and chick flicks. Olivia had already given her friend the lowdown on all things Erik Grady—thanks to that third glass of Cabernet—so when her phone screen lit up with the man's name, Angie insisted Olivia answer. From what she remembered, the exchange had been a madcap conversation between Erik, herself, and a none-too-quiet, overly opinionated Angie.

In the end, Erik had agreed to Olivia's (Angie's) idea of an afternoon at the aquarium based on Olivia's (Angie's) point that he wouldn't be able to use his "mad seduction skills" in a place where the walls were made of glass and little kids outnumbered the adults four to one. But he'd made his own concession, saying that since she'd picked the first activity, he could choose another one—keeping with the "in public" theme—for after the aquarium, to which she also agreed (Angie forced her to accept).

She hadn't given it much more than the occasional curious thought, but now that they'd concluded her portion of the day, Olivia wanted to know what he had up his sleeve.

"So what now?" she asked as they stepped from the dimly lit aquarium into the brightness of the early evening sun.

"Now I take you out for dinner."

Olivia's giddiness faltered. It never registered that their date would extend into the dinner hour, making his choice for a public outing rather obvious. Not good. She hated going to restaurants on dates. It didn't matter how many people occupied the dining room, it still felt intimate in a way that made her overly self-conscious and socially inept.

Until recently, she'd never thought of dating as one of life's many gauntlets. Her courtship with Brett had started organically, rather than formally, her freshman year in college, so she'd never gone on a real, honest-to-goodness date. When she finally got up the nerve to "put herself out there" a few months ago, she accumulated failed first dates like a string of social experiments gone wrong. She had all the right elements for success, but one ingredient kept reacting poorly with every subject.

Turned out that mentioning her former husband in casual conversation made for an uncomfortable environment. Of course, none of them had come right out and said as much, but they didn't have to. It was in the way their eyes sought out random things to focus on, and in the way they fidgeted in their seats and subtly checked the time whenever she said Brett's name.

Like any logical person, she thought all she had to do was remove the part causing the problem. She decided to give dating another try, only this time, she would omit Brett and mention of her marriage at all costs. It solved the original problem, however, once things turned physical, Olivia hadn't been able to separate what she'd shared with Brett years ago from the physical intimacy she'd attempted with her dates.

Until her last failed attempt led her to the delectably irresistible Erik Grady. He'd been the first man ever to make her feel something other than guilt in his arms. Now she was finally having fun on a date with a man she could *also* be intimate with, and he wanted to switch to a stuffy, formal, uncomfortable restaurant setting. Not an awkward-dating-woman's idea of a good time, but she could get through it.

"How do you feel about bar food?"

It took a few seconds for his question to worm its way through the fog of her wandering thoughts. "Excuse me?"

"Bar food." He pointed to the aquarium's waterfront bar and restaurant, The Reef. "Personally, I love their lobster salad BLT sandwiches. I thought we could grab something easy and watch the activity in the harbor. You know, people watch or whatever."

Olivia took a good look at The Reef through the eyes of her new idiosyncratic dating rules. It was little more than a large white party tent with a bar and outdoor seating set up along the edge of the inlet. The dining furniture was no-frills, black wrought iron with aquamarine blue table umbrellas for providing shade, and brushed metal Samuel Adams buckets that held the condiments and other essentials.

They'd have a perfect view of the activity on the Harborwalk and could watch the numerous tourist boats as they passed in front of the eyesore that was the Boston Marriott Long Wharf in all its timeworn glory.

*Casual. Outdoors. People watching.* Relief flooded her system and she offered him a smile to match. "That sounds great."

Erik glanced down to where she'd unknowingly pressed a hand to her stomach, concern etched in his brow. "You feeling okay?"

*"Yes,"* she said a little too emphatically. With a nervous laugh, she did her best to recover. "Trying to keep you from hearing it growl. I forgot to eat lunch and now I'm starving."

"Not on my watch. Come on."

Erik intertwined his fingers with hers as though they'd done it a hundred times and led her across Aquarium Plaza where they were soon seated right along the edge of the harbor. He ordered the lobster salad BLT and she chose the Margherita flatbread, and they both decided on starting with a bowl of the famous "chowdah" made with sustainable clams.

For a long time, they simply enjoyed their meals and the view in silence. Not an awkward or uncomfortable silence but one of easy companionship, simplistic and oddly natural for two people who were more strangers than acquaintances. It gave her time to reflect on their time together so far.

She'd been surprised to see him talking with a little boy and his distraught babysitter when she arrived. At the time, she wasn't sure if they knew each other, but she managed to get close enough to glean the situation from what she could hear. He'd been so sweet with the boy, giving him advice on how to be a man, the kind of advice Olivia imagined Erik might give his own son someday.

The scene had tugged at her heartstrings and even her uterine-strings, if such a metaphor existed. It'd been years since she felt the pangs of longing for children of her own, but at one time she'd had them on a pretty regular basis. She'd wanted to start a family with Brett, but "kids weren't written into the family plan" until well after the five-year mark. The goal was to ensure career and financial stability "before bringing anything new to the table." It had been one of the biggest points of contention and strain in their marriage.

Olivia wouldn't have pegged Erik as a kid magnet. He was just so...*intense*. Plus stubborn, domineering, and heavy-handed to name a few of his more prominent traits. But he was also intuitive, caring, and incredibly charming. He'd crouched down to the child's level and spoken to him in a way that made sense without sounding like a condescending adult. That babysitter would never have to worry about her ward leaving her side again because, instead of giving him a lecture he'd no doubt forget all about as soon as they walked away, Erik gave the boy a purpose and a desire to see it through. It was one thing to lead men into the fray but quite another to get a five-year-old to do something without protest.

Apparently, Erik had no problems leading in either situation, but she couldn't help but wonder if he'd have such an easy time with a whole pack of unruly children, like when classes visited the fire station. Angie was a teacher. Maybe she could set it up so Angie's class did a tour of Rescue 2 and Engine 42 and then tag along for maximum amusement.

"How did you get your call sign?"

Erik propped an elbow on the table, took a long drink of his beer, then let the bottle dangle from his fingers as he answered. "Dozer gave it to me during Basic. I had a piece of paper with a quote on it—something I'd learned during a short-story unit in English class—that I kept for motivation. To remind me of how I wanted to perform and someday lead."

"What was the quote?"

"It says, 'For the strength of the pack is the Wolf, and the strength of the Wolf is the pack.'"

"By Rudyard Kipling," she said.

A brilliant smile broke over his face, that lone dimple winking at her through the light scruff of his beard. "You know it."

She nodded. "It's a great quote. I can see why you chose it. Do all call signs hold so much meaning? I thought they were more or less playground names, like the kind kids get stuck with when something notably embarrassing happens."

The warm sound of his amusement slid into her ear and tightened her belly. She wanted to hear more of it; she wanted to make him smile and be the one he smiled at. His mirth could easily become her addiction.

"You're not wrong," he said. "Some of them are given out for things like that, and a lot of times we get other handles for things that can't be repeated in polite company—or any company other than ours, for that matter. Strictly barracks banter. Either way, no one picks his own call sign. It's not like we're in the UFC and get to pick out catchy nicknames that go between our first and last names. They're given to us mostly by our peers and, love it or hate it, it becomes part of your identity."

"Interesting," she said, smiling. "What about your friends?"

"Theirs are pretty straightforward. Dozer bulldozes through anything in his path, on or off the battlefield. Ashton is called Smoke because he's always been a bit of a pyro. He was my sapper, someone specially trained to facilitate movement in combat. If it needed to go boom and it didn't, he'd send it into orbit with the snap of a finger. There's a running joke that if he hadn't joined the army, he would have been an arsonist, which makes his current career choice pretty ironic."

"Remind me to never piss him off," she said wryly.

"Smoke's the least of your worries. He's the easygoing, fun-loving one in the group. Now Sean—better known as Bowie—he's a little harder to read. He has a great dry sense of humor, so unless you know him well, it might be unnerving when you hear him threaten to take one of his favorite knives and gut me like a fish."

Olivia gasped, a piece of her flatbread frozen halfway to her mouth. "Jesus, are you kidding? Is he balanced?"

Laughing, Erik said, "For the most part, yeah, he's balanced. If that ever changes, though, I'll slip him your card, Doc."

"You do that. What about Preacher? Is he actually a member of the clergy?"

"No, but his dad is. Tyler's a bit of a paradox—he's got levels of demons the rest of us don't have that started long before he joined the service."

Olivia frowned, her heart immediately going out to the man she'd never even laid eyes on. "I'm so sorry to hear that."

"Yeah, I worry about him sometimes, but I keep a close eye on him." Erik crumpled his napkin and dropped it on his plate. "Still, even with whatever he has going on inside that head of his, Preacher's one of the most loyal and compassionate men I've ever known."

"Did he get his name because of what his dad does for a living?"

"Indirectly, I suppose. Mostly it's because he's like a goddamn sage. He's always doling out advice when people need it, whether they want it or not. And the kid's always fucking right, which means he's perfected the 'I told you so' look, the righteous prick."

She chuckled and finished her dinner while he sipped his beer. When she was done, Erik moved his chair next to hers and slung an arm around her shoulders, angling his body close. She kept her eyes on the boats in the harbor, pretending she couldn't sense his intense gaze. He'd look away in a moment or so and then she'd be able to breathe normally again.

Several moments passed with no luck. If she didn't want

to turn blue, she had to be the one to break the tension. "You're staring at me, Lieutenant."

He ignored her statement with one of his own. "Tell me about yourself."

"What do you want to know?"

"Everything."

Olivia almost laughed until she spared a glance at him and realized he hadn't meant it as a joke at all. "That's a bit much right out of the gate. How about I stick with the basics?"

Erik gave her a clipped nod. "That'll work. For now."

A shudder of anticipation ran through her. This was a man used to having his orders followed without question. It was clear in the tone of his voice that he considered this a concession on his part. That if he wanted to, he could easily get her to spill a verbal memoir from her earliest memory to the night they met. She couldn't help but wonder what sort of methods he'd use.

"Livvie," he prodded.

Right. She'd just ignore the tingling heat swirling deep in her center. No problem. "I grew up in Cambridge and had a great childhood. My dad was a financial advisor and my mom stayed home with my older brother and me. When my dad retired, he had their finances set up so well that now they spend most of the year traveling all over the world. Their goal is to see every habitable country at least once. Seeing their pictures and talking to them always makes me jealous. I'd like to do that someday, too. Maybe not quite as extensively, but you know, travel to different countries and experience their culture."

The muscles in his neck and shoulders visibly tensed as he stared into the distance. "There are some places I don't ever want to see again." Erik's eyes were haunted, no doubt from the nightmares he survived while serving overseas in war-torn lands. Nightmares she hoped Uncle Eddie could help Erik banish enough that they no longer debilitated him.

"Hey," she said softly. She placed a hand on his cheek and he let her guide his face back to hers. When his eyes refocused, she brushed her thumb over the smooth skin of his cheekbone, right above his stubble. "Where'd you go just now?"

His attempt at a grin was little more than a stiff quirk of his mouth, and the single word he uttered sounded forced through gravel. "Nowhere." Erik covered her hand with his as he turned in to her, kissing her palm then the sensitive skin on the underside of her wrist, before lowering it to rest on his leg. "Did you always want to be a psychologist?"

Olivia let the subject change stand and continued to appease his curiosity. "No, but I've always had an affinity for helping people. When I was in high school, I volunteered at the children's hospital and loved it, so I chose Boston U to stay close to my family and continue working at the hospital when I could. Originally, I planned on becoming a middle school teacher, but I ended up changing my major to psychology my junior year."

"What made you change it?"

*My boyfriend at the time, who later became my husband, said it would be a better financial career choice for our ten-year plan.* Giving him a smile she hoped wasn't as tight as it felt, she waved a hand and tried for flippant. "I couldn't pass up the sixty-hour work weeks, working through my summers, and most of my colleagues being men who grow hair from their ears and keep Old Spice in business."

The deep rumble of his laugh warmed her from the inside. She loved the sound and the way it made her feel, knowing that he found levity in something, even if only for a short while. It struck her then that, more than anything, she wanted Erik to find inner peace and genuine happiness. She hadn't been exaggerating when she told him that at her core she wanted to help people, and though she originally planned on being a teacher, she'd found that helping individuals like him to take back control over their lives after traumatic experiences was a special calling all its own.

"And when you made the switch to psychology, did you always intend on specializing in PTSD with vets? Or did the idea of working with egotistical, pigheaded megalomaniacs struggling with reentry into society among the boring civilians sound like too much fun to pass up?"

"Come on, you're being too hard on yourself," she said with a sly grin. "You're not always pigheaded." He feigned affront, which made her laugh with an embarrassing snort, but it made him smile and chuckle in kind, so in the end, it was worth it. But she decided it would be best to move on before he said something to make her do it again. "To answer your question, though, after I received my Masters in clinical psych, I did my internship at the VA hospital. I have a lot of service members in my family, so I've always been passionate about the military and helping those who've sacrificed so much for us and our country."

*Like you.* Her concern and desire to help Erik had started the same as it did with everyone else who came to see her. But even though he wasn't one of her clients, over the days and weeks—and especially the past several hours—that basic concern had grown exponentially, to the point where part of her happiness hinged on his. Add in the three-hundred-pound-gorilla-awkward-first-night and more sexual tension than Amish teens on Rumspringa, and that about summed up her current relationship with one Lieutenant Erik Grady.

"After my internship was almost over, Uncle Eddie invited me to do my supervised clinic work with him, and whether he thinks I'm an asset to his clinic or he's obligated as my godfather to keep me on, I've been there ever since."

"I'm very impressed, Dr. Jones. That's one hell of a résumé

you have. I could never have gone to school all those years. Learning in a classroom setting never appealed to me. And by that, I mean I spent more of my time trying to figure out ways to play pranks on my teachers than I did taking notes. Luckily, I never had to study much to do well, so my parents wrote most of it off as 'boys being boys.'"

"Evil boy genius, huh? Interesting. Okay, your turn," she said, desperate to get herself out of the hot seat. "Hit me with the abridged version of how Little Erik became Big Erik."

One side of his mouth curled up and his eyes sparked with the boyish mischief she was beginning to recognize as his default setting. "Biologically speaking, it's a simple matter of my blood rushing to the center of my body. It's like when Little Mario eats the red and white mushroom and grows into Big Mario…"

Olivia laughed at his blatant misunderstanding, complete with Super Mario Bros. analogy. She loved that he laughed at his own jokes and that she never knew what would come out of his mouth next. He was predictably unpredictable.

"However, in my early years, my 'growth' was brought on by a multitude of things, by which of course I mean anything that even *remotely* made me think of sex. Or women. Or having sex with women." Erik narrowed his eyes at the sky and canted his head slightly as though considering his thoughts. "Or women having sex with other wo—"

"Okay!" She chuckled as she clapped her hand over his mouth. "I get the picture. You're a horny bastard who gets hard in the produce aisle because you see tits and cocks instead of melons and cucumbers."

"It's true; it never took much to get my flag to fly until about a month ago. Now the only time it happens is when I think of you, which wouldn't be all that bad—" Reaching up, he used a single finger to trace a light path from her temple, down and along her jawline. "Except everything makes me think of you."

Damn, this man was good. What was she supposed to say to that? It made her ridiculously giddy, but she wasn't about to unleash her inner cheerleader and giggle while twirling her hair and pushing out her chest to test his claim. The fact that she suddenly *had* an inner cheerleader because of him was disturbing enough without actually humiliating herself.

"That's, um…" Olivia searched her brain. Words, words, where were her *words*? "Wow." Nice. Her IQ was now lower than the number of people who thought the Marriott's antiquated appearance wasn't an eyesore.

"Yeah, that about sums it up. At first, I thought it was a pretty cool party trick, but it turns out that having a live-in erection as a roommate made things a little uncomfortable, a little tight, you know? So I went to the doctor, but he said that the over-four-hour-erection warning was only if you took a Viagra. Personally, I never touch the stuff; I'm a purist. Anyway, he said the only way to end my suffering is to fuck whatever's causing it out of my system."

"Oh, he did, did he?"

Somehow, he managed to keep his expression totally somber. "He did."

"It's strange, now that you mention it, because I went in for my yearly female visit the other day, and do you know what *my* doctor said?"

"Tell me."

"She said that I needed to close up shop for a while."

"Close up shop?"

"Yep, you know, just—" She clapped her hands together once. "Close it up. Something about a new study and living longer; I don't really remember all the specifics. But what I do know is that I signed a bunch of documents stating that I would indeed close up shop for a minimum of six months."

*"Six months?"*

Damn, the man was cute when pretending incredulity. "I know, it's terrible. But I have to go through with it because the documents state that I can be sued for breach of contract and other nasty stuff. Darn, right? If it weren't for those signed pieces of paper, I'd be jumping your bones, right here, right now."

Erik took out his cell phone, pushed a button, and held it to his ear.

"What are you doing?"

"Baby, I was special forces. I know at least a dozen people who can make those documents go away. Hold on, this'll only take a sec."

Olivia laughed and squealed, trying to grab his phone, but he easily evaded her. "Erik Grady, you better be joking. I swear if you tell one of your buddies that I signed contracts to close my vagina shop, I will murder you in your sleep."

A bark of laughter escaped the man she wouldn't have guessed possible of such levity. What a wonderful surprise. "Sorry, but anything you said was completely erased in my mind the second you said 'vagina shop.'"

He probably wasn't the only one if the side glances they'd gotten from at least half a dozen people around them were any indication. Normally, she'd be ten shades of embarrassed, but she was having too much fun to care if she scandalized any strangers.

She continued trying to swipe his phone (which never really had a call going through, thank God) while citing all sorts of absurd reasons for needing it. Then he started fighting fire with fire and made moves to confiscate hers. Considering everyone with a pulse kept their entire lives on their phones, it was a valid reason for playing a serious game of Keep Away, even if they were only joking around.

After they wore themselves out and called a phone truce, Erik checked the time on his large and very manly watch. Even the way he wore a watch was sexy. How was that possible? "Time to go, gorgeous."

"Go where?"

"To my portion of the date."

"I thought this was your portion."

"Then you need higher expectations," he said, linking his fingers with hers once again. "Come on. We have a boat to catch."

# Chapter Nine

"Can I rub your head?"

Erik almost choked on his beer but managed to keep his composure and swallow without mishap. "Come again?" Jesus, if the double-meaning phrases didn't stop, he'd be harder than the ship's anchor.

For his portion of their date, he'd brought her on one of the sunset cruises run by Boston Harbor Cruises. Another thing that locals like her usually had on their perpetual to-do lists but never actually got around to experiencing because they figured they could always do it another time. Aboard the triple-decker *Fort Independence*, it was a fully narrated (not that he was paying attention to a damn word unless it came out of Olivia's mouth), ninety-minute tour around the harbor with dozens of tourists enjoying drinks, snacks, and a stunning view of the sun setting over the Boston skyline.

But for as amazing as it was, Erik couldn't care less about any of it. All he could think about was the woman in front of him and how desperately he wanted her.

Olivia blushed but didn't point out the play on words. Her

gaze lifted to his hairline. "Your hair," she said. "I felt it a little bit, um…before, but not much because I was—"

He leaned in and spoke at her ear. "Highly distracted?" His cock twitched, remembering where his hair would have touched her that night. Like the inside of her thighs, for sure, as he kissed and licked and fucked her with his tongue.

She cleared her throat and sipped her drink. "Sorry, that was a stupid thing to ask. Must be the Long Island iced teas talking. Forget I said—"

Erik grabbed her free hand and pulled her in closer. "Two things," he said. "One, nothing you ask me is ever stupid, and two, you never have to ask permission to touch me. The answer will always be yes. Got it?"

One corner of her sensual mouth curved up the tiniest bit. "Got it."

Slowly, she raised her eyes to where her hand hovered. He felt the pads of her delicate fingers skim his hairline then glide lightly over his scalp and down the back. His head dipped forward of its own volition, leaning into her like a feral dog reveling in its first experience with a gentle touch. Erik locked down the rumble of pleasure in his chest and focused on keeping his breaths even as she sent tingles vibrating through his spine that settled heavily into his balls.

He couldn't look away from her. He'd spent all day—weeks, really—chipping away at the wall she kept between them. Now, as he studied her face and the emotions that skittered across, it looked as though he'd finally tumbled the damn thing down.

"It's so soft," she said with a sense of wonderment. "You'd think a buzz cut would feel prickly, but it doesn't. It feels… really good, actually."

Erik's voice came out thick and rough. "So damn good."

She, of course, caught on that he wasn't reiterating her statement as much as he was making one of his own. Lowering her eyes as a blush crept into her cheeks, she took her hand away. Erik missed her touch instantly. He could now relate to the Husky he had growing up who always nosed her way under his palm every time he stopped petting her.

If he had any supernatural powers, he would have made it so they were in her bed in the next moment. Then he'd nose his way between her thighs and revel in the double pleasure of eating her until she came on his tongue while she grabbed and clawed at his head and shoulders.

Olivia cleared her throat and offered a friendly smile, most likely in a futile attempt to make things less…intense. "Well, at any rate, I like your hair."

He liked *her*, and if he didn't get the subject onto something that had nothing to do with sex, or the innuendos thereof, they'd be shocking a lot of people when he bent her over the nearest flat surface and had his wicked way with her.

"I'm surprised you haven't asked me how my sessions are going with Dr. Marion."

She shrugged but didn't meet his eyes. "You aren't my client, so it's not my business."

"In the last few weeks, did you ever want to make it your business?"

Finally, she turned her face up to his and gave him a no-bullshit stare. "What I do or don't want is irrelevant, Erik; you know that."

"I disagree. I think what you want is extremely relevant. I want to know your every desire, from your favorite guilty pleasure to every sexual fantasy that's ever floated through that beautiful brain of yours."

*Way to stick to the plan, asshole.*
*Screw the plan. Ask about her fantasies.*

Olivia swallowed hard, yearning and uncertainty swirling in her hazel eyes. Erik tucked her hair behind her left ear, then his lips followed to ensure no one but her could hear the erotic musings ghosting over her skin. "There's nothing you can tell me that'll change the way I feel about you, Livvie." A tiny, helpless sound escaped her throat as his tongue traced a languorous path along the delicate shell of her ear. "All you have to do is tell me. If it's within my power, I'll give you whatever you want."

"Have you always been such a generous lover, Lieutenant Grady?"

"I haven't been for a long time, no. But there's something about you, Dr. Jones. From the first moment our eyes met, I craved you like a new addiction I couldn't shake."

"Oh."

She looked so incredible, the orange-and-pink-streaked sky behind her and the lanterns lining the ship reflecting in her eyes.

He couldn't put off tasting her any longer. Angling his body to block them from other passengers, he slipped his fingers into the hair at her nape, rested his thumbs along her jaw, and lowered his mouth to hers.

Instinct told him to take, to plunder, to conquer and claim, but he reined it in and locked it down. There'd be time to unleash all that later when they didn't have an audience. For now, he'd go slow and explore her in the ways he didn't get to that first night together, ways he'd fantasized of doing ever since.

Gently, he brushed his mouth over hers, their breaths mingling as he teased them both, never committing to the kiss they wanted. He nipped the pouty center of her lower lip and reveled in her quiet gasp. He felt her sharp intake of breath, felt her fingernails graze his sides through his shirt when she fisted the material tight enough that it pulled across his lower back. Erik wondered if she did it out of frustration from being teased, or shock from the pleasure-pain of the bite, but the cause wasn't as important as the outcome.

Right now, the only thing that mattered was her reaction. That she responded to him in ways that showed he wasn't crazy. That she wanted him every bit as much as he wanted her, despite the cat-and-mouse game they'd played over the last several weeks. And that's exactly what she was showing him as he continued to manipulate the non-kiss, using his hands to angle her head this way and that, letting his tongue dart out for quick tastes of her sweet lips.

Livvie's eyes were heavy-lidded with the lust building between them, but they never left his face and didn't completely close. Something he found to be hot as hell, which ramped things up a bit sooner than he'd planned. He killed the last of the controlled hesitation and dove in. One hand threaded into her hair, the other circled to the front and closed around the smooth column of her throat. He didn't dare squeeze, but he made sure she felt his grip, his claim.

*My Livvie. Mine.*

What started as a single flame was swiftly growing into an all-out conflagration. Olivia seemed to be just as lost in the moment, tugging on his shirt, his shoulders. Pressing the mound of her sex against him like a cat in heat.

"Fuck, you're killing me, gorgeous," he rasped into her mouth.

"Same," she said a little breathlessly.

Erik was about to show her just how dead he could make them when the captain's voice droned through the speaker mounted over their heads, directing everyone to the starboard side of the ship, reminding him all too well that they were still very much in public.

Pulling himself together, he maneuvered them back to their original place at the railing and nodded over her shoulder. "Look."

She turned in his arms and faced the city. The sun had finally slipped behind the line of skyscrapers, standing tall like silhouetted sentries, guarding the city. "Oh, wow. The way the bright orange glows in the sky, it almost looks like the city's on fire."

"It wouldn't matter if I was suspended or active and between tours; a blaze that big and I'd be heading in for sure. Let's be glad it's just a sunset."

Olivia chuckled and relaxed against his chest.

"I can't believe I've never done this before. It's so beautiful from out here," she said with an appreciative sigh. "And there's no such thing as 'just a sunset.' I'll have you know, sunsets are near the very top of my Favorite Things Ever list."

"Oh yeah? Tell me how one goes about getting on that list," he said, nuzzling her ear.

"One doesn't. I said favorite *things*, not people."

"You got a list for people, too?"

He felt her smile when her cheek bunched up under his. "Doesn't everyone?"

God, this woman was killing him. "What if I campaign to get on your list of favorite people by introducing you to some new things that'll make the top of that Favorite Things Ever list of yours?"

"Hmm. It would certainly be a first, but I suppose it's not entirely outside the realm of possibility. May I ask what sort of things you plan on introducing me to?"

"You may," he said, "but I don't think I'll answer."

"Why not?"

"Because I'd rather show you," he said in a gravelly voice. He moved his hands to her belly, pulling her back against him even more. Pressing his hips forward, he nestled his cock in the center of her round ass. Her head dropped back to his shoulder, and he ducked his head to kiss and lick the side of her neck. "God, I can't tell you how much I've been dying to taste you again. I told myself I was going to be a perfect gentleman today, but there's something about you that makes me so damn crazy I can't think straight."

"So let's not think at all," she whispered. "How much longer until we dock?"

He stilled. "Livvie, what are you proposing? I need you to spell it out for me, because if you don't, my libido will make its own assumptions. As hard up as I am to be with you—pun *very* intended, by the way—"

She chuckled and he felt the vibrations flow from her back and into his chest. "Yes," she said with a quick wiggle of her ass, "I can feel just how intended 'your pun' truly is."

He groaned softly. "You better stop teasing my pun with that sweet ass of yours, baby, or I'll make sure it gets punished later."

"I apologize, Lieutenant." *Jesus H. Christ.* Did she mean to say his rank all breathy and seductive like that? "Please continue."

He'd never had a thing for women calling him "sir" in the bedroom. Maybe it was because being an officer in the army desensitized him to the title. Maybe because he'd never labeled himself as a Dom. Hell, he still didn't want to label anything. He'd had enough of that in the military. Erik knew what he liked when it came to sex, and he made a habit of doing what he liked. No rules, no protocols.

But he'd be damned if his dick hadn't twitched when she called him "Lieutenant" like her tongue was fucking her teeth on every syllable. Yeah, he could get used to hearing her say that real quick. As in, immediately. First, though, he had to make sure they were on the same page.

"The last thing I want to do is misunderstand something and screw things up between us."

"Ah," she said knowingly as she turned to face him. Wrapping her arms around his neck, she molded the front of her body to his. "Then let me be crystal clear. I want you to drive me home, where I'll invite you up to my apartment and introduce you to Ben and Jerrys."

"Got a thing for their ice cream, huh? That why you wanted to meet at the cart in the plaza earlier?"

"Well, I figured if you stood me up, at the very least I could enjoy some ice cream."

"After everything you've put me through to get this date, nothing short of a nuclear disaster was stopping me from making it to the aquarium today. If anything, you were the one with a high risk of being a no-show. Then I would have had to buy out the entire ice-cream cart to drown my sorrows. See if that chick trick really works."

Olivia laughed. "I guess it's a good thing I showed, then. It'd be a shame to ruin such a remarkable physique with so many empty calories."

"Remarkable physique, I like that. You've got a real way with words, Doc. You make me hot when you start speaking all formal like that," he said with a wide smile.

Chuckling, she said, "Can't say I've heard that one before."

"And ain't that a shame. Okay, so you mentioned introductions. Do you always introduce people to your cartons of Chunky Monkey and Cherry Garcia, or am I a special case?"

She slapped him playfully on the shoulder. "Ben and Jerrys are my cats. If I don't formally introduce them to my guests, they get cranky, and they'll never leave us alone."

"And once they leave us alone, what'll we be doing?"

She smiled. "Well, I'm hoping you'll use your imagination for the specifics," she said, "but let's just say that if I don't end up with at least one less condom in my bedside drawer, I'm going to be *very* disappointed."

Erik turned, ready to drag her to his truck and call in a favor to a buddy on the BPD to make sure he wasn't stopped for breaking every traffic law from Central Wharf to the

Seaport District, when he realized where they were. *Fuck.* Catching the attention of a staff member, he asked how much longer until they docked.

"About a half hour, sir."

"Thirty minutes?" he growled through clenched teeth. "Why the hell so long? The sun's practically gone, show's over, back to home base."

The kid's eyes grew wide and his mouth gaped like a fish, uncertain how to answer. Erik wanted to bark at him, tell him to stand up straight and speak up like a man, but Olivia politely thanked Fishy and sent him on his way.

The woman tried hiding her amusement as she wrapped her arms around his neck again, but he could see it in her eyes and where the very corners of her mouth curled up. "At ease, soldier. We'll be back before you know it." He was about to scold her for taking that CO tone with him, but then her fingers started running through his buzzed hair and massaging his head, and his train of thought derailed. Goddamn, that felt so fucking good.

"Remind me never to take you anywhere that getting you naked and under me isn't an option in ten minutes or less."

"Has anyone ever told you how cute you are when you're grouchy?"

"Actually, yeah." He raised an eyebrow and narrowed his gaze a hair. "But you'd be the first one I put over my knees and spanked for it."

She feigned indignance with a sharp inhale. "Why am *I* the only one who gets punished?"

"Because I don't go anywhere near my mom's ass," he said with a lopsided grin and a wink. "Kind of a rule I have. But *yours*, on the other hand…" Erik reached down and squeezed big handfuls of each of her cheeks, pulling her into him and laughing as she squealed and squirmed.

For the next endless thirty minutes, Olivia distracted him

with kisses and touches that did nothing to dampen the fire between them but sure as hell sprayed it with a fire hose of fuel. Once they stepped foot on the mainland, he dragged Olivia behind him, and when she tried getting him to slow down, he swept her up in a fireman's carry all the way to where he'd parked his truck. Luckily, she was laughing as much as complaining, so no one bothered trying to rescue her.

Now all he had to do was get her back to her place before she changed her mind.

...

As soon as Olivia opened the door to her Waterside Place apartment, she scanned every visible surface to make sure she didn't have anything embarrassing lying around. When she'd left earlier, the possibility that she'd invite Erik over never crossed her mind. Okay, maybe it'd *crossed* her mind, but not long enough for her to take herself seriously. Now here they were, and for all she knew, one of her bras could be hanging off a kitchen chair.

Oblivious to their owner's concerns, her cats emerged from her bedroom and jogged over to welcome her home. "There's my boys," she said to them as she bent to give each a few halfhearted strokes before their curiosity led them to the man at her side. Erik crouched down, stopping the longhaired feline in his tracks. "The orange and white scaredycat is Ben," she said by way of introduction. "Any sudden movements make him freeze up or run away. Once he sees that you haven't tortured his brother, he'll warm up to you."

"Makes sense." No sooner had Erik held his left hand out than Ben tiptoed his way over to it. "There, see? You're not a scaredy-cat at all, are you, Ben? You're cautious, which means you're smart. And *you* must be Jerry," he said to the shorthaired tuxedo rubbing against his legs.

"His name is actually Jerrys. With an 's.'" While her boys kept Erik busy, Olivia walked a quick lap around the main areas to make small adjustments she thought made a big difference: throw pillows straightened, forgotten slipper socks collected, and last night's dishes into the dishwasher.

Straightening, he crossed to where she stood at the breakfast bar that separated the kitchen from her living room. "Does he have multiple personalities?"

She laughed and slid her hands up his chest and around his neck as he gathered her into his arms. "I named them after the heavenly ice cream, not the men who created it."

"Heavenly, huh? So what I'm hearing is that their ice cream is another thing at the top of your favorites list. That right?"

Erik dipped his head and skimmed his lips up the side of her neck. Her eyes drifted shut on a sigh that turned to a gasp when he nipped the sensitive skin behind her ear. Did he end with a question? Was it her turn to say something? Before she had a chance to remember, he thrust his hands into her hair and seized her mouth with his.

Holy shit, she couldn't think. His lips and tongue shorted out her brain and hijacked her senses. All she could see, hear, smell, feel, and taste was *him*. Kissing Erik Grady was her new favorite thing in the entire world.

Breaking apart to drag in deep lungfuls of air, she looked into his golden amber eyes and said, "Mission accomplished. You just made the number-one spot on the list."

A huge smile broke out on his face. "Happy to hear it, but you should probably break that list into a few sub-categories. I plan on making very specific things your new favorites."

"Sub-categories sound like a fantastic idea."

"Hell yeah, they do," he rumbled, then leaned in to resume their kiss. But before he made contact, his phone rang in his back pocket, startling her into pulling back. Cursing an apology, he silenced the ringer and placed it back in his pocket. "Nervous, sweetheart?"

Olivia lifted her chin a notch in defense. "I was the one who suggested you come over, remember?"

"Of course I do." Erik stepped into her space again, eclipsing the world around them. With her head tilted back to hold his steady gaze, she didn't know he'd lifted his hand until she felt the backs of his knuckles graze over her pebbled nipple. She gasped, and her body jolted as though he were made of electricity. A smirk tilted his lips. "Doesn't mean you're not a little on edge."

"Smart-ass. Maybe I *could* use a glass of wine. Want one?"

"Whiskey?"

"Let me see what I can find."

She gestured for him to make himself at home and moved back into the kitchen to hunt down the appropriate glasses. It wasn't often (okay, almost never) that she entertained guests and needed to use anything other than her casual ware. Grabbing a stemless wineglass and a highball tumbler from way in the back of a cabinet, she stole a brief glance in Erik's direction.

He'd settled onto her sectional sofa in front of the ten-foot windows that stretched from floor to ceiling. She wasn't lucky enough to have one of the units with a balcony, but her view of the harbor and the eastern exposure was her favorite feature of the small apartment. It made the pricey rent of living in the Seaport District well worth it to her.

"Is Johnnie Walker Black Label okay?" she asked, unsure. "I have a bottle my brother gave me. It was from two Christmases ago, but whiskey is supposed to get better with age, right?"

"If you don't drink it, why did he give it to you?"

"Because Robert has mastered the art of giving that's actually receiving. It's what *he* drinks, which works out well for him when he comes to visit." She smiled as she poured their drinks, remembering her brother's feigned look of shock when she called him out on it. Then the jokester had redeemed himself by giving her her real present.

"Is this him?"

Olivia picked up the glasses and started to bring them to him in the living room, but then froze midstep and she felt her smile falter. There were several pictures of Robert around her apartment, on the walls and on shelves, but the 5x7 frame Erik held from where he'd gotten it on the end table wasn't of her and her brother.

It was of her and her husband.

Brett's arms were wrapped around her from behind, their figures bulky in winter jackets, scarves, and knit caps that covered their heads. It'd been shot at the end of a snowball fight during Christmas break their last year in college. With bright eyes, red cheeks, and white puffs of laughter, the image perfectly captured their happiness—back when things, including their relationship, had been easier—frozen in time.

Jesus, how could she have been so stupid? Bringing a man back to the apartment that still looked as though Brett might walk through the door at any minute. She'd never even gotten rid of the navy blue papasan chair he'd had during college. The one that he always sat in and pulled her down to his lap so she could snuggle with him while he studied. The one that she cried in for weeks after he was gone, that could still be found in the corner of her bedroom and was now used by Ben and Jerrys as their preferred cat bed.

Bringing Erik here was a mistake. How could she expect to move on in a place where she'd stopped the hands of time? She needed to get both aspects of her life—the emotional and physical—on the same damn page before any of this could happen here. *Shit, shit, shit.*

Maybe they could finish their drinks and she could beg

off with a headache or something. Yeah, that was a great fricking plan. *Cliché much, Olivia?* She'd have to make it up as they went.

Pasting what she hoped appeared as a carefree expression on her face, Olivia walked over and handed Erik his whiskey. She lowered herself to the other corner of the couch and tucked her bare feet under her, then finally answered his question. "No, Robbie's the one with me over there next to the windows."

Erik followed her line of sight to the hanging frame and got a laugh out of it just like everyone else did. She and her brother were often mistaken for twins, they looked so much alike, but their personalities were almost complete opposites, and their outfits in that picture aptly portrayed that fact. Olivia wore a simple sundress with a lightweight sweater and a sweet smile, while Robbie's mischievous grin matched his faded black T-shirt that stated "I'm with Stupid" above an arrow pointing straight down to his crotch.

"I bet he's a riot at holiday gatherings."

"That's putting it mildly. I don't think he was born with a serious bone in his body, but for as big as his sense of humor is, his heart is even bigger. He's a great older brother."

"Doesn't surprise me that you have a wonderful family, considering how amazing I think you are." He stretched his arm out along the back of the couch and linked his fingers with hers. It scared her how much she craved his touch after not having it for only five minutes. After taking a sip of his drink, he nodded at the picture he'd replaced on the end table. "So who's that?"

Her stomach tightened into a knot and she eagerly lifted her wineglass and took several large swallows to stall for time. Though what good that would do, she had no idea. A distraction, that's what she needed. It was what they both needed; screw the headache idea. A distraction with no thoughts of the past. Only the here and now. Erik and her.

Rising, Olivia finished her drink and set the glass off to the side. Holding his gaze, she straddled his lap and fitted their bodies together. Whiskey all but forgotten on the end table, his large hands slid over her hips and around to squeeze her ass cheeks as he pulled her in to notch his hardness against her sex.

She leaned in to kiss him, but his head backed away at the last second. Golden eyes studied her for what seemed like forever, causing the knot in her belly to twist. "Why do I get the feeling you're avoiding my question?"

"Probably because you're thinking with the wrong head. Let's focus on what this one wants," she said with a roll of her pelvis.

The way he grunted in the back of his throat and closed his eyes gave her a thrill, that she could affect him so much with so little. Coming out of his brief moment of euphoria, he leveled her with a look that she imagined he gave subordinates right before having to repeat a command. "Who is he?"

Fuck! She couldn't do *this*—be with another man, especially in the apartment that held so many memories—if Erik kept bringing up her husband. *Former* husband, she corrected herself. "No one. Now stop making it a big deal, okay?"

"Olivia, I asked out of casual curiosity and expected a simple answer in return, after which I planned to act on all the things that've run through my mind in the last four hours, if not the last four weeks. You're the one making this a big deal by avoiding the question."

"Just because I don't want to give you a verbal slideshow of every photo in my apartment doesn't mean I'm avoiding anything," she bit out.

"He your ex-boyfriend? The one you wanted me to help you get over that night?"

She had no idea how to respond to that. Distraction hadn't worked. Denial? Deflection? Some other *D* word? Telling him the truth wasn't an option. This might only be one question, but it always led to a whole slew of questions, and she wasn't ready to have that conversation with her new—or *potentially* new—lover. It would ruin everything.

Men were territorial creatures, like domestic dogs, running around and marking what they considered to be theirs to warn off others.

But Erik...he was so much more than that. Fiercer, more intense, more loyal. His call sign fit him perfectly, for he truly was a wolf among dogs. How would he react when she told him she'd belonged to someone else as completely as she had to Brett? As ludicrous as it was—it's not like she'd done anything wrong by being previously married—she knew she wouldn't blame him if he showed any discontent because she already had the crazy feeling that Erik belonged to *her* more than Brett ever had.

*Oh my God, what am I thinking? That can't be right. No, no that's just...*insane.

Releasing a heavy exhale, Olivia stood up and paced several steps away before facing him again. She had really fucked this up. She should have ended the date after the sunset cruise while they were still ahead. The agreement was for three *dates*, not *hookups*. "Maybe this wasn't the best idea after all."

Erik rose and ate up the distance between them with two strides of his long legs. When his hands closed over her shoulders, she wanted to both break away and fall into his arms. Her body begged her to stop listening to her brain and give in to what it craved more than anything else in that moment. But it wasn't her head that kept throwing down roadblocks. It was her confused heart warring between remaining faithful to a husband who was no longer here...and wanting to be absolved of doing that very same thing.

"Livvie, don't shut me out. Not after finally starting to let me in."

She huffed. "I'm not shutting you out, Erik. We'd have to be '*a thing*' for me to do that, but that's not what this is. We hooked up once and we enjoy each other's company. Don't make it out to be more than that."

His hands fell away, and the muscles in his jaw ticked in agitation. Olivia hated watching the molten passion in his eyes harden, but she had to stand firm. She'd been fooling herself that she was ready to let go, and until she did, Brett's memory would always be a third wheel in any relationship she had.

"Whatever you say, Doc." Erik strode across the apartment and yanked the door open. He started to close it behind him but turned back at the last second. "I'll be in touch so we can work out the plans for our second date."

"You…still want to go out with me?" Her pulse raced like she was in the middle of running the Boston marathon and not standing in her living room, her body as immobile as the furniture around her.

He let out a quiet chuff of what she could only describe as mirth borne of frustration with a single shake of his head. "Sweetheart, it's gonna take a hell of a lot more than some issue with a guy in a picture to shake me. Sweet dreams, Livvie."

# Chapter Ten

All things considered, Erik didn't hate his sessions with Dr. Marion. He'd liked the older man before all of this, and now he also respected him as a fellow veteran even if he *was* a fucking jarhead. Erik tried not to hold that against him.

It helped that Marion knew what it was like to be in combat, in enemy territory, never knowing if each day you woke up might be your last. It helped that he understood how being deployed in a war zone for any length of time required a person to mentally compartmentalize things in order to do his job, no matter how hard or fucked up that job might be, when the time came. Without hesitation or reservation. When Erik had difficulty iterating certain things about his experiences downrange, Marion knew how to gently prod the words from him.

Probably the aspect that made Erik the most comfortable—as comfortable as he could be in a situation where he was required to repeatedly relive his nightmares and failures—was the sense of formal address and command. When given the option of using the man's title as doctor or major, Erik chose the latter. You can take the man out of the military, but you can't take the military out of the man. He guessed that's why he and the boys operated their team on Rescue 2 the way they did. It felt natural, like part of their government-issued DNA.

True to his military style, the major was a no-bullshit kind of guy. Instead of saying things like, "Tell me, how did that make you feel," he grunted and then stared until it got so awkward, Erik felt compelled to fill the silence by elaborating till he was fucking blue in the face.

Interrogation 101. *Crafty bastard.*

But just because Erik liked the major and felt more comfortable talking to him than he would most people didn't mean therapy was all sunshine and endless ammo. Fuck no. Mostly it downright sucked ass. He wasn't there to talk about their football games in the desert, or the music video parody they made to Nelly's hit song "Hot in Herre," or the time he shook habanero hot sauce into Dozer's mouth when he fell asleep on detail. (Fucker got him back good by shaving off one of Erik's eyebrows during rack time. Made it damn hard for any of his men to take him seriously with only one goddamn eyebrow.)

No, he was there to talk about the "bad shit" he'd worked to keep on lockdown since the day he signed his release papers. That meant tearing open the ugly scars to expose the wounds and hating himself when he cried, showing weakness almost every fucking session. But, like the major reminded him every time, without that continued progress, Erik would never make it back to active duty with Rescue 2. So if he had to hate himself a little every week to get back in rotation, he'd deal with it.

They'd already gone through all of that this session, so Erik felt on edge and restless to get the hell out of there and head to the firehouse. He'd been going there a few times a week to work out with the boys during their tours. Being at the house both calmed and upset him, but at least they hadn't had any calls while he'd been there.

"Let's talk about the present for a bit," the major said. "You and Olivia saw each other over the weekend?"

Erik braced his hands above his knees, pressed back into the couch, and adjusted his position. As difficult as it was to talk about his time in Iraq, he'd almost prefer that than broaching this topic with Marion. Failure didn't sit well with him, and that's what Saturday ultimately felt like. One step forward and two leaps back. "Yes, sir, we had our first date."

"And did you talk about yourselves, get to know each other better?"

Thinking of how to answer, he scratched at the beard growth on his jaw and made a mental note to trim it down later. Now that he no longer had to be clean-shaven for work—anything more than a mustache was prohibited because it affected the seal of a SCBA mask—he sported anything from a five o'clock shadow to full-on scruff depending on his mood. Since his mood had pretty much been shit since his failed evening with Olivia, he hadn't bothered with it at all. Another day and he'd be reaching hobo status.

"Son?" the major prompted.

Clearing his throat, Erik answered honestly. "Some. I told her I wanted to know everything about her. She laughed like I'd meant it as a joke, but I didn't." One of the things that unnerved him was the realization that he'd happily listen to her tell her life story, beginning to present. Livvie took all his hard and fast rules—about women, dating, and permanency—and fragged them all to fuck, like she'd tossed a grenade at his feet. Normally, he would've been Oscar Mike—on the move—covering as much ground as possible before he got caught in the blast. But with Olivia, he didn't seem to care what the woman blew up. "She told me about her family and how she became a psychologist, basic things like that. She was hedging, though. There's something important she's not telling me."

"What makes you say that?"

"It might be her job to read people, but I honed my own skills in the service, much like I expect you did, sir."

"True enough," Marion said with a nod. "Important like what?"

"I think it has to do with her ex."

"Ex?"

"Ex-boyfriend. The one she's trying to get over. I think he messed with her head about something and she doesn't want to tell me."

"I see," the older man said against his steepled fingers. "And did you tell her about you? Your family, your time in the service or as a firefighter?"

"Not exactly." The major stared at him until Erik felt like a bug under a microscope. He sighed. "Not at all. I changed the subject."

"Why? Don't you think she deserves to know you like you want to know her? You can't expect someone else to open up if you won't do the same."

"I couldn't, not then," he said, swallowing hard. More staring. *Fuck.* "Something she said…it triggered me, and she noticed. Hazard of dating a shrink, I suppose. She was kind and let it drop without making anything of it."

"So it was a minor reaction?"

Erik drew his brows together and recalled the minutes in question. "Now that I think about it, I don't know that it was necessarily minor. I mean, I remember feeling like I was getting sucked into the memories, the tunnel vision started… but then her hand was on my face. Her touch grounded me somehow. Like a lifeline, pulling me back to the present. I think she actually kept me from sinking."

"That's good, Erik, but we need to work on *you* keeping yourself from sinking. Olivia isn't a service dog. You can't have her with you twenty-four-seven."

*And ain't that a shame.*

Dr. Marion pushed a disapproving, bushy gray brow toward his receding high-and-tight and put a stop to Erik's line of thought that had been on its way down in a hurry. Hell, was the man a psychologist or a psychic? Thankfully, the doc didn't comment, and Erik wasn't about to share.

"Keeping the guidelines we've established in mind," the doctor continued, "tell me how you think the rest of the date went. Did Olivia seem…present? In the moment with you?"

At his first session, the major had made it clear that due to his connection to Olivia as both her boss and godfather, hearing Erik talk about any part of their relationship would be walking more than one "fine line." Erik had agreed that any discussions involving her would remain focused on him. In other words, asking the good doctor for any inside intel on the enigmatic woman was a definite no-go, as was going into even the vaguest of details about anything physical that happened between them.

That's why Erik wasn't sure as to how questions about Olivia's demeanor related to him, but what the hell did he know? He wasn't the one with the fancy degree hanging on the wall. "She started out that way," he said, "but everything went to shit after we got to her apartment."

Concern flashed in the old man's eyes before he covered it up with his usual mask. "How do you mean?"

"She wouldn't tell me about a guy in a picture she had." No response. Fair enough. That wasn't a lot of info to go on. "She kept trying to change the subject, telling me it was nobody, but you don't keep framed pictures of nobodies. I'd bet ten-to-one odds it's her ex."

Dr. Marion shrugged. "So what if it is? What difference

does that make?"

"Fuck, I don't know. I mean, I didn't want to make a big deal about it—I even told myself that if she said that's who it was, I'd calmly put the frame down and leave the topic alone—but the more she didn't want to tell me, the more I wanted her to, until I pushed her too far. She put an end to the night before we finished our first drink." Then, because Erik knew what the follow-up question would be, he added, "And I've been an ornery son of a bitch ever since."

"Hmm." Dr. Marion's eagle-sharp eyes drilled into him as he rubbed two fingers over his chin. Erik had learned it meant the old marine was turning things over in that big brain of his before imparting words of wisdom. "You've heard the phrase never judge a book by its cover, yes?"

"I'm pretty sure my two-year-old niece has heard that phrase, sir," he answered wryly.

Dr. Marion grinned. "Exactly. It's one we all know, and yet we forget the lesson more often than not. You're here because you need help working through things from your past, but people who aren't aware of your situation would probably never assume you need therapy, much less that you're in it. Do you feel that's a fair statement?"

It was true enough. Erik liked to think that no one outside of the department would suspect he was cracking up. "I suppose so," he said, "but what does that have to do with Olivia or the fact that she wouldn't even tell me about the guy in the picture?"

"The point I'm trying to make is that you shouldn't make assumptions about the mental or emotional well-being of others. You're living proof that you can't look at someone and know whether they're fine or struggling with something. In other words, you shouldn't assume that something is easy to talk about simply because you think it should be."

Erik cursed and leaned forward, bracing his elbows on

his knees and scrubbing his hands over his head a few times before peering back up at the major. "I acted like a total ass, didn't I? I wasn't thinking about *why* she wouldn't tell me. I just kept pushing her."

As usual, the man didn't answer, but rather let Erik marinate in his own thoughts.

He couldn't deny that it had pissed him off to be faced with the reality that Livvie had belonged to someone before him—not that she belonged to Erik now, but that wasn't the point—and that that *someone* was still smiling in framed pictures with her that she apparently couldn't bear to take down. His sense of propriety, when it came to her, was irrational, but then again, nothing about the way he felt for her was anywhere near the realm of rational.

Damn it, he'd known she'd been hurting. She'd said as much that first night in the elevator, that she'd been trying to get over someone. Somewhere along the line, he stopped being sensitive to that fact, as though the few weeks they'd been talking would have automatically cured any heartache incurred from her past relationship. *Heartache.* The idea that some asshole caused her pain made him violent. He needed to check that shit at the door if he wanted a shot at making things better with her.

Better. He wondered if that was even possible. Being defeatist wasn't usually his way, but he couldn't help feeling like his inability to connect with Livvie, to get past her barriers, was somehow intertwined with the darkness in his past. Like the universe had put the perfect woman in his path just to fuck with him, to tempt him with a future he'd never have. The kind of future the men he'd let down in Iraq would never have. The epic karmic payback.

Dr. Marion finally decided to speak, interrupting Erik's thoughts that were starting to spiral downward fast. "I'm going to take my therapist hat off for a moment, son, and speak plainly for your sake and Olivia's."

Erik straightened on the couch like a dog whose ears perked up. If it had to do with him and Olivia, he wanted to hear it.

"I know I agreed the dates with Olivia were a good idea—and I still think they can be, under the right circumstances—but if your intentions don't reach beyond your belt buckle, I think it'd be best if you set your sights elsewhere. Understand?"

Okay, so not words of wisdom this time. A warning. The alpha in Erik wanted to tell Uncle Eddie to kindly fuck off in a not-so-kind way. But the man raised by Norma Grady—who pulled the hairs on her sons' heads as punishment for saying or doing anything considered rude or lacking in compassion—understood and respected the protective nature Olivia's godfather would have for a woman who was like a daughter to him.

"Yes, sir, I do."

"Good." A quick glance at his watch signaled the end of the session, and Dr. Marion went through the usual reminders and final thoughts. They stood, shook hands, and Erik made his way to the door.

As an afterthought, Erik paused with his hand on the doorknob and met his therapist's steady gaze. "For the record, Major, I don't have any intentions on going anywhere unless she's with me."

Surprise flitted over the old man's face, but he hid it quickly. "That's quite a statement, young man. Tell me, does my goddaughter agree with those terms?"

"I'm working on it, sir."

...

Since Olivia's last client of the day had canceled, she'd decided to leave the office early and work from the comfort of home. It had absolutely nothing to do with Erik's weekly appointment being scheduled for that afternoon and wanting to avoid him after the disastrous end to their date.

Nope. She simply felt like going home. She loved her office at the Pru, but sometimes she enjoyed the quiet of her apartment, knowing coworkers wouldn't disturb her if she needed so much as a restroom break. Her desk was in her bedroom in the extra sitting area space and faced the large windows that shared the same view of the harbor as her living room.

Usually, she got so much done in her little home office—but not today. Today, Olivia couldn't focus to save her life.

She'd tried doing the things that usually helped her relax and refocus—drinking her favorite hot tea, meditating, a quick run down in the fitness room—but nothing worked. Her mind was like a playlist with a single track on it, stuck on repeat: Erik Grady, Erik Grady, Erik Grady…

It seemed as though nothing would relieve her of this new obsession her brain had. At any given point in the day, she wondered what he might be up to. If he was doing well or struggling with his past. Hanging out at home or out with his friends. Whether he spent his nights alone…or with other women.

And *those* thoughts in particular always gave her the sudden urge to claw the eyes out of every female in a three-block radius. That sort of thing was more Angie's style, not Olivia's. Olivia had always been the picture of calm and reason to her Latina friend's displays of emotionally driven melodrama. That was, until recently.

For the hundredth time in five days, she wished she could go back in time to when Erik asked who the man was in the photo. She'd tell him this time. She'd bite the bullet and open herself up and take the chance that it might ruin things between them, because *not* telling him hadn't been any better.

Part of her balked at the idea of opening herself up beyond the basic new date chitchat. It wasn't like Erik had given her even that much on Saturday. She didn't know much about him other than what was in his psychiatric file and the little things she'd picked up on from his messages to her over the last month.

But then the other part of her said it shouldn't matter that he hadn't given her anything personal yet. Growing up with her father and Uncle Eddie, both former Marines, Olivia understood that people who served in the military were often incredibly private, and the only people who truly knew them were family and their fellow service members. They ate, slept, and breathed esprit de corps, and if you weren't a part of that group, you might as well be the enemy. So it wasn't probable that a man like Erik would willingly offer up anything that could make him vulnerable, which, to a man like Erik, was pretty much everything.

Sighing, Olivia closed her laptop. It was after ten o'clock at night, and she could already tell a certain man-slash-wolf would be running through her mind instead of sinking into a deep slumber if she tried turning in for the night. Maybe another cup of chamomile (with a splash of Robbie's whiskey) would help things along. If that didn't work, she'd need to break out the big guns: Benadryl.

Satisfied with her new plan, she shoved her feet into her fuzzy slippers, pulled her lightweight robe on over her thin tank and sleep shorts, and shuffled into the kitchen. She flipped the switch on her electric teakettle to start the water and almost had heart failure when her cell phone rang from where she'd left it on the coffee table. Figuring Angie wanted to firm up their lunch plans for the next day, Olivia hurried over and swiped to connect the call before she lost it to voicemail. Angie *hated* going into voicemail.

"Hey, babe, what's up?" she said as she flopped onto the

couch, earning an annoyed look from a previously sleeping Jerrys.

"I thought that was my line."

Olivia froze. That was not the lively, chipper voice of her best friend. Low and gruff, it caused things that couldn't possibly exist to take flight in her stomach. "Erik?"

"Hey, gorgeous. Good to hear your voice again. Sorry it took so long for me to call."

"Oh, that's okay. I mean, no, I wasn't expecting you to call so— There's just no reason for you to apologize, is what I'm saying." *God, Livvie, talk much? For shit's sake, you sound like an idiot.*

"That's where you're wrong, Livvie," he said with a hint of a sigh. "I do need to apologize. That's why I'm calling. I acted like an asshole the other night. I should've never pushed about that picture. It's none of my business, and I'm sorry."

"No, I'm the one who should be apologizing," she said. "You were right. It was an innocent question that should have had a simple answer."

The tension from not speaking to him for so long drained from her body as she tucked herself into the corner of the couch and pulled her favorite fuzzy throw over her legs. Jerrys instantly moved to the nicer real estate on her lap and then curled back into a ball before promptly going back to sleep. Taking a deep breath, Olivia took a leap of faith. "He was my husband."

Silence rang out louder than the cannons from the *USS Constitution*. "Husband," he repeated slowly, almost as though he couldn't quite process the information, then she heard him blow out a breath. "What happened between you? Because I have to tell you, it feels like he hurt you somehow. Like you have pieces of you that are damaged, and it drives me crazy to see that, Livvie."

She didn't realize he'd thought that about her, but it made

sense considering how they'd met, and she'd never corrected his assumption that she'd simply had a relationship end badly. Then again, it didn't get much worse when your other half was suddenly taken from you.

"It's not what you think," she said. "Brett was killed in a car accident two years ago."

"Fuck, baby, I'm so goddamn sorry." The rasp of his hand dragging over his stubble came through the phone. "I understand if you don't feel comfortable talking to me about this yet, but…I hope that someday you will be."

Olivia's heart melted. Erik Grady was more compassionate than she ever could have hoped for, and suddenly she couldn't hold things back from him any longer. Everything spilled out.

She told him how they'd met her freshman year in college and been friends and study partners for six months before they even had their first date, but then were pretty much inseparable: a power couple, their friends liked to tease. After years of dating, marriage became a forgone conclusion, the next step in the ten-year plan Brett had plotted out. One that she'd helped make but didn't necessarily agree with every step—like the one about having children that was set for years later than she preferred.

"Part of me will always mourn him, but I've worked through the worst of it. Brett and I were college sweethearts and got married at a young age. In retrospect, we probably wouldn't have made it into our thirties as a married couple. I loved him—he was a great man, and an even better friend—but we just weren't compatible in a lot of ways.

"Regardless, I was devastated when I lost him, and it wasn't until recently that I even started dating again. Any physical intimacy made me feel like I was being disloyal to Brett. I just couldn't seem to get past it, but…" Olivia paused. "When I'm with you, Erik, you're the only one I'm thinking about. You consume all of my senses," she said softly. "There's no room for anything or anyone else."

She heard him curse softly on the other end. "I can't tell you how fucking glad I am to hear that, Livvie."

He hadn't run. He was still on the phone, still talking to her. The crushing weight no longer sat on her chest. She had no more secrets. She felt light…and free. Free to finally be with someone on a deeper level. To be with Erik. "I wanted to tell you before, but in the past—well, let's just say the conversation has a tendency to chase men away."

A warm chuckle floated through her phone. "I don't know if you've noticed, sweetheart, but I'm kind of hard to get rid of where you're concerned. I'm like a dog with a very sexy bone."

"Or a wolf," she said to herself in the barest of whispers.

"Exactly. Just like a wolf, when I see something I want, I go after it with a single-minded purpose. And I want you, Livvie. All of you."

The air in her apartment suddenly felt thin, and taking a full breath was more of a struggle than it ought to be while immobile. His words made her hope for things she thought she'd never have again, and it rendered her momentarily speechless. Thankfully, he didn't mention the lull in conversation and continued talking.

"I want to ask you something, but I realize it might be too personal, so tell me if you'd rather not answer."

Clearing her throat, she finally managed, "Okay."

"What was your love life like with him? Because someone as beautiful as you shouldn't be as insecure as you are."

Olivia dragged her lower lip across her teeth as she thought of what to tell him. Her relationship with Brett had never been the kind that burned bright and hot with passion, whether in the bedroom or out. It was more like having the steady warmth of an electric blanket, knowing it would always feel the same—comfortable and reliable. It hadn't been bad; it just hadn't been great.

"I guess I'd say it was average?" Crap, she didn't mean that to sound like a question. "I mean, it wasn't anything like, um… It was, you know, good."

"Has any man ever told you you're the most breathtaking woman on the planet, that the curve of your waist was made for his hands or the delicate skin of your neck calls to him like a drug to an addict?" Erik had pressed. "Ever had a man worship your body with his hands and his mouth until you felt boneless with pleasure?"

Hearing those words, gruff and sensual, made her breath catch in surprise, and before she could release it, lust spread through her chest and much lower until she had to squeeze her legs to relieve some of the aching there.

"No," she'd whispered.

"Ever grab you from behind, remind you who you belong to, and then devour you up against the wall like a man starved?"

She shook her head, forgetting he couldn't see her. "No."

That's when his tone became a tad acrimonious. "Part of me is pissed off at that, Livvie. You deserved to hear those things, deserved to feel special and desired. But another part of me is glad as hell that I'll be the first one to make you feel like the goddess you are. And I can't fucking wait to show you all the ways I can make you melt beneath me."

"Me, either," she rasped. Erik exhaled sharply and cursed under his breath. "What's wrong?"

"Nothing, I just got carried away is all. It's damn near impossible to control myself where you're concerned. I called to apologize and tell you that I'm going to give you space or time or whatever it is you need. When you're ready, you let me know, and we'll go from there."

Before she could overthink it and change her mind, she blurted out, "I don't want that."

He spoke slowly, like his words were navigating an audible minefield. "Don't want what, exactly?"

"I don't want you to give me space. I've been kicking myself all week for being so bullheaded, and I wanted to be the one to call and apologize, but I was afraid you wouldn't want to talk to me anymore, and—"

"Livvie." He practically barked her name to get her to shut up, but she responded instantly. "You seem to have a real problem with believing me. How many times do I have to tell you that I'm not giving up that easily?"

Olivia bit the tip of her thumb in a variation of the pinch-for-reality-verification trick, then spoke hesitantly. "Maybe once more?" She couldn't be sure, but she thought it sounded like he might be growling on his end of the line. In her limited Wolf experience, that was either very bad…or very good.

"Tell you what. I have offsite Rapid Intervention training all day tomorrow, but after that I think I should come over."

"You do?" she asked, all breathy and…well, just breathy was bad enough. She cleared her throat and tried sounding like a normal human. "You do?"

"I do," he repeated. "We have some business to take care of."

"And what kind of business would that be?"

"The kind where I make sure you understand, once and for all, just how serious I am about being with you." Olivia's stomach clenched. But then his voice turned even gruffer and his next statement made a part of her lower than that clench, too. "The kind that'll make your ass pink and your pussy wet, and that's only the foreplay."

*Holy shit.* If he kept talking like that, this would be yet another round of foreplay to the hot-as-hell sex. *Holy double shit.* Tomorrow night, there would be hot-as-hell sex. And not the anonymous strangers in a one-night stand kind of sex. The kind that had been building up for weeks with every voicemail, email, text, and encounter they'd had. It'd be like touching a match to a gasoline-soaked pile of wood.

"I'll be there by six, Livvie. Be waiting for me. And make sure you're not wearing anything you want to keep intact."

"Okay," she answered breathily. Squeezing her legs together ceased offering any sort of relief. At this point, she'd have to take care of things herself as soon as they were off the phone. But somehow he sensed her frustration, and whether it was a damn good guess or his wolfish instincts, he put an end to that plan instantly.

"Don't you dare touch yourself tonight, Livvie," he growled. "That orgasm belongs to me. And when I'm good and ready to watch you come undone for me, I'm going to take it from you."

# Chapter Eleven

Olivia tried to concentrate on the book in her hands, but she'd already read the same page four times and still had no idea what the hell it said. Worrying her lip with her teeth, she pushed the button on her phone to illuminate the screen. Erik was supposed to have showed up an hour ago so they could pick up where they left off the week before. At least that's what he'd said last night.

Just the thought of their conversation the night before made butterflies erupt in her belly.

*Damn, damn, damn…* Just thinking about that part of the call was getting her worked up all over again. Where the hell was he? Maybe he had reconsidered…?

No, if he could make it, he would. She needed to stop doubting him every time her insecurities wanted to toss in their two cents. She needed to stop having insecurities, period. Unfortunately, that was easier said than done, but definitely something she'd work on.

The problem was that she was a worrier by nature. So if he wasn't purposely standing her up, then her mind automatically switched to thinking that something bad happened, which didn't help her frayed nerves in the least.

Taking a long, steadying breath, Olivia brainstormed a logical reason as to why Erik wasn't there. She exhaled slowly and decided that after a hard day of training, he sat on the couch at the station to relax for a few minutes and then passed out from exhaustion. Yes, that was it. And *that* was completely understandable.

She just wished he'd have made it to her apartment first. She'd gladly take care of him as he unwound; maybe she'd rub tension out of his shoulders or let him rest his head in her lap so she could absentmindedly trail her fingertips over his soft buzz cut while they watched TV.

She'd gotten home earlier than usual today and had already taken her nervous energy out on her apartment—it could now pass for one of the model apartments that no one lived in—and then she'd attacked poor Ben and Jerrys with a brush. It was true they were overdue for a good grooming, but judging by the plastic bag filled with black, white, and orange fur, they were lucky they had any still attached to their bodies. Her beloved pets had been hunkered together under her bed for the last two hours, probably fearing for what little fur they had left.

Crap, this was driving her crazy. Her fingers itched to call him and put herself out of her neurotic misery, but she'd managed to restrain herself thus far, and she'd continue to do so, damn it. She needed something that could take her mind off of the waiting and wondering.

That's when her gaze snagged on the bottle of Jameson she'd picked up for when Erik arrived. Maybe drinking a few fingers of whiskey would take the edge off. At the very least, it would take all her concentration to get it down without choking to death. Perfect.

Thirty minutes later, she needed a distraction from her

distraction (she was pretty sure her throat was literally on fire) and took that opportunity to glance at the time on her phone when someone pounded on her door, followed by a booming voice that easily penetrated the solid barrier. "Fire department, open up."

Jumping up in giddy relief from the bar stool, she almost knocked over the glass of whiskey that still held one and a half of the two fingers she poured herself (seriously, that stuff was nasty) before composing herself to react like the mature adult she was. But mature or not, she wasn't above holding out on him and making him squirm—just a *little*—to get back at him for her shot nerves.

"I'm sorry, but you must be mistaken," she called back. "I didn't call the fire department. Mrs. Peters down the hall probably did, though. You should check with her."

Olivia heard the distant sound of a door slamming—oddly enough in the direction of where Mrs. Peters's apartment was located—and then heard a low command uttered barely loud enough for her to make out the words. "Unlock this door, gorgeous, or I'm breaking it down."

Okay, screw payback, she'd waited for him long enough. She reached out, threw the deadbolt, and immediately hopped back when the door swung open like a gale-force wind was behind it. She was dimly aware of it being kicked shut, but most of her brainpower was totally focused on taking in the sight of the hottest thing she'd ever seen: Erik, standing in her neat little apartment, larger than life and fully dressed in his bunker gear.

*Ho...ly...shit.* She'd imagined him in his ranger kit before, certain it would melt her panties to see him geared up and ready for battle, but she never thought she'd find his turnout gear so damn sexy. He stood there, massive, like a first-responder god, dressed head to toe in bulky black attire striped with bands of reflective yellow. The coat hung open, revealing a tucked-in navy blue BFD T-shirt, and his helmet dangled from the fingertips of one hand.

"Why are you dressed like that?" she rasped through a suddenly dry throat.

"Training took for-fucking-ever." Setting his helmet on the counter, he pulled his cell from a pocket and held it up before tossing it on the counter. "Totally dead, or I would've called. Couldn't wait. Guys dropped me off."

One of her favorite things about Erik was how well-spoken he was. As primal as his characteristics might be, he wasn't a Neanderthal grunting his likes and dislikes in disjointed phrases. But tonight was obviously no ordinary night. Since walking through the door, he hadn't uttered a single complete sentence, and his whiskey-colored eyes might as well be saying *Me, Tarzan. You, Jane* for all the civility she saw in them.

"The fuck are you wearing?" he asked, heat flickering in his eyes.

Unable to remember, she glanced down. Oh, right. "An oversize sleep shirt I've had for years." She frowned, rethinking her choice. "Not the sexiest thing, I know."

He'd said she shouldn't wear anything she wanted intact, and this thing was a handful of washes away from dissolving into the ether. The white cotton shirt, which hit her at mid-thigh, was threadbare and transparent enough that the dusky rose color of her nipples showed through without the aid of special lighting, and the neck was so wide it was forever sliding off one shoulder or the other. Underneath, she wore a white lacey thong. She almost hadn't worn any panties at all, but she couldn't bring herself to be quite that bold.

"No," he said, "it's perfect." Rolling his shoulders back, he shucked the heavy coat and tossed it over one of the kitchen bar stools, then advanced, ambling toward her and causing warmth to pool in her belly.

Dark stubble covered his jaw and part of his neck, and she remembered loving the way it softly abraded her skin as he roamed down her body or scratched along her inner thighs when he buried his face between her legs and launched her into the heavens with lips, teeth, and tongue.

"You're blushing. Tell me what you're thinking." Like a trained animal, her body reacted to the command and strength in his tone. Her skin tingled and her nipples pebbled in anticipation of his hands, his mouth; good Lord, what the man could do with his mouth.

"I'm thinking about how devilishly handsome you are," she answered hesitantly. "That's not exactly right, but what I'm thinking is…well, lewder than I'm comfortable articulating at this juncture of the evening."

"Christ, Livvie, I love the way you say things. When you talk all proper like that, it makes my dick get so fucking hard."

Good thing, because she didn't know how else to talk—something she would have iterated to him if she didn't find herself rendered speechless as she watched him come toward her with lithe movements that belied his size. He shrugged out of the suspenders attached to his bunker pants and let them fall to hang at the sides of his legs. Then he started pulling his shirt up and out of his waistband, and her throat went dry.

"I love that you're thinking dirty inside that sexy brain of yours, Doc," he said, his voice deep and gravelly. "Have I turned my sweet, innocent Livvie into a sexual deviant already?"

Reaching one hand back between his shoulder blades, he yanked off his T-shirt and dropped it to the floor, discarded as thoroughly as every last thought in her head. It was the first time she'd seen his entire torso shirtless since the hotel, and her memory should be ashamed of itself, because it hadn't done the real thing a shred of justice.

Perfectly formed pectorals tipped with flat brown

nipples sat over two columns of eight—yes, *eight*—blocks of abdominal muscles that disappeared into his pants that rode low on his hips, along with the slashing *V*s of his obliques. All of that framed by round shoulders and muscular arms... Sweet baby Jesus. *No* one with a body that perfect should ever be allowed to cover it up.

At last he stood directly in front of her, mere inches apart that still seemed like miles. "I asked you a question."

Did he? She tried to rewind the last thirty seconds... something about...*sexual deviant*. Oh, definitely, but... "Only with you."

"Good answer," he growled as he caught her up against the hard planes of his body, then he crushed his mouth to hers and all sense of time and place evaporated.

Erik devoured her, consumed her. His hands were everywhere all at once—fisting her hair, kneading her breasts and the globes of her ass—then his kiss went rogue, running over her jaw to her ear to the place where neck met shoulder.

She felt him grab the top of her shirt a split second before the sound of it being rent in two filled the air. It was now ripped down the front far enough to expose her to her naval. He pushed the sides apart and attacked her breasts with his mouth, lavishing each of them in turn with a ferocity that made her feel worshipped and helpless in the same breath.

"Erik, please," she begged, staring down at the top of his head in a dizzying reverie. "I need you."

His gaze snapped up at her plea. He reminded her of a feral creature standing over his meal, wary and unhappy at the interruption. But then awareness flickered in his eyes and he straightened to his full height, which placed the tempting hollow of his throat in her direct line of sight. Giving in to temptation, she leaned in and laved the indentation, intending on continuing all the way up, but he halted those plans when he fisted her hair and forced her eyes to meet his.

"How? Where?" he demanded. "Tell me, Livvie. Tell me how to make you forget your own name. Tell me what you need."

She tried shaking her head, but he held her hair fast. "Anything, everything, I don't care. So long as it's here and now, all I need is you."

Holding his gaze, she slipped her hand inside his bunker pants then cupped his thick erection over the heavy cargos he wore underneath. Hissing through clenched teeth, he wrenched her hair back even more. She gasped, both startled and exhilarated as the pleasuring sting at her scalp swept over her skin and left trails of goose flesh in its wake.

Erik's nostrils flared with shallow breaths and his pupils had long since swallowed their amber counterparts. Still, he held himself back. Like he was waiting for her to say the one thing that would snap the leash on his control and release the man he'd been with her in their hotel room, the man she'd known only as one thing.

"Take me, Wolf."

That's all it took.

Whether it was her complete submission or using the name she'd called him that first impassioned night together, he went from stock-still to explosive in the blink of an eye.

He spun her around in his arms and bent her over the small dining room table. Pressing a hand between her shoulder blades, he growled a single command of "Stay" before crouching behind her. He shoved the bottom of her shirt up around her waist then tore her thong clear off. Rough hands grabbed the cheeks of her ass and spread them, exposing her even farther. She felt the cool air hit her a moment before the warmth of his breath feathered over her swollen sex.

"Swear to Christ, Livvie, you have the prettiest pussy I've ever seen." He slid one finger through her folds, from entrance to clit and back again, stimulating her precisely enough to make her insane.

She whimpered, ready to beg if that's what he wanted. Hell, she'd beg, grovel, plead, and promise damn near anything under the sun to get him to do more than merely tease her with his finger. Unable to control the urge, Olivia's hips arched up, her pussy literally seeking out the contact it needed so desperately. But that only earned her a sharp smack to her right cheek, making her gasp as the heat from his hand seeped into her skin.

"That was for trying to manipulate me into giving you more than I wanted. Now hold still or I'll drag this out even longer."

Oh God, if he did that she wouldn't survive it. Never in her life had she experienced even a hundredth of the sexual tension—the desire, the feverish *need*—coursing through her body. She'd do anything in this moment to feel him filling her, stretching her, claiming her.

"Please," she whispered.

"Shhhhh…" Again he stroked along her inner lips, lighting up the zillions of sensitive nerve endings and killing her a little more with every passing second. She bit down on her lip, her body vibrating with the discipline it took to not move a single muscle as he tortured her with one long finger. "So perfect. So pink and wet," he grated. "So fucking *mine*."

With that, Erik finally—blessedly—delved between her legs, his mouth assaulting her in the most carnally delicious ways. She cried out, overwhelmed by the ministrations of his wicked tongue lapping and swirling and flicking. The stubble on his jaw scratched along the inside of her thighs and the calluses on his hands rasped her sensitive skin as he pulled her open to give him better access to the most intimate parts of her.

Though she was still lying prone on the table, Olivia swore she was floating. The world around her felt fluid and in constant motion, like a zero-gravity chamber. Erik pulled back, breaking contact with her, and she thought she'd cry from the separation until he drove two fingers deep inside of her and started pumping them in and out, priming her body for him. Then he curled his fingers and used quick, shallow strokes to rub along the ridged surface of her G-spot, and suddenly she was that much closer to heaven.

"Yes!" she cried out. "Oh God, that feels so good. Don't stop, don't ever stop."

The sensation of a rubber band twisting in her belly grew tighter and tighter as she chased her orgasm. But she couldn't seem to catch it. It hung there, suspended and just out of reach. Sweat dampened her hairline, and somewhere in the back of her mind she was cognizant of the mumbling pleas spilling from her lips, begging him to give her that sweet release.

"Good girl, Livvie," he said, the vibrations of his deep voice radiating through her overly sensitized flesh. "Go ahead, you've earned it. Come for me."

She felt the rough pad of his thumb press on her clit, and the double stimulation (and maybe his command) finally, *finally* sent her flying. Her back arched sharply, her entire body pulled taut like a bowstring as he continued to milk her climax, and the waves of it crashed over her like a stormy tide.

"That's it, baby. Fuck, you're so tight. I can't wait anymore."

Olivia heard the foil wrapper of a condom being torn, then felt the blunt head of Erik's cock part her swollen lips and poise at her entrance. Relief and anticipation swirled together at the culmination of what she'd fantasized about more times than what could be considered healthy. She was about to be filled by the man who'd haunted her dreams and even her daydreams; the man who'd obliterated every misconception she'd had of how sex *should* be; the man who did, in fact, make her feel like a goddess and knew exactly how to make her melt beneath him.

"You'd better hold on, gorgeous. This is going to be a bumpy fucking ride."

Her pleasure-addled brain had only one response. *It's about damn time.*

...

Erik barely gave her time to grab the opposite edge of the table before he thrust home, burying himself so deeply he couldn't tell where he ended and she began. Hell, he wasn't sure he even wanted to. He might play the dominant role, the one who held all the power, but in truth it was Olivia. Thank fuck she wasn't the type to get off on control but preferred having it taken. Because if she knew just how badly he had it for her, she'd have him pinned to the ground under a spiked heel faster than he could say Oscar Mike.

Leaning over her, he blanketed her body with his and kissed his way up from shoulder to ear. "Livvie, Livvie, my Livvie," he said, his voice strained from holding himself still inside her hot sheath. "You feel so goddamn good, Livvie. I'm not going to last."

"I don't care. Just fuck me, Erik," she said. *"Please."*

Hottest thing ever? This strong and beautiful woman literally begging him to fuck her, and he'd be damned if he'd keep her waiting any longer. "My pleasure."

Erik withdrew almost entirely before slamming all the way back in to the hilt, forcing a grunt from his chest and an exultant cry from her lips. He didn't pause or break stride as he pistoned his hips again and again, seating her on the length of his dick with reckless abandon.

Part of him wanted to straighten up so he could watch himself enter her, watch as her sweet cunt swallowed every last inch of his cock. But he couldn't bring himself to put that much space between them; he'd prefer it if nothing, not even air, separated him from Olivia's body. Already he regretted not taking the time to shuck the rest of his clothes and bunker pants, since he could feel them preventing his groin and thighs from making contact with the smooth skin of her backside.

Although he had to admit, fucking her in part of his turnout gear was hot as shit. Talk about a fantasy come true, this couldn't have been better than if one of those smut-pedaling romance novelists had written it for him.

"Harder," she gasped. "Fuck me harder."

"Hell yes." He kept the steady rhythm but threw all his weight behind his thrusts, acting like a battering ram breaking down any remaining walls she'd built to keep him out. "You're going to feel me inside of you for days. And every time it'll remind you of who owns your sweet pussy."

Needing more leverage to make good on that claim, he slipped his arm beneath her, then anchored his hand on her opposite shoulder. He used his other hand to wrap around the length of her hair. With one hand pulling in and the other pulling back, Erik doubled his efforts and reveled in her moans and cries of utter satisfaction as he pounded into her like his life depended on it.

"Feel that, baby? This is where you belong. Under me, with my cock filling you up. Isn't that right?"

"Yes."

"Say it," he growled. "Say this is where you belong."

"It's where I belong," she panted. "However you want me. I'm yours."

*I'm yours.* Those words echoed in his head and reverberated through his chest, somewhere in the vicinity of his heart. They made him feel like an indestructible force, a Sherman tank in human form. As long as she was his, he could do anything, beat anything—even this PTSD shit—because just being with her was motivation enough to be the best self he could be.

She'd been one hell of a catch to reel in, damn near fighting him the entire way, but now that he had her—and he *did* finally have her—he wasn't about to let her slip away from him again.

"That's right, baby. No more running. Not from this. Not from us. You. Are. *Mine*."

As they hurtled toward the finish line, he got faster and faster, like a runaway train with a busted accelerator. He felt the muscles in her cunt flutter around him, felt the white-hot lightning of his own orgasm shoot down his back to pool at the base of his spine, gathering strength and drawing his balls in tight. If she didn't come soon, he'd be going off without her and that was un-fucking-acceptable.

Releasing his hold on her shoulder, Erik drove his hand between her pelvis and the table. He found her clit with the tips of his fingers and began to rub circles over the distended nub. Her mouth fell slack and her eyes rolled back. She was right there, hovering at the edge, but not yet falling over.

"Told you last night. I own your orgasms, baby, and I want your cunt milking my cock right fucking *now*," he said, giving her hair a quick yank for emphasis. "Give yourself over to me, Livvie. *Come for me.*"

Obedient as ever, her inner muscles responded to his command and clenched him so tight he thought he might pass out. She tried to scream through her climax, but he wrenched her head to the side and swallowed it with a bruising kiss just as his own cum rocketed up his dick and emptied into her convulsing channel.

Breathing being a necessity for sustaining life, they were eventually forced to break apart and draw in long gulps of air. Other than the heavy panting, they could've passed for dead, lying lifeless over her dining room table.

"Am I crushing you?" he asked, his face buried in her neck.

"Uh-uh."

She may have answered in the negative, but she sounded like she had an elephant sitting on her chest. "Liar." Reluctantly, Erik pushed himself up. He had to take care of the condom and get them both cleaned up so they could move on to the Netflix part of their date…so they could do more of the "chill" part later, after they recovered. Despite not being cleared for active duty yet, he still had another seven-hour day of training ahead of him, so he'd have to suck up the lack of sleep. He'd done a lot harder shit on a lot less sleep as a ranger, and he had a lot of wasted time to make up for with this woman.

The sad little sound she made when his softening erection slipped from her tight sheath made him want to gather her up and hold her, reassure her that even if they weren't physically connected, he'd keep her as close to him as humanly possible.

Instead, he bent to kiss her sweat-dampened temple and told her he'd be right back. After turning the shower on to let the water warm up, he finally got out of his boots and the last of his attire, bunker pants and all. He went back to Livvie, who hadn't moved a muscle other than the satiated smile now gracing her beautiful face, and tore the rest of the shirt from her before lifting her into his arms and carrying her into the bathroom.

When he set her gently on her feet, his eyes immediately caught on the light purple marks marring the creamy skin in the front of her hip bones. What…? *The edge of the table.* Cursing a blue streak, Erik dropped to his knees to study the bruises. "Fuck, Livvie, I'm so sorry," he said, his voice raspy with tension. "I was too rough with you; you should have said something."

Anger boiled in his veins; anger at her for not telling him he was hurting her and anger at himself for not keeping his head on straight and realizing what the repercussions would be from their position and the force he was using.

"I would have said something if I needed to, Erik."

Delicate fingers with trim nails skated over his buzzed head. As always, her touch instantly soothed him and calmed the beast rioting inside his mind, but he didn't want to be soothed or calm. He didn't deserve it after doing this to her. He was a fucking monster who couldn't be trusted to keep his own brothers alive, much less an angel safe from harm. Why did everyone in his care always get hurt?

"Erik." She pushed back on his head to get him to look up at her, which he allowed and found himself staring into hazel eyes that had the power to condemn or exonerate. "You didn't hurt me."

"But—"

"No," she said firmly. "You did *not* hurt me. I would have told you if you were. I get bruises all the time. Look at me, I'm like Casper the Friendly Ghost. You can't be worried about leaving your marks on me or this relationship is going to have a very boring sex life."

He searched her face for signs that she wasn't as okay as she claimed, but all he saw was sincerity. *She's okay. She's fine.* The knot of dread unfurled in his chest, allowing the last part of what she said to finally sink in. A slow smile spread over his face. "Are you conceding that we're in a relationship? Not that I'm giving you a choice, understand. I just want to hear you agree."

"I don't know," she said with a half grin. "I guess I'll consid—" Erik delivered a quick smack to her backside, making her draw in a sharp breath before chuckling. "Yes, Lieutenant Wolf, I concede. I'm agreeing to a relationship."

"'Bout damn time you got on board, woman," he growled. He kissed her just above the belly button to punctuate his approval, then shifted to place a gentle trail of healing kisses along each of her bruises.

Olivia's fingers were back on his scalp, causing tingles to

run down his spine. He was so lost in the moment he almost didn't hear her speak. "Does it make me kind of weird that I like having them?"

She was referring to the purpling marks on her skin. Ones that would be tender and sore and remind her of him every time she felt them. With his hands at her hips and his thumbs softly grazing the bruises in question, he told her the absolute truth. "It makes you kind of perfect."

Blushing, she bit down on the corner of her lip. A sight that made him greedy and selfish, wanting it for himself, so he rocked up to his full height, framed her face with his hands, and *took*. Took her kiss, her mouth with its swollen lips, red as cherries and her tongue that still tasted of the Jameson he'd noticed she had earlier.

He felt like an addict. He'd had her mere minutes ago and already he craved her taste on his tongue and harbored a soul-deep need to watch her fall apart in his arms again. But another part of him—a part he hadn't known existed until Olivia—wanted to care for her, protect her. Even if that meant protecting her from his own insatiable appetite.

Using the last remnants of his control, Erik broke away. "Come on, sweetheart. We've got about ten minutes before the pizza I ordered on my way over gets here. I need you cleaned up and dressed because if the delivery guy catches even a glimpse of what's mine, I'm guaranteed to lose my shit."

Laughing, she let him lead her into the stall and under the spray, and even with as much as his dick protested, Erik managed to keep the shower quick and PG-13. Later, though, after they'd eaten and relaxed a little, he'd make sure they worked off the carbs and alcohol with a marathon bedroom session for the books.

He'd have to stop for a sixer of Red Bull and a bottle of Advil on his way in to training tomorrow morning, but he had no doubt in his mind it would be totally fucking worth it.

# Chapter Twelve

"Come on, Wolf, get it up here. Being away from the house turning you into a pussy or what?"

Air hissed out between Erik's teeth as he glared up at a shirtless Smoke—a rare occurrence due to the cosmetic damage his body suffered from an explosion downrange—and pushed the free bar the last few inches before racking the weight. Breathing heavy as a motherfucker, Erik crunched up into a sitting position on the black padded bench that sported several manly patch jobs with silver duct tape.

Smoke ran a hand through his sweat-dampened blond hair and scoffed. "My fucking grandmother benches more than that. You're getting soft, old man."

Erik grabbed the small towel by his feet and wiped the sweat dripping down his face as he turned to his overly critical spotter. Smoke, wearing white basketball shorts and his trademark shit-eating grin, was now hunched over with elbows out and forearms stretched along the racked bar, casual as could be.

"Not what your grandma says, brother." Pushing up to his

feet, Erik said, "And her strength comes from handling my giant fucking cock all day."

Shouts and laughter erupted in the firehouse gym as the guys rated the "burn" handed to the golden boy. With a final swipe down his chest, Erik winked and tossed the sweaty towel on Smoke before smacking him upside the head.

Chuckling, Erik turned and ignored the scuffling sounds that told him "the kids" were probably roughhousing behind him, and made his way over to the pull-up bars. Dozer joined him, having just finished an eternity with the jump rope. For as huge as the man was, when he worked with the rope, he was extremely nimble and light on his feet. Training as an amateur boxer for years did that.

They chalked up their hands in silence and jumped to grip the adjacent metal bars, immediately starting a set of nonstop butterfly pull-ups. At the end of the set, they dropped to their feet and then their asses to do the abs routine they used to do in the army.

Hands behind his head, Erik continued his sit-ups as he spoke. "Ask."

Dozer didn't break his stride, either. "Ask what?"

"You know what, so ask."

"Fine. You getting serious with this chick?"

"First of all, she's a woman, a lady, and you'll respect her as such, whether she's around or not."

Dozer chuckled under his breath. "No need for a 'second of all,' Grady. You just answered my question."

"Very funny, wiseass. It's too new to be considered serious," Erik said. "But it's a lot more serious than any of the one-nighters we've been having for the last however many years."

"Hey, just because you got attached to someone doesn't mean you can knock the crazy-hot sex that's been keeping our dicks wet with no strings for years. Some things are sacred, brother."

Erik chuckled, but then sobered as he asked, "Don't you ever get sick of it, though, man? Wouldn't you like to know you have someone who cares about you; someone to come home to at the end of a long tour? Because I gotta tell ya, this thing with Livvie might be new, but she fills this part of me I didn't even know was empty until I met her. Being with her makes me…"

"Horny?" he supplied with a smirk.

"Happy, dumbass," Erik said, unable to hide the smile his friend's ribbing brought out. Erik knew all too well what it was like to lose his friends, and he was constantly aware that any one of them could be taken from him on any given day with their jobs. He appreciated every minute he had with them, even when they acted like cranky two-year-olds or like pre-pubescent boys. "She makes me happy, D. I know it's still early, but I'm fucking crazy about her."

"If that's the case, then I'm happy for you, man." The humor slipped from Dozer's face as he stared at Erik, the strength of their bond—forged in the fire of more life-or-death situations than they could count—pierced through all the bullshit jokes. "If she turns out to be the one, she'll always be treated as one of our own."

A thick lump formed in Erik's throat. That wasn't a simple statement from one friend to another promising to be nice to his new girlfriend. No, that was a vow from one brother to another that if anything happened to Erik in the line of duty, his brothers would take care of the woman he left behind. Erik didn't know if this thing between him and Livvie had what it took to go the distance, but he *did* know that he was already in deep. She was special, and if it were up to him, he'd spend every moment of every day with her.

A flash of guilt speared through him at the thought of him dying on the job and leaving her to pick up the pieces—just like she'd had to do with her husband—but it was the reality of his position and all he could do was be as safe as possible to make sure he came home every time. But in the event something happened, knowing his brothers would always be there for her eased some of the tension in his chest.

*You're getting ahead of yourself, Grady. Rein it the fuck in.*

Swallowing to banish the lump in his throat, Erik held his hand out for Dozer to grasp in a symbol of solidarity. One quick squeeze conveyed the myriad emotions of both men, and then it was over.

Needing to get back to their normal footing, Erik challenged D to a timed set of pull ups when a few appreciative whistles drew their attention to the gym entrance. Smoke stood in a wide stance, the muscles in his back rippling with tension. He blocked most of Erik's view, but the gender of their guests was obvious from the reactions of the men.

"Sorry, sweet cheeks," Smoke said with an exaggerated southern drawl tinged in acid. "Rules say no chicks allowed in the cock-house. But my tour ends at six. I'd be happy to meet you at your place and give you a ride on my private rig."

"As inviting as that sounds, I think I'll stick with the cock I'm already seeing, but thanks anyway."

Erik got to his feet and grinned as shit flipped around in his gut at hearing Olivia's voice. He'd almost laughed at her candid response to Smoke's attempt at crude-and-rude, but hearing her publicly claim Erik *or* his cock (he wasn't particularly picky at the moment) made his chest swell with pride and a sense of rightness.

"Suit yourself," Smoke said, shrugging. "How 'bout you, baby? You're *muy caliente* and lucky for you, I happen to like playing with fire."

"Ooh, sorry, *mijo*, this chick is strictly free-range. But I'll be sure to let you know the moment that changes."

At the sound of the second female's voice—one that Erik

recognized as Olivia's feisty Latina friend, Angie—Dozer's head snapped up, and the color drained from his face like he'd seen a ghost. Erik was about to ask him what was up, but then Smoke continued talking to the women, and the acrimonious tone in his voice snagged Erik's attention.

"Sure you will, honey. Nice try, but I own a fucking mirror." Crossing his arms over his chest, Smoke delivered a warning. "I don't know who you're here to see, but you'll have to wait till he's off duty. No civilians allowed, so kindly get the *fuck out*."

Erik's vision was bathed in red. *"Smoke,"* Erik bellowed, the echo bouncing off the walls of the sparse room. Ashton's head snapped to the side and watched with wary curiosity as Erik's strides ate up the distance between them.

Seconds before Erik reached him, Bowie and Preacher blocked Erik's path, stepping in before shit hit the fan. It still might, if Erik had his way. The cocksucker needed to be taught some fucking manners.

"Whoa, there, Wolf," Preacher said in his soothing let's-not-do-anything-rash voice. "You're already not supposed to be in here until you're released to come back to work. You start any shit and things'll get even uglier for you, and none of us want that."

*Fucking Preacher.* Sometimes Erik hated how much sense he made.

Erik jabbed a finger in Smoke's direction between the shoulders of his team members. "Watch your goddamn mouth, soldier. Or I'll be watching it spit out your bloody teeth after my fist goes through it."

"Erik," Olivia said, maneuvering herself in front of him and closing her hand over his to pull it into her chest. "It's okay, it's not a big deal."

He continued to glare at Smoke. "When one of my brothers disrespects my woman, it's a *huge* fucking deal."

Smoke's blue eyes pinged back and forth from him to Olivia and back. That the man had the decency to look ashamed for the way he acted went a long way to quiet the storm raging in Erik. "Fuck, Wolf, I'm sorry," he said. "I didn't know, I swear."

Smoke tried to advance between Bowie and Preacher, but they held their positions until Erik gave them a slight nod, letting them know he had his shit under control.

Smoke moved in close and spoke low so the women wouldn't hear. "I wasn't thinking, man. When they walked in, I was right there, and I just reacted. But that's no excuse. I'll make it up to you—both of you—I promise."

Pulling back to level his sincere gaze at Erik, Smoke waited for his CO and friend to damn him or absolve him. But Erik would have to be a grade-A asshole to come down too hard on Smoke for going on the defensive after the women saw him with so much of his body exposed.

In the army, Smoke had been Erik's artillery platoon sergeant on his last tour. Smoke had the mother of all artillery collections and frequented the shooting range almost as often as he was at the firehouse. The guy was a weapons expert, with a rep for loving anything that went *boom* and left a cloud of smoke behind, hence his call sign.

But irony was just as big of a bitch as karma sometimes, and she'd done one hell of a number on Smoke. He'd gotten caught by an IED that lit up the whole left side of his body from shoulder to ankle. Angry, puckered scars blanketed half of his body and he had plenty of raised scars in other areas where shrapnel had torn through him. Thankfully, after all the surgeries and healing was complete, the only residual damage had been cosmetic. But it was that damage that caused the man's insecurities about anyone, other than the men and women he worked with, seeing him without his scars covered.

The man with the golden boy looks, who once had more

confidence than all of Hollywood's A-list actors combined, had become something he considered the equivalent of a hideous beast in a children's story.

And it was all Erik's doing.

There wasn't a day that went by that Erik saw Smoke and didn't feel guilt for what he'd caused. His only consolation was that Smoke hadn't been killed in the blast that took two of their brothers that day. Having their blood on his hands sometimes felt like he'd been buried alive with six feet of earth slowly suffocating him…

"Erik," Olivia whispered in his ear. "Come on back to me, baby."

…And he did. Thank God for Livvie. Whenever she saw him start to slide, she used her touch and her words to instantly draw him back to her. The wave of relief that washed over him every time she did was indescribable. Squeezing her hand to let her know he was okay, Erik gave his friend a reassuring nod then jerked his head toward the locker room. "Hit the showers," Erik rasped through a tight throat.

Smoke acknowledged the order, which they both knew wasn't an order at all but a way to give the man an easy way to excuse himself. He offered a quick apology to both women and then stalked off in the opposite direction with Bowie, Preacher, and a few of the men from Engine 42 following him in.

"Sorry, ladies," Erik offered as he pressed one of Olivia's hands between both of his and brought it up to place a kiss on her palm.

Olivia's brows drew together. "I wish you wouldn't have been so hard on him, Erik."

Erik pushed out a heavy exhale and rubbed the back of his neck. "I know, I'll talk to him. He's not normally an asshole, but he's…sensitive about his scars."

"Who, *that* hottie? The one with the Brad Pitt, Ivy League

good looks?" Angie asked with incredulity, pointing to where Smoke had disappeared into the locker room.

Chuckling, Erik said, "I can't wait to tell him you called him Brad Pitt. That should bring his ego back to its usual over-inflated state in no time."

"I suppose I should make the official introductions," Olivia said. "Erik, I'd like you to meet my friend—who you've already spoken with on the phone—Angie. Angie this is my... um...Erik."

Erik laughed as the color crept into Livvie's cheeks. "I like the sound of that," he said to her with a wink, then smiled at Angie, extending a hand. "Nice to finally meet you in person, Angie. I appreciate all the nudges you gave Livvie in my direction."

The petite Latina was beautiful and had killer curves, reminding him of a young Salma Hayek, and a playful personality to rival Smoke's on his best day with a side of spitfire. Grasping his hand firmly, Angie arched a brow and tipped the corner of her mouth up in a saucy grin. "Maybe someday I'll let you show your appreciation by hooking me up with one of your hottie firefighter buddies."

Erik chuckled. "Will do. Actually, that reminds me." Turning back to the gym, he scanned the room for his friend—who Erik just realized had been suspiciously MIA when the shit went down with Smoke—and found Dozer in the back, talking with a few of the guys from 42. "Hey, D! Come here, man."

Dozer met his gaze and gave him a nod that said he'd be over in a second. In the meantime...

Erik grabbed Livvie's hips and pulled her in close enough for a proper hello without transferring his sweat to her expensive work clothes. Her hands came up to frame his face as her smiling mouth melded to his in a kiss that was over way too quickly. Whipping his libido into a temporary submission, he asked, "Now, to what do I owe the pleasure of this impromptu visit?"

Olivia's hazel eyes lit up. "Angie and I were at lunch and concocted plans to have a Fourth of July barbecue at my parents' place in Cambridge. They'll still be traveling, but it's a great place to host a small gathering of friends, away from the craziness of the city. I'll invite a few of my friends—" Angie interrupted with a cough. "Okay, fine, coworkers—whatever—and of course your team and anyone else you want. What do you say?"

"I say, as long as I get to be in charge of the grill, I'm in."

"That'd be a mistake," Dozer said, stopping next to Erik. "You can't grill for shit."

"Says the man who likes his meat so rare it's still fucking kicking."

Arms crossed, Dozer shrugged a shoulder and said, "I like what I like," as he brazenly locked eyes with Angie a lot longer than what was polite.

Erik thought for sure she'd respond with something flirtatious or maybe some sass to put the big man in his place. What he didn't expect was to see the same stricken expression on her face that Dozer had when he'd heard her voice earlier. They knew each other, and from the looks of things, this might not be a happy reunion.

Glancing over at his right-hand man, D appeared stoic and unflappable. But Erik knew better. He saw the tension in the man's shoulders, the rapid pulse fluttering in his thick neck, and the way his feet were braced like he was expecting a physical blow. Or maybe an emotional one.

Olivia smiled brightly and held out her hand. "You must be the infamous Dozer I've been hearing so much about."

The Latina recovered her snark and snorted. "Dozer? If that isn't truth in advertising, I don't what it is."

"This is one of those times you should use your filter,"

Olivia said to her friend wryly. "Dozer, this is my obnoxious best friend—"

"Hello, Angel." Dozer's deep voice held an edge of strain. "Been a long time."

Angie narrowed her eyes at him. "Not nearly long enough."

"Come on, we have to talk." He reached for her arm to lead her away, but she yanked it back.

"Like *hell* we do." Angie planted her hands on her hips and burned twin holes into Dozer with flame-throwers for eyes. "We have nothing to talk about, but if you head into the locker room, you can tell Tall, Blond, and Gorgeous I've reconsidered his offer for a ride on his rig."

"Over my dead body."

"I can agree to those terms," she said, her voice frosty. "And don't call me Angel, *Dozer*."

Dozer's jaw muscle ticced. "Then don't call me Dozer, *Angel*."

What the hell? Erik had known his best friend for seventeen long years, and not once did he ever tell anyone not to use his call sign. He probably would have made it his legal name, but it required paperwork, so he refused to do it on principle. Even more intriguing was the fact he and Angie obviously had a history that Erik knew nothing about. Not that Dozer was required to tell him every detail of his life, but it wasn't like him not to. If anything, the man tended to *over*share.

The two glared at each other for several seconds, their eyes volleying silent arguments back and forth, before Olivia finally spoke up. "Okay, what the hell is with you two? Angie, how do you know Dozer, and why don't I know about it?"

"We had a thing a long time ago. Wasn't worth mentioning." Angie severed eye contact with Dozer and turned to Olivia. "Sorry, *mija*, but I suddenly remembered I have something

I have to do this weekend. Looks like I can't make it to the barbeque after all."

Olivia frowned, disappointed with the strange turn of events. Dozer's entire body clamped down on his bones like it did right before a battle or a fight. "Don't bother making shit up on my account, Angel. I promised to cover someone's shifts, so I won't be there."

"And just like that, I'm free again." Angie's lips curled into a devilish smile. "I gotta go. The barbecue's only a week away, and I need to find a date. Loveyoucallme," she sang out as she left the room.

Seconds later, Dozer stalked off in the opposite direction, shoving the door open to the locker room so hard it bounced off the wall behind it and slammed shut instead of easing closed.

"That is not how I pictured this going when I thought of surprising you," Olivia said, concern marring her brow.

"Well, look on the bright side." Erik used the pad of his thumb to smooth the lines on her forehead. "Even without the real ones, we'll have plenty of fireworks at the barbecue."

"And why is that?"

"Because I know for a fact Dozer isn't covering any shifts, and I'm guessing wild horses couldn't keep him from turning up wherever your friend is that weekend."

"Ah, good to know," she said. "I highly doubt she's going to bring a guy, but just in case, I'll make sure the fire extinguisher is handy."

"Sounds like a plan. Actually, it sounds like a date. Our second official one, to be exact."

Olivia chuckled. "What are you talking about? We've had dozens of dates."

"On the contrary, Dr. Jones, watching movies and hooking up at our respective apartments is not a proper date. Attending a party at your parents' house, however, is definitely a date-type thing."

"But my parents won't even be there."

"What about your godfather?"

A slow smile curved her lips. "Yes, I suppose Uncle Eddie and Aunt Tish will be in attendance."

"There, you see? Anything that includes your family and my therapist is definitely an official date." Erik gave her a sly grin and crowded her into the corner where the equipment lockers met the wall. "Come on, humor me. Calling it a date makes me feel like I'm not only a piece of meat being used for my body."

"Fine," she said with an exaggerated sigh and roll of those sexy hazel eyes. "It'll officially be our second date. But just so we're clear, I *am* only using you for your body." Peering up at him coyly through the dark fringe of her lashes, Olivia placed a single manicured nail at the hollow of his throat and dragged it down the center of his body.

The muscles of his torso flexed and shuddered in its wake, shooting signals to his cock and balls that it was time to play. Thankfully, he still had a small supply of blood in his brain that prevented him from hauling her into his office and fucking her over his desk. *Christ, that's getting added to the fantasy bucket list.* For now, though, he had to postpone the fun until later.

"Oddly enough, I'm very okay with being your boy toy, and I encourage you to get as much use out of me as you can. Now, I don't know if you know this, but I also happen to be a firefighter. So if you've got any *hot spots* you need checked, I'd be more than happy to bring my hose by later and check them out thoroughly."

"Mmm, that's the best idea I've heard all day. You're such a do-gooder, Lieutenant Grady."

"Just doing my civic duty, ma'am. But you better get out of here before I decide you need to take the afternoon off so

I can do some initial inspections."

Laughing, she bussed him on the lips quickly and ducked under his arm, giving him a sexy wink before leaving him with the biggest hard-on that'd ever graced the firehouse gym. *Fuck me.* Time for a cold shower.

After showering and dressing, he went in search of his team. He wanted to make things right with Smoke and talk to Dozer about Angie before he left. He found Dozer in his bunk, ankles crossed and hands behind his head, staring at the ceiling. Taking a seat on his own bed, Erik leaned his elbows on his knees and studied the tension in his friend's body. For D's sake, Erik hoped it wouldn't be a slow night or he wouldn't have any way of expending it.

"Wanna tell me what the hell that was with you and Angie?"

"You heard her," he ground out. "Nothing to tell."

"If I believed that, I wouldn't be sitting here and you wouldn't look like you're about to smash my face in just for asking." Silence. "I'm not the enemy here, D."

Releasing a heavy sigh, he sat up and swung his legs around, mimicking Erik's position. "We were a thing back in high school."

"She's from Rockland?"

"Fuck no, man, Rockland is the 'wrong side of the tracks' from where she grew up in Hingham. Towns are right next to each other, though, and kids all share the same hangouts, so…"

Dozer purposely let the sentence hang, not needing to elaborate on how he'd met Angie, just that he had.

"Shit, the odds of her ending up in Boston and running into you have to be a fucking million to one," Erik said in amazement. Dozer grunted in agreement. "What happened after high school?"

"Joined the army. End of story."

"You must be mistaking me for someone else. I know you better than anyone, and you're full of shit. Wanna try again?"

"Nope."

"Do it anyway. Turnabout is fair play, my friend," Erik quipped, referring to the grilling he got in the gym earlier.

Dozer scrubbed a hand over his short, sandy blond hair in irritation. "Angie was the closest thing I ever felt to love. I thought I loved her, anyway, but we were just kids, so fuck if I know."

Erik had a feeling his macho friend was minimizing what he'd felt for her, but he didn't push. "She cut you loose when you enlisted?"

D shook his head and looked at the floor between his legs. "Hell no. She wanted to get married and start a family, even knowing I'd be deployed who knew how many times. I was enough of a selfish prick that I let her believe we were on the same page so I could have that last summer with her. Then if that wasn't bad enough, the night before I left for Basic, I made love to her and held her while she slept. Then I woke her up, took her home, and did something unforgiveable."

"Unforgiveable's a pretty strong word. I'm sure it wasn't that bad, bro."

Dozer raised eyes laden with regret the likes Erik had never seen in his friend. "That night, I took her virginity, then told her we were over the very next morning."

"Fucking hell, D. That's bad."

"Thanks, Sherlock, I hadn't figured that one out," he said drily. "It's the only time in my life I've ever acted like a coward, and I've regretted that day ever since."

"Jesus, no wonder she wanted to murder your ass. That the first time you've seen her since?"

"Yeah. Hence the de la Vega wrath," he said, ire grating his voice. "Whatever, man. I tried talking to her—I owe her an apology, figured I'd clear the air, especially considering the circumstances—but she made her stance abundantly clear."

"You were both blindsided, bro. Give her some time, she'll come around." Giving him a sly grin, he added, "We both know there's not a woman alive who can withstand your charms."

That dragged a chuckle from the big man. Dozer probably had the least amount of charm in the group. His style was more primitive caveman. "We'll see."

The tones sounded, and both men shot to their feet. It only took a moment for them to realize that only one of them would be riding The Animal to the call. Dozer clapped a hand on Erik's arm and gave a supportive squeeze. "You'll be back before you know it, Wolf."

Tipping his head in acknowledgement, he watched with a bitter taste in his mouth as D disappeared to join the rest of the men in the house. Fucking hell. It killed him to see his men go out without him. He couldn't get back here fast enough. Until then, he'd focus on getting through his sessions with Dr. Marion and spending as much time as he could with one Dr. Olivia J. Jones.

# Chapter Thirteen

If a day could be perfect, this particular July Fourth was the epitome of perfection.

It'd started when she woke up to a sexy fireman burning her up with his mouth between her legs. Olivia didn't have the words to describe how that felt.

She'd been hovering in the mist between sleep and wakefulness when one of her own moans pulled her through. Her eyes opened to see the sun's pinkish-orange rays streaking across her ceiling as her back arched of its own volition from the intense pleasure vibrating through her pussy.

"Holy fuck." Her voice was raspy with disuse, adding to the raw sensuality of her reality.

"Mmmmm…"

Olivia's entire body jerked and her hands fisted into the sheets. *That's* what had caused her to moan: the vibrations from his mouth buzzing her clit closer to climax. "Oh my God, that…I…*uhn*…"

Okay, so sentences were no longer possible. Good to know. Now she could stop trying to string one together.

Peering down her naked body, she saw Erik lying between her legs, eyes closed as he feasted on her slowly and languidly as though he wasn't quite awake. He was so damn primal and beautiful. The muscles in his back rippled with the slightest of movements and his exquisite glutes, paler than the rest of him from lack of sun, flexed with his lazy thrusts against the mattress.

When she raked her nails over his buzzed head, his eyes drifted open and locked on her without so much as a hitch in his ministrations to her sex. The early morning light struck the side of his body and made the amber of his irises glow like that of an otherworldly being. Neither spoke, but then neither had to. His eyes said everything she wanted to hear, and she hoped hers did the same.

Everything about that moment had been perfect. He'd used his entire mouth — lips, teeth, and tongue — to make love to her wet sex. Laving through her folds, French kissing the shallow depths of her entrance. He'd built her climax in thin layers, one atop the other, then again and again. A thousand layers laid and still her orgasm felt hours away, making frustration set in and her hips rock against his face in an effort to gain more friction. But the sadist just narrowed his eyes at her, used one of his large paws to press down on her pelvis, and kept right on going.

Then, when he was satisfied she'd ceded control, he went for the kill.

Keeping the one hand just above her pubic bone, he entered her with the middle two fingers of the other. Curling them up, he rubbed the pads of his fingers over her G-spot. Pleasure, intense and instant, flooded her body, and the layers started flipping down like a deck of bridged cards. A sheen of sweat shone on their skin in the sunlight and her breathing alternated between hyperventilating and stopping altogether.

The devil of a man held her at the crossroads of sheer

rapture and utter torture, not allowing her to yet choose the former without first taking more of the latter. Her keening cries had probably roused the neighbors, but she didn't care if the whole damn world heard. She couldn't control them any more than she could control the lightning in a storm.

At last, Erik took sweet pity on her. Sucking her clit between his teeth, he gently bit down and released her to chase her orgasm. It crashed over her, causing tingles just below the surface of her skin as it rushed to her extremities and filled her up with wave after wave of pleasure. Too soon it began to ebb and fade, but in its wake, Olivia was left with a sated body swept free of tension, like the midnight tide erases the day's footprints from the sand.

He'd made her soar, folded her into the warm comfort of his strong embrace, and then whispered beautiful things as she drifted off to sleep once more.

When the smell of fresh coffee knocked on her brain, she opened her eyes and stretched with two words poised on the tip of her tongue. "Utter bliss," she'd whispered to herself, then threw on Erik's worn T-shirt and practically bounced out to the kitchen to join him.

What remained of their morning had been spent cooking together and eating—thank God he knew his way around a kitchen because that was one domestic talent she'd never gotten the hang of. By the time they'd managed to leave her apartment, they only had a couple of hours to get groceries and head over to Cambridge for their Fourth of July party. She wasn't sure what Erik's level of triggering was since he'd been in therapy, but there wasn't a fireworks display anywhere near her parents' quiet, affluent neighborhood. The theme of the day was all about good food and good friends.

"You need to tell me what has you grinning like a loon over there," Angie said. "As your best friend in the whole world, I deserve to know."

"Yes, and as your nosy assistant, I insist on knowing. So spill it, lady."

Olivia blatantly ignored the gazes of Angie and Cindi sitting on the settee perpendicular to her lounge chair on her parents' flagstone patio and checked on her other guests (made up an excuse to catch a glimpse of her über-hottie boyfriend across the yard).

Erik and Uncle Eddie were manning the grill and telling stories about their mutual friend, Chief Bill Marshall, who was due to arrive soon with his wife. Mike, Cindi's fiancé, was playing a game of horseshoes with "the kids," Ashton, Sean, and Tyler—also known as Smoke, Bowie, and Preacher. Dozer stood with the "man pack," too, but chose to merely look on instead of participate in the revelry. He divided his attention between the game and the barbecue conversation while nursing a Sam Adams and flicking heated glances over at Angie every few minutes.

He'd arrived fashionably late, and as soon as he pushed through the backyard gate, Angie's laughing smile turned instantly to a frown. Not necessarily one of distaste, like she tried so hard to play off, but one of disappointment and maybe a hint of regret. It made Olivia even more curious about the story behind her best friend and the man who was closer than a brother to Erik. Whatever it was, Angie apparently preferred to brush it under the rug and throw a damn couch over it, because she wasn't coughing up an explanation any time soon.

Olivia respected that, both as a friend and a psychologist. She knew Angie would tell her when she was ready. Until then, Olivia had given her a subtle pep talk about needing to at least act civil around him for the sake of the group. Now that she and Erik were a couple, their best friends were bound to run into each other at social functions. They had to play nice like adults or avoid each other, which no one wanted. Angie had agreed, albeit begrudgingly, but it was good enough for now.

"Hell-oooo. Earth to Olivia."

She tried pulling in the corners of her mouth, but her attempts were futile. There simply wasn't anything that could take away her smile when the one responsible for it kept shooting her lopsided grins from across the yard.

"You both know this is my favorite holiday," Olivia finally answered. "It's a beautiful day and I'm celebrating with my friends, old and new. Why *wouldn't* I be smiling?"

Angie snorted. "You're not just smiling, *mija*, you're glowing. If I didn't love you so much, I'd probably throw up in my mouth a little every time you two looked at each other."

Cindi busted out in belly laughs, two of Angie's famous blood orange margaritas aiding her mirth. Meanwhile, Olivia's jaw dropped in her friend's direction, the shock partly authentic but mostly mocking. After all, Olivia was more than used to Angie's colorful way of speaking. Her middle name might as well be Frank, because that's what she was to a fault. The woman never pulled her punches.

"You should see her in the office," her assistant piped in.

"Cindi, you know I can fire you, right?" Olivia gave the perky woman her best *think before you speak* look, but as expected, Cindi completely ignored her.

"She walks around humming and I can't count how many times I've caught her staring into space." Angie made a big *aha* deal out of it and then Cindi asked, "Do you even listen to your clients anymore, or do you just smile and nod with a 'that's nice' after everything they say?"

Angie and Cindi laughed louder than ever and took turns pretending to be Olivia's clients trying to get her attention with outrageous confessions.

"Oh, ha ha, you're both *so* hysterical," she said drily. She pointed an accusing finger at Cindi. "Do I need to remind you of how you acted when you first met Mike? You couldn't even mention his name without your eyes going all starry, and the number of times I caught you daydreaming with that goofy-ass look on your face probably added up to a week's worth of vacation time."

The humor fell from Cindi's face and was replaced with a sudden flush, causing Angie to laugh even harder. But her bestie wasn't getting off that easily. "And *you*, Miss Thing, have no room to talk."

Like a record scratch, Angie stopped laughing and crossed her arms over her ample chest, then lifted a challenging brow. "You don't have any dirt to dig up on me, bitch. At least not when it comes to men. I'm perfectly happy going home to play with my B.O.B. He doesn't make false promises and he doesn't require reciprocation. He's the perfect partner."

"A Battery Operated Boyfriend can't be the perfect partner," Olivia argued. "It's not even *a* partner, much less a perfect one."

Cindi made a *mm!* sound to grab their attention as she sucked down the last of her margarita. "Fun fact," she said excitedly, as though she believed this fact might *actually* be fun. "In Dutch, a B.O.B. is a Bewust Onbeschonken Bestuurder, which is a designated driver."

Angie raised an eyebrow. "And what exactly makes that fact so fun?"

Cindi laughed. "Well, if you ever party in the Netherlands and announce to the crowd at large, in your sassy Latina way, that you're leaving to go play with your B.O.B., they'd think you were going home to play with your designated driver."

Now that everyone in the area was in on the joke, they joined Cindi in laughing at the idea of how many guys Angie would have suddenly volunteering to be her sober chauffeur for the evening.

"Whatever," Angie said as the chuckling started to wind

down. "My only point is that I'm not a hearts and flowers kind of girl."

"Maybe not anymore, but I'm remembering a drunken GNO with enough tequila shots to put a few holes in that tough-girl exterior of yours."

"Nope," Angie said. "Never happened."

Olivia laughed. "Oh, yes it *did*. And *in* said weakened condition—"

"Stop changing the subject, Dr. Jones," Angie said, leaning forward in her seat.

"—you told me all about your first love from high school, who I, in my professional opinion, think—"

"That's it, bitch, you're cut off. No more margaritas for you." Angie sat back and folded her arms across her body. "You always get doctory when you drink."

"Stop interrupting me, Angie-Pangie-Pumpkin-Pie, kissed the boys and made 'em cry." Uh-oh, she was nursery rhyming. Maybe she should slow down on the margaritas, too… Nah. "*I* think," Olivia said again for emphasis, "you never really got over him, and *that's* why you're not a hearts and flowers kind of girl."

Angie's light brown eyes narrowed, almost fusing her long, dark lashes together. "You're *loco*, chica, you know that?"

Olivia tapped a finger on her chin as she thought aloud. "Now what was his name? Hmmm…I know it started with a hard G. Garret? No. Gaelen?"

Cindi held her margarita high and shouted, "Gandalf!"

"Nice try, Cin, but no. Surprisingly, Angie's first love was not Gandalf the Grey."

"Gavin," came a deep voice from behind them.

"That's *it*," Olivia repeated triumphantly. "Gavin." Turning in her seat, she smiled up at Dozer, who'd tossed her the assist, and another one of Erik's team members, Sean, aka

Bowie. "Thank you, Dozer. That was an excellent guess."

Bowie huffed a bark of laughter. "You'd be a lot less impressed if you knew D-man's real name, Doc. One hell of a coincidence, though, I'll give you that."

*Coincidence?* Olivia looked at Dozer. "Your name is Gavin?" She racked her brain, trying to remember a time when Erik had referred to his right-hand man as anything other than Dozer, but she couldn't think of a single one. Erik used the other men's first names interchangeably when talking with her, but Dozer had always just been…Dozer.

"Bowie has a big mouth," said the man in question.

Bowie opened his arms wide. "I'm just saying let's not give the big guy too much credit for guessing his own name. His gigantic ego doesn't need any stroking."

"I wouldn't stroke him if my life depended on it." Angie rose and turned a flirtatious smile Bowie's way. "Now you, on the other hand… Got anything *you* need stroked, handsome?"

An animalistic growl rumbled from deep in Dozer's barrel of a chest. Bowie chuckled, seemingly unaware of Dozer's unsettling reaction. "Always did like a woman who gets straight to the point."

But when he went to take a step forward, Dozer's hand shot out and slapped dead center against Bowie's chest. The men exchanged a glance that could have meant anything, but that glance was all it took to communicate one very important message.

Bowie placed a hand over his heart and put on a mock look of pain. "Sorry, babe. Looks like you're spoken for."

"The *hell* I am," Angie said through clenched teeth as she aimed her barely suppressed rage right at Dozer.

"No one's touching you while I'm around, sweetheart. Get used to it."

"Let me get this straight," Angie said, her eyes sparking with fire. "You don't want me, but you plan on cock-blocking me from anyone who does?"

"You don't know the first goddamn thing about what I want, Angel."

Olivia's jaw dropped as the last piece of the puzzle slid into place. "Holy shit, Angie, *Dozer* is your Gavin?"

Cindi's drama radar must have hit soap opera level because she was suddenly an eager participant. If she was any more visibly excited, she'd be bouncing in her seat and clapping. "Oh *shit*," she squealed with glee. "Dozer is *your* Gavin. This. Is. *Awesome*."

Was it awesome? As her gaze darted from the beast of a man to her fun-size friend, Olivia wasn't so sure. It was like witnessing the initial stare down at the battle of David and Goliath. Only "David" didn't express determination as much as she did hurt and disbelief. From what she knew of Dozer, Olivia liked the gruff man, but her loyalty was to her best friend, and right now Angie needed her.

"Come on, girl," Olivia said, grabbing Angie's hand. "I need your help in the kitchen with some obscure and random tasks."

"Oh good," Angie said drily. "I love obscure and random."

Dozer stepped into their path, and his eyes made Angie silent promises to aid his verbal one. "This isn't over."

"Funny, I seem to remember you saying something similar to me a long time ago, but that wasn't quite it, was it? Do you remember what you said to me that day? No?" Ever the proud Latina, Angie raised her chin. "Let me refresh your memory. Your exact words were '*It's over.*' Now you want to bulldoze your way back into my life and change the fucking rule *you* set to begin with? Hell no. So, you're wrong, Gavin. This is *very* over." And with that, Angie stalked into the safety of the big house, Olivia trailing close behind her.

• • •

Several hours later, Olivia and Angie plopped onto the stools at the breakfast bar after getting the last of the food put away and cleaning the kitchen. They'd insisted on everyone else staying outside to enjoy the bonfire, assuring them that they'd be out to join them momentarily.

Just as soon as they polished off the last piece of Olivia's mom's famous Death by Chocolate seven-layer cake.

"Oh my God," Olivia said, pulling the small plate between them. "I'll have to run all damn weekend to work this off."

"It's so worth it, though," Angie replied before indulging in her first bite and moaning around her fork. "Besides, with all the hot sex you have these days, you'll probably burn off half of it as soon as Mr. Perfect gets you alone."

Olivia felt her cheeks burn, and she quickly reached for her glass of water, hoping the cool liquid would help before—

"You're blushing, which means you're feeling either guilty or embarrassed about something."

"What? No, I'm not."

"Uh-uh, *mija*, don't even. Spill it or I'll start guessing, and you know my imagination is always way worse."

With bravado she didn't feel, Olivia raised her eyebrows in a challenging *see if I care* manner and ate a bite of the cake.

"Okay, you asked for it." Angie set her fork down and rubbed her hands together with a truly devious look in her eyes. "Let's see…you went cherry when I mentioned your hot sex, so my first guess is that it made you think of his huge, thick—"

"OhmyGodshutthefuckup," Olivia hissed at her friend, who she was seriously considering *un*friending at the moment. "I give, I'll tell you."

"Good choice." Angie gave her a playful wink and ate another bite. Her eyes nearly rolled into the back of her head. "Jesus, I can't believe how sinfully good this is. Your mom's skills are out of this world. I'd gladly give up sex if I could eat this every day without gaining weight. I'm not even joking."

"Still on a bad streak, huh?"

"Epically bad. The only reason I haven't thrown myself in front of a bus is because I can finally fuck vicariously through you. So if you love me at all, you'll get back to the story."

Olivia chuckled but humored her best friend and spilled about the night Erik had gone straight to her apartment after his training. "He was an hour later than I was expecting and his phone was dead, so he had the guys drop him off on the way back to the station."

"Wait, so he basically used Rescue 2 like his own personal Uber?" Olivia laughed at that but had to agree it was sort of true. "This is already awesome. Please tell me he kept some of his gear on. And by that I mean, if he didn't, I want you to lie to me."

"I don't have to lie," Olivia said with a half grin. "He left it all on and then pounded on my door, announced himself as the BFD, and demanded entry for my own safety."

Angie stared, a look of awe on her face. "Sweet Jesus, you role played. Who were you? No wait, let me guess. You were experiencing shortness of breath and needed mouth-to-mouth with the new tongue-sweep technique when checking for objects."

Olivia laughed. "What? No."

"Your clothes were on fire and he had to pat you down all over and cover your body with his to smother the flames."

"Not even close."

"Okay, there's always my personal favorite: he was answering a call about a gas leak and busted in to find you collapsed on the floor and not breathing, so he had to check you for a pulse..." A wicked gleam lit up her eyes as she leaned forward and whispered, "In your vagina."

Olivia laughed so hard she almost choked on a bite of cake and had a damn hard time making sure she didn't need *real* emergency response. "You have an overactive imagination, you know that?"

"I beg to differ," she said, pointing her fork in Olivia's direction. "The problem is my *under*active sex life, which leads to excessive fantasizing during my daily runs, *which*, thanks to your new beau, have all been fireman related."

"Yeah, I'm sure that's the reason."

"What's that supposed to mean?"

"Seriously, Angie? I know this is my field of expertise and all, but a ten-year-old would know the reason for your firefighter fixation."

"Okay, Freud, tell me why, if it isn't because my best friend is always talking about, to, or with her super-hot—pun intended—BFD boyfriend."

"Oh, I don't know," Olivia said with more than a hint of sarcasm, "could it have anything to do with a certain gigantic member of my boyfriend's squad whose nickname rhymes with Hozer?"

"Now I know you're crazy. I told you what happened. What part of 'he broke my heart and left me and now I hate his frigging guts' don't you understand?"

"It's not a question of understanding it, it's a question of believing it. You might be able to convince yourself that you hate Dozer, but I think deep down you know it's bullshit. I know you too well, and I know how you work when you're scared. And, sweetie, your feelings for that man scare you shitless."

"That's *loco*," she said with a forced chuckle as she cleared their place. "The only thing I'm scared of is ending up in prison orange when I decide to let him know how I really feel."

Olivia's heart went out to Angie as she needlessly busied herself with hand-washing the plate instead of putting it in the dishwasher with the rest. The strain around her eyes belied her flippant comment, but Olivia knew when to let something go. Now was not the time or place to coax the truth from her friend.

After drying her hands, Angie dropped the towel and rounded the counter to link arms with Olivia. "Come on, *mija*, let's go make some s'mores."

"Are you kidding me?" Olivia said as they stepped outside and started walking toward the back of the large yard where the rest of the guests were sitting around the fire. "We just ate our weight in chocolate cake."

"Yeah, but *they* don't know that. So now we get to have 'second dessert.'"

Olivia giggled at the typical Angie nonsensical logic. "What are we, hobbits?"

"I don't care what we're called as long as we pretend it's normal to eat cake with roasted marshmallow chasers. But you might want to do the roasting for me."

"Why's that?"

Angie's eyes narrowed and locked onto Dozer as they approached. Lowering her voice, she said, "Because if you give me a sharp, pointy object while drinking, I'm liable to try roasting something other than the marshmallows."

Olivia mentally cringed at the image of the double-pronged metal skewers sticking out from the crotch of Dozer's jeans. She nodded and patted her friend's hand. "You grab the crackers and chocolate. I'll handle the marshmallows."

・・・

"Jesus, how much time do you think we have before it's here?" Erik hid his smirk with his Heineken as he took a pull from the green bottle. He was riding an emotional high and it made him want to screw with his best friend, who was having a less-than-stellar evening. It was his brotherly duty.

The day had been fucking fantastic, from the moment he opened his eyes and saw the beautiful angel sleeping soundly next to him, naked and flawless, to now as the small group of friends that remained—the major and the chief having left about an hour earlier—sat around a sunken fire pit, talking and laughing. All day long, Erik had been aware of Olivia, like their love-making that morning had tethered them in some cosmic way. Even when she hadn't been in his line of sight, it was like he could *feel* her exact location and how long it would take to get to her, bare her to him, and bury himself deep inside her.

The little minx knew it, too. Whenever she thought no one would notice, Olivia's eyes blazed a path to his as she bit her lip and then slowly dropped her gaze until it settled on his dick, so heavy it felt like she used her hand to stroke it and cup his balls. More than once he'd cornered her with very little privacy and retaliated with a little teasing of his own. Only *his* kind *did* stroke and cup her pussy, thanks to her Daisy Dukes giving him easy access. Payback's a bitch.

Dozer's brows slashed into a *V* between his eyes, the light from the dancing flames casting shadows across his face. "Before what's here?"

"Armageddon, brother," he said, clapping a hand on the man's giant shoulder. "Figure the end of the world's coming if you finally found a woman capable of telling you no."

Erik tipped his beer in the direction of where Angie held everyone's rapt attention as she told a story in dramatic fashion. The woman had a presence much larger than her small stature when she was sober, but after her brief encounter with Dozer that he'd witnessed from the grilling area, she'd had a steady flow of margaritas in her hand. The alcohol had taken care of that huge chip on her shoulder with Dozer's name on it, and she'd eventually relaxed enough to have a good time, but not so much that she didn't consciously avoid D.

Dozer followed Erik's line of sight and, for a split second, Erik saw longing and pain flash in his brother's eyes before the stone mask settled back into place. "Don't worry, partner. When it comes to Angie, Armageddon would be more likely if she ever said yes."

Well, shit. That little thing had one of the biggest dudes he'd ever known turned inside out in a way Erik never thought he'd see. He felt sorry for the poor bastard and more than a little guilty for giving him shit, not that Dozer would want an apology. Even the *thought* of not being with Olivia made him fucking violent.

Good thing he didn't have to worry about it. He didn't plan on making Dozer's mistake by pushing Livvie away, and may God have mercy on the soul of anyone who tried to take her from him.

In his periph, he saw her rounding the fire toward him. He turned his head in time to receive a kiss as she perched her pretty ass on his lap and wrapped her arms around his neck.

"Mmmm, what did I do to deserve that? Tell me so I know to do it again," he said.

"When I looked over at you, you seemed…" She had several words swimming in that genius head of hers, but he could tell by her reservation that she was searching for the right one. "Angry, in a way. Like you were preparing for battle."

He had been, in his mind. Ready to battle anyone or anything for this woman who'd come to mean so much to him in such a short time. "You thought I could use a distraction."

Olivia gave a small nod. "Are you feeling okay? Do you want to call my uncle for anything?"

"No, baby, I'm good. All I need is you. The rest'll work itself out."

She smiled and stroked the side of his face. Erik buried a hand at her nape and pulled her in for another kiss, a kiss less innocent than the one she'd greeted him with seconds before. Unfortunately, Olivia's sense of decorum didn't let him get very far before she broke away, leaving him needy and desperate.

Using the fall of her golden hair to hide his words from any lip readers in the group, Erik spoke plainly. "I've been staring at you all day in these poor excuses for shorts, knowing I could have my fingers buried inside you in a heartbeat." She didn't say anything, but her fingers spasmed behind his neck and her breath rasped out through parted lips. "I say we let your guests continue to enjoy their evening out here while we go in and start a fire of our own. What do you say?"

"Hmmm...I say..." She screwed up her face into one of deep consideration, pretending to think about his offer. He loved that she felt comfortable enough with him to tease, but teasing or not, that she didn't answer immediately was a smack upside his inner caveman's head. There was too much testosterone coursing through him after wanting to fuck her for the last eight hours. If she didn't answer him correctly—and *soon*—he'd go into hair-dragging mode.

At last she locked those hypnotic eyes on him, the mischief replaced with desire. "I don't think I can stand another minute without feeling you inside me," she whispered.

"That's the answer I was waiting for, baby." Erik stood them up and grabbed Olivia's hand. "We'll be inside if anyone needs us." While leading her away from the group, he reconsidered his parting statement and paused just long enough to make himself clear. "Don't need us for at least two hours."

*"Erik,"* Olivia scolded through the giggle she couldn't help. She dug her heels in and called back over her shoulder. "We'll be right back."

"No we won't." Dipping his shoulder, he tossed her over as easily as a bag of sand. A very light bag of sand that smelled of rosewater and the slick honey of her arousal. *Fucking hell.*

"Eventually?" she asked as she held onto his belt to keep from bouncing into his back.

"Not likely." A smile spread across his face when he heard her sigh of contentment, and her arms came around his waist to embrace him in the only way she could while upside down. Erik couldn't think of a single woman he knew who'd be okay with what he was doing. Olivia, on the other hand, wasn't the least bit pissy about being dragged away from her guests to satisfy his sexual hunger. *Their* sexual hunger.

*Fuck me. I'm crazy about this woman.*

Once he stepped into the kitchen, he set her on her feet and gave her a quick kiss before heading to the fridge to retrieve the bottle of Merlot he'd brought over. He'd been imagining the two of them in a hot bath and him drinking the red wine from the tips of her pointed nipples. Holding the bottle up, he asked, "Your dad have glasses? If not, I'm perfectly fine licking it from your body."

Olivia sauntered over to him and dragged a finger down the front of his shirt. "Why choose when we can do both?"

A growl of anticipation and growing impatience rumbled in his chest. She winked and turned to open one of the cabinets. He was considering giving her a warning smack on her perfect ass when the all-too-familiar rapport of a .50 cal going cyclic rent the air.

His world exploded, horrifically underscored by the sound of shattering glass and a woman's scream. Huge clouds of dust from the explosion hung in the air, making his range of visibility no more than a few meters in any direction. Off to his left, a female civilian stood in shock with blood splattered across her front and the mangled body—or what was left of it—of one of his men at her feet.

"Goddammit, Jazz. *Fuck.* Preacher, we need a medic! Jazz is down! Preacher, you hear me?" Erik shouted so loud his vocal chords burned, but he needed Preacher for Jazz, even though he knew the man was beyond help. Anguish ripped through him like bullets, shredding his heart as he tried to gather up the gruesome remains of his fallen brother.

The guns kept firing, the sound like thunder raining down from above, and yet the woman didn't run or take cover. "Get down!" Erik yanked her behind the Humvee with him and pushed her to the ground. Bullets sprayed the dirt-packed route that passed for a street in these parts of the world. Men shouted from every direction, some in English—his men— and some in Arabic—their enemy. But from somewhere in the melee he heard Bowie yell out the status of two more of their team. Smoke was fucked up but alive, which was more than they could say for Harley.

Jazz and Harley had been the ones to hit the door of the compound first, following Erik's orders based on intel he'd trusted. Their blood was on his hands, the same as if he'd been the one to trigger the bomb that took their lives.

*"Fuck!"* He banged his head back against the Humvee and squeezed his eyes shut. He had to get his men out of there. Sweat poured from his brow, down the center of his back. His heart slammed so hard and fast he expected to feel the sharp pain of his ribs cracking at any second.

He scrambled to draw his M4, to feel the comfort of the cold, blued steel in his grip, but it wasn't there. Where the hell was it? Not having his rifle was the same as not having his right arm; it was just as much a part of him as any God-given appendage. *Fuck, fuck, fuck!*

"Erik, baby, talk to me. What's going on? What are you seeing?"

The woman he'd dragged to cover pushed herself up from the ground to kneel next to him. She had blood everywhere; he didn't know if it was all from Jazz or if any of it belonged to her. God, what in the hell was she doing in the middle of a goddamn war zone? He needed to get her to safety and get Preacher to look at her, too. If he could get Dozer and Bowie to lay down some cover, Erik could get her to the RP—

"Baby, please," she begged, "talk to me."

"I'm going to get you out of here, but I need you to listen to me and do exactly what I fucking say, when I fucking say it. Got it?" Tears swam in her eyes. He wanted to tell her everything would be all right, but he couldn't bring himself to make that promise. "Do you understand me?"

Finally, she nodded. "Yes, I understand."

"Good. Now keep your head down. I'm going to redirect the boys to lay in and provide some covering fire so I can get you to the rally point where you'll be safe. Then I'm unleashing hell on these motherfuckers."

...

The kitchen floor was covered in red wine and shattered glass. Most of the shards had scattered away from them, but not all, and when Erik had shoved her to the floor, she'd caught herself with her hands. She spared herself a concussion but now had several cuts staining her hands with blood the way the spray of wine had stained her clothes.

But those details were a mere blip in her mind compared to what mattered most as she knelt next to Erik in the corner of the L-shaped counter, and that was coaxing him out of the nightmarish flashback he was steeped in.

Olivia winced as the sound of fireworks continued to pop from a neighboring yard. She'd considered the possibility that the loud bangs might trigger something for him, even if he'd never had problems on the Fourth of July before, which was the sole purpose for hosting the party at her parents' house; it was far enough away from any city fireworks display. What she hadn't thought of was that the sound of the smaller ones—

the kind people bought to set off at their own parties—might trigger him as well.

Olivia's specialty was treating individuals with PTSD. She'd seen many of her clients experience flashbacks, and she knew exactly what to do when they did. How to speak to them, how to guide them through and eventually out of it. She loved her job, and she was damn good at it.

But none of those people had been teasing and flirting with her one second and sinking into a flashback so fast in the next that it took her a full fifteen seconds to get over the shock.

None of them had been her boyfriend, the man she'd fallen for faster than she ever thought humanly possible.

None of them had been Erik.

*"Dozerrrrr!"*

Olivia jumped at Erik's sudden shout for his friend. Before she had a chance to react, she heard the French doors to the patio whip open with what sounded like a stampede rushing through. Erik heard them, too, but based on his reaction, his mind told him their friends were members of Al-Qaeda advancing on their position.

Angling his body to better cover Olivia in the corner he wouldn't let her out from, Erik snatched up the broken bottleneck and yelled out a warning. "Don't you fuckers come any closer, or I swear you'll be eating this grenade as a last meal!"

The action seemed to have stopped on the other side of the breakfast bar with lots of loud whispers and concerned murmuring, but Erik didn't react to it, making Olivia wonder if he couldn't hear things that would be abnormal on a battlefield. She could only imagine whatever was going on in his head.

"What the fuck is going on?" That was Dozer's voice. "Grady, what are you doing, man?"

"D! I have a civilian, possible injuries. Taking her to RP Lone Wolf, but I need some cover, copy?"

She couldn't see them from her crouched position, but she had no problem hearing the strings of agitated curse words from the guys mixing with the concerned whispers from the women. "Erik," Olivia said in her calm therapist tone, trying to get his attention. "I need you to listen to me. You're not in Iraq anymore. You're home now and it's safe."

More fireworks crackled like gunfire, acting like an audible "fuck you" to what she'd just promised. Erik reacted by pulling her to his chest and huddling over her.

"Goddammit, Dozer, do you fucking copy?"

"Dozer," she interrupted as she eased her way out of his arms, "don't answer him, and everyone needs to stay out of his line of sight. In fact, you should all go back outside and let me handle this."

"You're insane if you think I'm leaving." The big man's words sounded like they were being pushed through clenched teeth. "How about you leave, and I'll handle it. I know him better than anyone." More fireworks, more shouted orders from Erik to his team. "Smoke, take the guys and make that shit stop. I don't care if you have to go house to house in a two-block radius and confiscate every last firecracker you see. Everyone else, out."

"Copy that," Smoke said. "Let's go, boys."

Olivia heard the sounds of people exiting through the back doors, but she wasn't yet alone with Erik. "You, too, Dozer."

"No can do, Doc," Dozer said as he rounded the corner and stood several feet in front of them.

"Dozer, can you see Smoke?" Erik asked, pain clearly etched on his face. "Is Preacher with him? Fuck, D, we lost Harley and Jazz. *Motherfucker*, we lost them."

"I know, brother. It was bad intel; there's nothing we

could have done. It happens."

"It *happened* because of me. I fucking sent them to die, man. *Me*. But no one else, do you hear me? No one else fucking dies. We need to get to the RP and pull out *now*."

"Erik," Olivia said, placing her hands on his face, no longer caring if she bled on him. She needed him to focus on her. "Sweetie, what you're seeing isn't real. You're safe, in my parents' kitchen." His erratic breaths started to slow down; he braceleted her wrists, holding her hands in place, and his eyes showed faint hints of recognition. "We're in Cambridge, Massachusetts, because we hosted a party for our friends, remember?"

"Wolf, you need to snap out of it, brother."

As soon as he heard Dozer's voice, everything in Erik tensed back up.

"Dozer, you need to leave. Your presence isn't helping to pull him out; it's anchoring him there. *Please*."

The man was primed to argue, but Angie, who had apparently been standing off to the side, stepped in and slipped an arm through his. "Come on, Gavin," she said. "Olivia knows what she's doing. She'll help him."

Dozer appeared conflicted, clearly torn between leaving a man he considered his brother and getting a chance to talk with Angie, which Olivia assumed was something Dozer had wanted since that day at the firehouse. But when Angie tugged on his arm, his resolve crumbled, and with a last pleading glance in Olivia's direction, he followed her out of the house.

*Finally.*

"Erik, baby, look at me." His gaze had been darting around the room, seeing things only visible to him. She shuddered to think about what it might be, considering the things he'd been saying about his men dying. Again, she held his blood-streaked face with her hands. His eyes darted to the front of her shirt.

"There's blood. You're injured. You need—"

"Baby, no, it's not blood; it's red wine. We were about to go take a bath and drink some wine, but you dropped the bottle and some of it sprayed me, that's all."

He furrowed his brow as though trying to decipher a foreign language. "Wine?"

"Yes, only wine." Ducking her head to lock eyes with him, she said, "Look at me, Erik, and focus on my voice. It's me, Olivia. There's no battle; you're having a flashback. We're in the kitchen and the sounds you heard were fireworks for the Fourth of July, not gunfire."

"Fourth of July," he murmured. His whiskey eyes darted back and forth on hers, the struggle to understand the current situation apparent. At last, she saw a flicker of recognition. "Livvie?"

She smiled in relief and drew in a deep breath, the first since hearing the bottle smash to pieces. "Yes, I'm here, baby. You're okay, I promise."

Full realization dawned on his face as he looked around and saw the reality of his surroundings as opposed to his hallucination. "Oh God, what the hell just happened? What did I do?"

"Some fireworks triggered a flashback from when you were in Iraq. It's completely normal, nothing to worry about. You can talk about it with the major next week, or if you'd like, you can call him right now from my father's office."

His attention snapped back to her, a mix of horror and outrage hardening his features when he took in her state. He gathered her hands in his and turned them palms up. "You're bleeding. Oh, Jesus, did I—"

"No," she answered vehemently. "This is from me falling on the glass. You didn't hurt me, Erik. You wouldn't."

He narrowed his eyes at her, his sharp mind doing double-time to put the missing pieces together. "You didn't fall, did you? What happened?"

"Erik, it doesn't matter."

"Bullshit, it doesn't matter," he said, his agitation growing. "If I hurt you—"

"You thought I was a civilian and pushed me down to avoid getting shot. You were trying to save me, not hurt me, and they're not even deep. A couple of Band-Aids and I'll be good as new." Olivia offered him a reassuring smile, but he wasn't buying it.

"I hurt you. Your hands are bleeding because of something I did. Bottom line."

She'd been afraid of this. He considered what happened his fault, and it would continue to eat at him if she couldn't get him to let it go. "We can talk about it later if you want, but right now I think you should go to our room downstairs and take a long, hot shower. I'll clean up in here and meet you in there when you're done."

He pushed up to his feet and pulled her up with him. "No, first we bandage your hands, then *I'll* clean the fucking mess *I* made while you go relax in the tub."

Ugh, the man was so damn stubborn! She wanted to scold him or swear at him or rail at him or all of the above, but Olivia knew it wouldn't get her anywhere. All that would do would be to bring out his caveman, and she'd find herself tossed over his shoulder and hauled off to be put through the paces he instructed her to do. No, to make any headway with a wolf, you had to fight dirty.

Stepping in close, she wrapped her arms around his waist and stared up into his eyes. As their bodies connected, he instinctively held her in his warm embrace, offering each other some much-needed affection. "Please, Erik. I know you love taking care of me, and it makes you the greatest guy on the planet, but this time let me do it for you. I know where everything is and it won't take me long. All I want is for you to go take some time for yourself, decompress. Please, will you do that for me?"

He blew out a sigh of frustration and scrubbed an agitated palm over his head a few times. "Fine. But only if you promise to call one of the girls in to help you."

"I will, I promise."

Nodding once, he kissed her forehead and made his way toward the basement guest room where they'd placed their overnight bags. She needed to recruit Cindi's help with her hands and the mess on the floor so she could get to the room. He'd have a hard enough time being with his thoughts during the shower; she didn't want to give him any more time than necessary where he could blame himself or feel as though he'd failed her. The truth couldn't be more opposite, and she'd do everything in her power to make him see that.

Before they went to sleep tonight, Erik Grady would know exactly where they stood: together, no matter what.

# Chapter Fourteen

Dozer followed Angie across the backyard to a small shed at the edge of the property that housed all the gardening and lawn-care tools. He glanced back at the house, hating that his brother was in there suffering. The only reason he agreed to leave was because he knew Erik wasn't in actual danger and he trusted Olivia to take care of him.

"He's going to be fine, you know. Olivia's very good at her job, and she loves him."

Her voice flowed around him like a caress from a soft breeze. She hadn't spoken to him like that since before he left for Basic. He'd almost forgotten how melodic and soothing it was, especially when her emotions brought out the lilt of her accent.

"I know." His words sounded like they'd passed through the shards of glass blanketing the kitchen floor. "But real or not, turning my back on him feels ten kinds of wrong. He's my brother, and right now, he thinks I abandoned him during a firefight. I'd sooner gut myself with a dull, rusty knife before ever doing that."

"How long have you been together?"

"First day of Basic." Dozer swallowed thickly. "Other than my mom and sister, that man's the most important person in my life. It's those three, followed by the other three guys on our squad. Then there's everyone else."

"I see."

The wooden answer snagged his attention. Distance covered her eyes and her face held no hint of her thoughts. But he didn't need a hint. He knew her inside and out, and his words had hurt her. *Nice move, asshole.* "Angelina, I didn't mean—"

She held up her hand. "No, don't," she said. "You don't need to explain yourself to me. You made my place in your life abundantly clear more than fifteen years ago, which is why you have no place in mine now."

"You think I *wanted* to let you go? All I ever wanted, from the first moment I saw you, was to make you mine and keep you with me."

She let out a sarcastic huff and crossed her arms over her chest. "You didn't want it enough, or you never would have broken things off."

"You're wrong. I loved you too much to let you waste your life waiting for me. I knew it would be years before I came back to the civilian life, and I also knew that I'd return a different man than the one you fell in love with…if I came back at all."

He heard Angie's sharp inhale, then nothing. No rush of released air or sounds of her breathing. Dozer was ready to reach out and shake her to make sure she was okay when she finally exhaled and spoke, her tone defeated. "I mourned you, you know. Not right away. For a year, I kept thinking you'd realize what a mistake you made and you'd show up to take me in your arms and promise to never push me away again."

Damn, she was killing him. He didn't think a night had

passed that first year that he didn't dream of the same thing. It'd been harder than he ever imagined to stay away from her after he got out of basic training.

"That year took a toll on me. So much hoping and waiting, it wore me down so much that my mother finally intervened. She forced me to realize I was holding onto something that no longer existed. That what we had was gone forever, and I wouldn't be able to move on until I accepted it, mourned the loss, and found closure."

"Sounds like you pretended I was dead. Wishful thinking?" His words had a sharp edge he regretted. He had no right to be angry with her, but the idea that she made herself forget him pissed him off.

"Even if it was, you don't have the right to judge me for it. We each handled things in our own way. You ran away from my love, and eventually, I accepted that and moved on just as you did. End of story."

Rage bubbled beneath the surface like a hot spring preparing to erupt into a geyser. Rage that deserved to be directed at himself rather than the innocent beauty in front of him. "You want that to be the end of the story so badly? Fine." He slapped his palms together like the covers of a book. "It's done. Consider it ended."

Angie studied him through narrowed eyes. "Really. Just like that?" She sounded like she expected the other shoe to drop at any second. *There's my smart angel.*

"Just like that. You're right," he said casually, "it was a long time ago. We're different people now. Time to close up that part of our lives and move on."

A flash of disappointment sparked in her golden-brown eyes before disappearing just as quickly, but not before Dozer saw it and held onto it for all he was worth. "Exactly," she agreed. "We need to move on. Finally, you're seeing reason."

Dozer altered his position to slowly maneuver her back

against the side of the shed. It took her a second to realize his movements weren't random. When she looked up at him with questions in her eyes, his only response was the predatory gaze he kept leveled on her as he advanced.

"Gav—Dozer, w-what are you doing?"

Goddamn it, it pissed him off that she corrected herself from calling him by his given name. He hadn't let anyone other than his mom and sister use it since he left Angie. It hadn't seemed right. In the army, people only addressed each other by their last names, call signs, or ranks, and after becoming a different man from when he'd been with Angelina, it made sense to leave the name he'd gone by back then in the past with the rest of it.

But hearing anything other than "Gavin" come from her sweet lips was like acid dripping into his ears. He'd let it go this time. As much as he hated it, it wasn't mission one right now. "Doing like you said. I'm moving on."

Her back hit the shed. Her only option for escape was to go around him, and if she took the slightest step in either direction, he'd let her go. This wasn't about trapping, tricking, or manipulating. It was about proving to her that she wasn't as done with him as she thought or claimed.

"Moving on to what?"

Mouth curling into a wicked grin, he said, "Our sequel."

"You're crazy, you know that?" she whispered.

"You're right about that." Dozer leaned forward enough to brace his hands on either side of her head. Her scent, spicy and exotic, just like her, hit him with a barrage of memories of all the nights he'd buried his face in her neck while holding her close. "Because ever since I saw you at the station, I've been slowly going out of my mind. I remember everything, Angel. How you taste, the little sighs you make when I close my lips over the pulse point in your neck, every curve of that luscious body, and the way it arches into me when I suck those dark nipples into my mouth."

It didn't matter how many years had passed. Dozer still knew how to read Angelina de la Vega. Pupils dilated, heartbeat rapid, shallow breaths through parted lips. His girl was turned on as fuck.

"You're not playing fair," she said, swallowing thickly.

"All is fair in love and war, baby. And this?" His eyes dropped to feast on the vision of her glossy lips before lifting to pin her with his hungry gaze. "This is both."

In perfect sync, they crashed together, ravaging each other with tongues, teeth, and hands. More than a decade of built-up longing and desire swelled and broke through the years of separation. Dozer grabbed her under the ass and lifted. Angie instinctively wrapped her legs around his waist, lining up her sex with the erection he'd been carrying around ever since he'd seen her a week ago.

"Gavin."

*Fuck yes.* Her whisper of his given name was like an answered prayer. "Right here, Angel," he ground out between kisses. "Not going anywhere."

His body pinned hers against the shed, freeing his hands to sink into her hair. Thick and heavy, it felt like silk on his skin as he held her head and angled it to take the kiss deeper. Nails scraped the back of his neck. Barely a notch on the general pain scale, but powerful as hell in the pleasure/pain category. The tingles burned down his spine and into his balls.

Dozer couldn't remember needing anything as badly as this woman. Claiming her as his once and for all. Marking her so that every man who came near would know she belonged to a strong male they didn't want to fuck with.

She was his. Always had been, always would be.

The bright lights of a car turning onto their street swung over them like a prison spotlight. An RPG could blow up the shed behind them and Dozer wouldn't have given a shit, but the brief interruption startled Angie enough that she pulled back.

Realization of what they'd done, what they might've ended up doing had that car not come, filled her eyes. "Oh God, what are we doing?"

"Ang—"

"Put me down, please," she said, her pitch climbing. Slowly, he lowered her to the ground, but he didn't take his hands from the curves of her hips. "Thank you. I have to go."

"No, you don't. You're overthinking this, Angel. Focus on how great it felt to be like that with each other again. The chemistry between us is still off the fucking charts."

"I'd be a fool to argue that point after what just happened. But chemistry is all we have left, and that's not good enough, not for me." She moved around him, and he turned to watch her take careful steps backward. "There's no sequel for us. The faster you accept that, the better off we'll be. Good-bye, Dozer."

Forcing himself to stay rooted to his position, Dozer watched as she spun on her heel and started to walk back to the house with her arms wrapped around her middle, like she was trying to hold herself together, trying to prevent everything from breaking apart, and it fucking killed him. Because he was the one who'd been holding the sledgehammer.

# Chapter Fifteen

The small bathroom was so thick with steam, he could barely see the white marble vanity as he stepped out of the shower. Typically, Erik preferred his bathing water on the cooler side—especially after a hard tour at the firehouse—but this time he cranked that fucking handle all the way over, hoping to burn away the memories as sure as the water scalded his skin. Even then, he'd had to scrub himself three times before the grime and grit of the desert no longer covered his body and the smell of soap finally replaced the stench of blood in his nostrils. Then he'd braced his hands on the tiled wall and didn't move a muscle until the water sluicing over him had turned frigid.

Jazz and Harley were gone. The sharp loss continued to slice through his heart, the pain as fresh now as the day it happened. It was Erik's fault his men had returned home in caskets draped in the flag of their country. Not the enemy's fault. Not friendly fire's. Not an accident's.

*His.*

His fault that Jazz never made it back to his young wife

and the six-month-old son he'd never had the chance to hold. His fault Harley's parents lost their only son and his fiancée was made a widow before she ever got to call him her husband.

Still dripping, he gripped the edge of the damp counter and hung his head low between his shoulders. He took slow, deep breaths and tried the positive-thinking exercise the major had taught him, running through the list of people and things he was thankful for: his family, the BFD brotherhood, and each of his team brothers.

Then he got to Olivia.

Sweet, funny, smart, sexy Olivia. She was everything he wasn't. Light, innocent, pure. If any of those had existed in him at one time, they'd been long gone. Since returning from that last tour, where everything had gone so fucking wrong, he'd struggled to keep the darkness pushed down far enough that it couldn't pierce his consciousness. Tried to keep the faces of his dead brothers out of his dreams and the sound of hundreds of guns from between his ears.

Then he'd met Olivia and everything seemed to change. Before her, he'd never laughed so often, smiled so easily. She made him feel lighter, less burdened. He hadn't even realized it until one of his recent sessions when Dr. Marion asked him to describe in one word how Olivia made that part of him feel, the part where he kept all of the bad shit in his head. After careful consideration, he'd smiled and answered, "Quiet."

It was like her presence muted that darkness with her incredible light and let him feel the good stuff that was still left. Around her, he felt almost whole again. Not necessarily the man he once was—war had irreparably obliterated that version of himself—but the man he was capable of being now and the desire to become the man she deserved.

Erik cursed and shook his head. It was a damn good thing being naive didn't get you killed in the civilian world. He'd actually believed he had a chance at becoming that man. He'd foolishly thought that all it took to quiet his demons was her presence.

Then he came to, huddled on the kitchen floor with Olivia talking him down from the proverbial ledge like a terrified child. If *that* wasn't a kick in his fucking balls. When a deadly—or at least *formerly* deadly—soldier needed his girlfriend to save his ass from a hallucination... *Fuck*.

Erik was starting to understand why so many servicemen and -women survived the war only to come home and punch their own clocks. If he had more of this shit to look forward to, getting a one-way ticket to eternal damnation would be the lesser of two evils. Because acting like a helpless pussy in front of Olivia? *That* shit he couldn't deal with. No goddamn way. Not if something like cheap Walmart noisemakers could convince him he was taking on enemy fire. What if the next time it happened, he grabbed her, thinking he was going hand-to-hand with a Tango, and wrapped his big fingers around her delicate throat?

He saw himself strangling the life from the woman he loved, the horrifying image flickering in his mind like an epileptic premonition. *"Oh Christ,"* he rasped. It kicked him square in the chest, sucking all the air from his lungs. It roiled in his gut like rancid meat, and he shivered with a cold sweat that defied the humidity in the room.

His stomach cramped, urging him to vomit, and he briefly considered collapsing over the toilet. Maybe the physical purge would do the same for his mind. Then he could drain that bottle of whiskey he noticed on Mr. Jones's wet bar upstairs and hope to Christ he passed out into a void of nothingness until the morning.

Running the cold water, Erik splashed himself in the face, over his head, and on the back of his neck, trying to eliminate the fevered flash. He dragged in deep breaths through his nose and exhaled through his mouth to fight the waves of nausea rolling through him. Once he got past the worst of it, he shut off the water and lifted his gaze to the steam-covered mirror.

With a quick swipe of his hand, Erik cleared a line of fog and stared into his dark amber eyes, assessing the man reflected there. The man who couldn't control his own brain, his own reactions. Couldn't trust himself around anyone who didn't have the strength and ability to take him down whenever he was too weak to fight against the terrors in his head.

He wanted to shatter the glass with his fists, to reel from the pain and feel the sticky warmth of his blood coating his scarred flesh. He was amped as fuck, every inch of his body battle-hard, like he was fresh off a firefight and riding a mission high.

*Weak. Too weak.*

*Weakness only leads to more weakness.*

Fuck that shit. He wasn't about to give those extremist bastards the satisfaction of breaking him. He'd survived their hell over and fucking over again; he'd be damned if he'd lie down on his home turf and let it kill him now. And when he came out on the other side, maybe Olivia would still be there waiting for him.

Then again, maybe not. Now that she'd finally had a relationship after the death of her husband, if Erik wasn't in the picture anymore, she'd probably move on. Date other men. Men who didn't have to worry every minute of every day whether something would trigger a debilitating flashback.

*FUCK!*

Erik made the decision right then and there that he'd be on death's door before he'd accept that he lost her forever because of four fucking letters. PTSD. He didn't care what he had to do or how many times he had to do it. He'd beat this thing. And then he was coming back to claim Livvie once and for all. If she found someone else in the meantime, he'd fight for her, fight to get her back.

"Erik?" He tensed at the sound of her voice through the bathroom door, every muscle tight enough to make him shake with the exertion. Steeling himself for the conversation to come, he wrapped a towel around his waist, rolled his shoulders in a futile attempt to get them to relax, then walked out of the bathroom…and froze.

The overhead light was off, but a group of pillar candles held dancing flames on the dresser across the room. They provided adequate light to see by as the mirror behind them doubled their efforts. Music—some kind of easy listening shit that doctors' offices played in their lobbies—piped in from hidden speakers in the corners of the bedroom, and Olivia stood at the foot of the bed, absently wringing her hands in front of her.

Fuck. Either she wanted to teach him how to do meditative yoga or she wanted to set the mood for a slow seduction. Neither option sounded good to him. Not now, when his blood flowed hot. When his head was filled with ghosts. When his muscles literally vibrated from an overdose of testosterone and endorphins, a volatile cocktail he needed to work off in one of two ways: a punishing workout or punishing sex.

He'd be damned if he'd let himself anywhere near her in this manic state.

Olivia took a step toward him, but he held a hand out to halt her. "Don't." His voice, low and tight from using every ounce of his restraint, held a bite he hadn't intended. The hurt and confusion on her face might as well be a gunshot wound to the gut because if he didn't fix it, it'd be a slow and painful death. "I'm sorry, I can't be around anyone right now. I'm not in a good place, and I need time to sort through my shit. Give me the night. We can talk in the morning."

Her softly arched brows pulled down in a *V*. "The last thing I plan on doing is leaving you alone tonight," she said.

"We don't have to make love if you don't want. We can lie in bed and watch a movie, talk, or just go to sleep. But I won't leave you."

He tried like hell to gentle his tone, but every time he opened his mouth, his words dripped with the acid of his shame. "Sorry, sweetheart, but none of those options are going to work for me. Not tonight or any night until I can get my shit together."

"What do you mean by that?"

"Exactly like it sounds, Doc. I've been fooling myself, walking around like nothing's fucking wrong with me. Like I'm on vacation and not suspended from my job for being a goddamn mental case." His chest heaved with agitation. Fists clenched at his sides, Erik forced the next statement past his lips. "Like I'm good enough to be the man you deserve."

"Erik, I don't want to hear you put yourself down like that again, do you hear me?"

Her indignance seemed to strengthen her resolve to fight him on this. Her spine straightened and chin lifted like a woman who expected to be obeyed. He hadn't noticed her move, but when she rested her hand on his heart, he realized she must have been walking as she spoke. He wanted to place his hand over hers, to pull her against him and wrap her up tight so she couldn't leave. But he held his position and kept his gaze steely with his shields up.

"You've already come so far," she said, her tone gentler. "You can't discredit all the hard work you've put in just because you had a setback."

"A *setback*?" he rumbled. "You make it sound like I forgot to add the eggs in a cookie recipe and have to start over. *That's* a setback. I fucking *hallucinated*, Olivia. I could have seriously hurt you. Hell, I could have *killed* you."

"No," she said firmly, shaking her head. "If you were that far under I would have known, and I would have stayed out of reach. I'm not an ignorant bystander, Erik. I'm a specialist, so trying to scare me away won't work. You'll just have to deal with me sticking around and helping you through this."

He usually loved seeing her bossy side. It turned him on when she unleashed it on other people, and normally he found it amusing when she tried it with him. But he was too jacked up to be anything other than frustrated as fuck, and he needed her to understand that and then get out before he said or did something they'd both regret.

"So *now* you want to help me. You didn't *want* to help me, remember, Doc? I tried to get you to treat me. I told you I only wanted to see you, but you insisted I see Dr. Marion. Forgive me if I don't feel like stretching out on your couch now that we've been fucking on a regular basis."

Turning, he made his way to his pile of clothes on the floor and grabbed up the black boxer briefs. Keeping his back to her—more so he didn't have to see the hurt in her eyes from his asshole comments than from any faux sense of modesty—he unhooked the towel and let it drop. The quick intake of breath behind him made his cock twitch, but he forced himself not to outwardly react as he bent to shove his legs through his underwear.

He'd been so focused on holding his shit together that he hadn't heard her bare feet pad across the carpet, didn't know she'd moved to step behind him, until he straightened and her hands stopped his before he had the chance to drag the waistband over his ass and cock.

"What are you doing?" Jesus, that came out so rough it didn't even sound human.

She placed a kiss in the center of his back, and her hands left his to skate over the curves of his glutes. "Loving you." Her hands changed direction and moved to the front, getting closer and closer to his straining cock pressed against his stomach. Her fingertips traced the ridges of his obliques that veed toward the base. Erik released a strangled grunt and his eyes slid closed as he dropped his head back. He wanted more. *Needed* more. Needed to feel her score his flesh with her nails, the sting of his skin giving way…

"That's it, baby," she whispered. "Let me make love to you."

That snapped him out of it. *Shit.* She wanted to make love and he'd only be able to control himself for a few minutes, max, before the poison inside him demanded attention. He couldn't allow that to happen. Not to her. Not ever.

"Stop." Manacling her wrists, he pulled her hands from him and stepped away, snapping the elastic of his boxers at his waist where it belonged. More. He needed more clothes between them. His turnout gear would be a good start.

"Why? It's not like you can claim you're not in the mood," she said, pointedly looking at the club he'd adjusted off to the left, hoping it'd go down. Fat fucking chance.

"Never said I wasn't. But I'm not fit for making love right now, Doc." Using the less personal nickname he had for her was his lame attempt to mentally hold her at arm's length. "The only thing I'm good for in this state is a rough fuck."

In this lighting, he couldn't see if her eyes darkened, but it was hard to miss the way her pupils dilated. She lifted a bare shoulder and offered a sly grin. "Sounds good to me, Lieutenant."

He shook his head and let his voice drip with condescension. Insulting her was infinitely better than showing her the beast lying in wait, so close he could feel its fur rippling just beneath the surface. "You don't get it. I'm amped way beyond anything you've seen from me. *Miles* beyond. Only two things can bring me down from this. Either I fuck it out of my system or I work it out in the gym, and you don't want me to do the former. It won't be pretty."

"Who the hell said I want pretty?"

"Seriously? You lit candles and have your iTunes set to a love song playlist."

Eyes narrowed, she planted her hands on her hips. "Fine, so I guessed wrong about your preferred mood after an episode. Big fucking deal. It's not irreversible, you know. I don't care if you turn on floodlights and blast Marilyn Manson, if that's what you want, because all *I* want is to be with you. And in case you've forgotten, you self-absorbed prick, I like it when you're rough."

He gnashed his teeth. This wasn't going the way he needed. She was supposed to be backing down. Hightailing it the hell out of there. "Self-absorbed prick? Every decision I make is in *your* best interest."

"Bullshit," she snapped. "This isn't about me or what I want. It's about what you think I want or what you think I *should* want." She laughed without mirth. "*My* best interest? What a joke."

"Well, it sure as hell isn't mine, because if it was, I wouldn't let you go for a goddamn minute, not even when the darkness takes me."

"Good," she said, crossing her arms over her perfect tits, "we're on the same page, then."

Cursing her stubborn streak—the one he found hot as hell—he stalked to the wall and hit the light switch. The room filled with sudden brightness, making them squint as their eyes adjusted. Then he blew out the candles on the dresser and changed out her phone for his in the docking station. He chose the playlist he used whenever he needed the punishing workout after bad calls to keep the past out of his head until he could pass out from exhaustion. The music was all fast and hard, the kind that blasted during car chases or fight scenes in an action flick. The songs were about fighting, or fucking, or fucking while fighting.

*This* was his preferred mood after what she referred to

as an "episode." Now she'd see exactly what she was asking for…and then she'd run.

As the bass and guitar riffs came through of Nickelback's "Something In Your Mouth"—a crude song about exactly what the title suggested—Erik turned to face Olivia, his hands flexing and fisting. They ached to dive into her long blond hair and control where he wanted her and what he wanted her taking from him.

*Hold, Grady. You're not trying to let it get that far, remember? Just give her a glimpse, enough to scare her a bit and rethink her position.*

Pointing to the floor in front of him, he issued his command. "Get your ass over here." She stared at him, then flicked her eyes down to his erection and swallowed. He almost groaned as he remembered how it felt when her throat swallowed on his sensitized head, but her refusal to follow orders overpowered his lust. "I gave you an order, gorgeous. If you're not front and center in the next three seconds, your ass will feel the sting of my palm until I'm satisfied you'll have to stand during all your sessions next week."

This time, she complied, moving to the spot he'd indicated. The darkness swelled inside him, but he only let it get so close. Still, he craved to see her eyes go wild with lust from the anticipation and uncertainty of what would happen next.

He grabbed her by the shoulders and whipped her around him as he spun, then shoved her back against the wall. She gasped in shock, but he didn't give her a chance to recover before he pinned her with his body and locked her wrists high above her head with his left hand, leaving his right free to grope and squeeze.

"If you're trying to scare me, it won't work," she said, eyes narrowed. "It'd take a lot more than tossing me around the room and holding me down."

"What, this? This is nothing, Doc. Child's play. I highly

suggest you call me off before we get to the hard stuff."

"Thanks for the warning, but I think I'll take my chances."

Working his jaw muscles in frustration, he forced himself to take a deep breath through his nose and exhale before speaking. "You don't want to do that, Livvie." Though he kept his voice strong, Erik had taken the acid out of his tone and used his name for her, hoping he'd get through to her that way because he was running out of time. Like a firefighter low on air, it wouldn't be much longer before Erik used up the last ounce of his control.

And then God help them both.

"Don't presume to know what I want, Erik, because you don't know the first thing about it. If you did, you'd know that this is *exactly* what I want. You, uninhibited and unrestrained."

Sighing, he released her arms and rested his forehead on hers. "Baby, please don't. Don't tell me things like that just so I take what you think I need from you. You don't understand what you're asking."

"Then explain it to me."

"Before I met you, when I got like this, I'd seek out women who enjoyed things rough. And not just from me. They gave as good as they got. Do you know what I'm saying?"

"Meaning they were rough with you?"

He closed his eyes, nodded, and took a breath before continuing. "The pain helps me purge everything, helps me atone. But I can't ask you to do that. You deserve to be made love to, soft and slow and reverent."

Erik felt Olivia's soft hands frame his face and her thumbs caress his cheekbones. "You're trembling," she whispered.

His eyes opened to see his fears reflected back at him in hers, and he hated himself more than ever in that moment. "It's the bad shit in me, Livvie. Usually it's contained, but when it gets stirred up... Goddammit, I don't want it touching you. I need you to go upstairs, baby, and let me work this out in your dad's gym. Alone. *Please.*"

She hesitated, her eyes searching his to find the answer to a puzzle that was missing too many pieces. He was like that poor bastard Humpty Dumpty. There was no putting him back together again. At least not completely.

"I'll go," she said finally. "But you have to promise me that next time, you won't push me away."

"That's a negative, sweetheart," he said softly, shaking his head. "I have to get myself under control before we can be together. Once I'm cleared for duty, if I can go six whole months without any problems, then I'll trust myself around you. And I promise that as soon as those six months are up, you won't be able to get rid of me. Not until I'm six feet under."

"You're serious," she said in wonder. "You're breaking up with me until you pass some sort of self-imposed test of your mental health? Erik, I—"

"Don't try to talk me out of it, Olivia." The edge was back in his voice and he sounded like a scornful parent using her real name to make his point. He'd managed to let the tenderness he felt for her peek through the black tar coating his soul for a few minutes, but how long would it be before he lost control? If he didn't get her out of there fast, she'd see a side of him she'd never be able to forget, and then they'd be over for good. "Even if I can be certain I'd never hurt you during a flashback, I still don't want you around me when I'm unstable like this. I swear that I will do everything in my power to beat this and come back to you, but you need to go, right the fuck now."

Defiance flashed in her blue eyes. He tensed, preparing for the verbal onslaught she'd no doubt unleash. But suddenly her features eased with acceptance. "Okay," she said. "I don't like it, but I understand that you feel it's for the best."

Erik's stomach twisted into a knot, which was fucking ridiculous. He couldn't be disappointed when she finally agreed to do what he wanted. *Man the fuck up, Grady.* "I do," he answered gruffly.

"Kiss me before I go?"

God, yes, he needed to kiss her. As long as he held himself in check… He flattened his palms against the wall and bent his head to take her lips. Her hands slid around his neck and she pulled herself into him. He opened his mouth to her and she dived in, stroking his tongue with an urgency that fueled his own. When the desire to toss her on the bed nearly choked him, Erik pulled the intensity back and gentled the kiss until he was only allowing himself small sips between their heaving breaths.

Olivia suckled on his lower lip, then used her blunt teeth to tease and nip and—

"Ah *fuck!*" Erik pulled away and glared at her smug expression through narrowed eyes. His lip throbbed, along with his dick, the pain getting him even harder. Before she wiped it off with the back of her hand, he noticed a dark red smear on her lips. He touched his mouth and came away with blood on his fingertips. "You fucking *bit me*. What the hell was that for?"

He immediately wanted to take those words back. There was nothing wrong with her. It was him. He was the twisted bastard who got off on the pain she'd inflicted.

She used both hands to shove at his chest. The fact that he didn't so much as sway an inch seemed to piss her off even more. So she did it again, with equally disappointing results. "To prove to you that I have no issues kicking your ass all over this bedroom if that's what you need. You gave me what I needed the first night we met. Let me do the same thing for you. I'm not as fragile as you seem to think. This might be hard for your ego to accept, but I'm not with you because you dragged me off to your cave by my hair. I'm with you because I *want* to be, because I care about you. Every. Single. Part of you. I'm not afraid of the big, bad wolf."

A mirthless chuckle rumbled in his chest. "The wolf I've shown you is tame," he ground out. "You haven't even glimpsed my 'big, bad' yet, gorgeous."

Clearly at the end of her rope, Olivia escalated to shouting, which did nothing to quell his growing temper. "So *show me*. You've been holding back with me, and I'm sick of it. I *want* your 'big, bad,' so give it to me already!"

*"Goddammit, woman."* Before she could blink, he crowded her back to the wall and crushed her lips to his. It stung where she'd drawn blood, but he reveled in the pain, the endorphins flowing like a drug through his veins.

His brain screamed at him to release her, lock himself in the gym and stay there until he could make his escape in the morning. But then Olivia scored her nails over his back and he felt a light burn travel down in eight identical rows, from traps to ass. The stinging grounded him in the here and now, made him remember he was alive, that he could still *feel*. And that's all it took for his dick to flip off his brain in a double "fuck you" salute.

Wrenching his mouth away from hers, he bent to lick and scrape a path up the side of her neck. Her hot breaths and wanton whimpers bathed his ear and drove him toward the brink of insanity.

Erik never felt as weak in his life than he did in this moment as he consciously made the decision to give in. To give in to his demons, to Olivia, to the promise of release and the temporary peace that came with it.

"I hope to fucking God we don't regret this, Livvie," he growled. Shedding the last bit of his humanity, he dropped the floodgates in his mind and let the darkness crash over him. "Brace yourself, baby, and get ready to sharpen your claws. You're about to meet the big, bad wolf."

# Chapter Sixteen

Erik grabbed the scoop neck of her thin tank and tore it in two, then made quick work of her bra in the same manner. He descended to engulf one breast in his mouth while he grabbed and squeezed the other, rolling her nipple between his fingers, then switched sides.

She sighed and arched into him, scraped her nails over his buzzed scalp, and pulled his head into her chest, encouraging him to feast. When at last he straightened, she whimpered, but he cut it off with an all-consuming kiss, his tongue delving in to taste every last bit of her.

Their hands flew over each other, groping and grabbing, her nails scratching and stabbing. With each sting of physical pain she inflicted, Erik's emotional pain lessened a little bit more. He needed to be hurt, to be marked, to be reminded, to not walk away unscathed. For his body to reflect the wounds on his heart, the scars on his soul.

He used one hand to fist her hair close to her scalp and yanked down to fully expose her throat as he ran his nose up the smooth column, from shoulder to jawline, drawing her scent deep into his lungs. She grabbed at his boxer briefs and shoved them down over his ass so they fell to the floor. Erik kicked them aside as he divested her of her jean shorts and panties.

Leaning his forehead against hers, he held her gaze and trailed a hand up the inside of her thighs until he cupped her sweet pussy. His fingers delved between her swollen lips, testing her, then he curled the middle two and slipped them into her slick entrance. A mewl of need tripped off her lips as he lifted up, sinking his fingers in deep enough to lift her onto her toes.

"Yes," she said on an exhale.

He didn't need to see her expression or hear her sounds of pleasure to know she was turned on. The only proof he needed was her drenched cunt.

Christ, his dick had never been so hard in his life, and every time the head glanced over her hip or even bobbed against his stomach, he thought he'd fucking explode on the spot. He needed inside her, and he needed it now.

Erik stepped in close, grabbed her ass, and hoisted her up. She wrapped her legs around his waist and he reached beneath her to grab his cock and drag it through her pouting flesh. He felt the head slide into place at the slick entrance of her pussy, and it wrapped him in welcoming heat. For the hundredth time, he was thankful they'd had the birth control/medical records talk a week ago and made the decision to nix the damn condoms. He'd never gone bareback with anyone before Livvie, and if she hadn't already ruined him for all other women, that would have done it.

"Please, Erik," she begged sweetly, and he thrust up, burying himself so deep he swore he saw stars. Usually, he held still after first entering her. To revel in the way she squeezed him and fit him so perfectly. To take in the moment and prolong things as much as possible.

But not this time.

Not with the anguish drowning him, the need to punish and be punished, to find sharp relief in every sensation allowed him as his fallen brothers would never feel again. Not with the driving need to come inside her nipping at his heels like the hounds of hell themselves.

No, this wasn't a marathon, it was a fucking sprint. And when they crossed the finish line, they'd both be boneless, gasping for air, and slick with sweat.

Erik moved, his hips pumping in time with the pulse galloping in his ears, hating every retreat and reveling in every return. Her face was the definition of rapture, eyes heavy-lidded, pupils blown, and mouth opened wide like she was waiting for him to fill it with his cock. And the strings of whispered *please*s and *oh God, yes*es mixed in among the moans was the audible assurance that she was as lost to this as he was.

Her nails dug into his triceps and yet he barely felt them. He wanted to tell her *more*, tell her *harder*, but he didn't want to scare her or ask for too much. The sex would be enough. It had to be enough.

No sooner did he finish the mantra than she lowered her head, latched on to the tendon where his shoulder and neck merged, and clamped down with her teeth. Erik hissed in a breath through a clenched jaw and growled on the exhale as the endorphins he craved flooded his system.

If he'd thought he could shock her with his need for rough treatment, he'd been dead wrong. Not only did she not shy away from it, but she gave every bit as good as she got. Releasing her hold on him, she gave him a feral smile right before pulling him in and crushing her lips to his.

Fucking perfection. That's what his Livvie was.

Without breaking their wild kiss, he moved away from the wall and walked them to the dresser. He perched her ass at the edge, palmed the sides of her head, and continued his assault on both her mouth and tight little pussy. After several minutes, or fuck, maybe it was an hour, they wrenched apart to catch their breath, and what he saw stopped him in his tracks.

Her lips were red and puffy, hazel eyes bright with lust, and cheeks flushed pink. Sweat dampened her face and smudged her mascara. Staring at her, he used the pads of his thumbs to further smear the black makeup over her alabaster skin. She was breathtaking, like a tormented angel, reveling in her own torment, and maybe even his.

"So fucking perfect," he said as he stroked her long hair back from her face.

Her eyes went all soft, and she leaned in to his touch on a long sigh. That's when everything clicked into place for him. He loved Olivia, was *in* love with her. Wholly and completely—heart, mind, body, and soul. His love reflected back at him in her eyes, in the way she looked at him, as if he was the *only* thing and *every*thing all rolled into one. And he wanted her to see.

Gritting his teeth, he pulled out of her and helped her down before turning her to face the large mirror over the dresser. One of his hands splayed over her belly while the other wrapped around the front of her throat, protective and possessive. "Look how beautiful you are, baby," he said all raspy and next to her ear. "You're mine, Livvie. You belong to me."

"Yes," she whispered. She slipped her right hand along the back of his head and pulled him down even more, offering her neck to him like a sacrificial lamb. He attacked her shoulder, blazing a trail of licks and bites up the length of her neck and back again.

Unable to hold back another second, he kicked her feet apart, lined himself up, and in a single thrust, shoved home.

*Home.*

For so long now, the place he most considered home was the Roxbury firehouse where he and his band of brothers lived and worked. But this…being inside this woman—hell, Olivia herself—felt more like home than anything else he'd had in his life. It's where he belonged. Where he wanted to stay. Now and for always.

As he set up a steady rhythm, Erik watched her face in the mirror, watched as the sensations of being filled and stretched by him burned in her eyes. He fisted a handful of her hair and pulled, banding his free arm around her middle to hold her against him. He fucked her in front of the mirror and committed every detail to memory. Him larger and darker, her smaller and fairer. Sweat made their skin glisten under the glaring overhead light. With every thrust, her tits bounced on his forearm and his balls slapped the swollen lips of her pussy. Carnality at its basest, its finest.

*"Yes, yes, yes!"* Her cries spurred him on, faster and faster. The noises they made mixed with the blaring music still playing, creating a soundtrack of grunts, pants, and moans with the staccato sounds of wet flesh smacking together.

She reached back and he felt her nails bite into the sensitive skin on the backs of his thighs, right under his ass. "Fuck!" Erik couldn't hold on much longer. The fire raced down his spine, and his balls pulled in tight. Using the fingers of one hand, he pinched and twisted a nipple, making sure to keep the pressure on. His other hand moved to her mound, the heel of his hand pressing in just above her pubic bone to create more friction on her G-spot while he rubbed and slapped her clit, pushing her toward that razor's edge between pain and utter bliss.

*"OhGod—ohGod—ohG—"*

He nipped her earlobe hard enough to make her gasp. "Wrong name," he growled. "Who's fucking you?"

"Erik."

He rubbed over her clit harder, faster. "Who do you belong to?" He gave her pussy a sharp smack for emphasis, making her jump on his cock. *Jesus fuck!*

"Erik!"

"Goddamn right. Now come for me, Livvie baby."

With that, Erik released his hold on her nipple, letting the blood rush back to the distended nub, and pinched her clit to finally send her over. Throwing her head back on his shoulder, she screamed as her body rocked with tremors, and her cunt gripped his cock, convulsing and dragging him over the brink. He buried himself to the hilt one last time and roared through the orgasm that exploded through him like a mortar tearing through a tank cannon.

As they slowly came back to the real world, Erik wished they'd ended up in the bed. His leg muscles burned from the exertion of staying slightly bent to compensate for her shorter height, and all he wanted to do was roll over and hold her while they fell asleep. But first he had to get them there.

Pulling out of her was a special form of torture, but he forced himself to step back and let his semi-soft dick slip from her heat. "Come here, sweetheart," he said softly, placing a kiss at her temple before scooping her up against his chest.

She wrapped her arms around his neck as she tucked her face into the crook of his shoulder. He laid her on the bed and covered her up, then turned the music and lights off on his way to the bathroom to clean up.

He did a cursory check in the vanity mirror, taking inventory of the physical damage. He had multiple scratches and dozens of tiny crescent-shaped indentations from her nails, but none of them were quite as impressive as the teeth impressions near his shoulder. Raising a hand, he traced the pattern with the tip of a finger, the sight of her mark on him was like a balm on an ache only she could touch. Only his

Livvie.

When he returned with a damp washcloth, his heart swelled to near bursting in his chest at the sight of her, lying on her stomach and hugging a pillow with a sleepy smile, waiting for him to come back. And he would, now and for always. He knew it as sure as he knew his own name. He'd never do anything to put her at risk, and he'd do everything he could to make her feel loved and cherished.

But after gently cleaning her, he had to make sure she was okay with everything. Setting the cloth off to the side, he said, "Hey, gorgeous."

"Hmm?"

"You don't regret what we did? Not freaked out by any of it?"

Olivia's features softened; it was a look he'd come to know well. A woman with a heart as big as hers, who empathized to a fault, couldn't not wear that look at least once a day. Her compassion was one of the many things he loved about her.

"C'mere," she said, rocking to her side to make room for him under the sheet with her.

Eager to have her in his arms, he stretched out and tucked her against him. Her head rested on his shoulder, but she lifted it to meet his gaze. She appeared rumpled with that freshly fucked look, and if he wasn't so exhausted, it'd probably stir his libido for another round.

"Hear me when I tell you this, Erik." She brought her hand up to cradle the side of his face, the gesture at once soothing and upsetting because of the bandage on her palm. "Are you listening?"

He raised his eyes back to hers as he stroked her hair and nodded, wary of attempting to push any words past the lump in his throat for fear they'd come out cracked.

"Good," she said warmly. "I don't regret a *single moment*. You gave yourself to me every bit as much as I gave myself to you. There's nothing more beautiful than that. As long as we give each other what we need, nothing is considered wrong. A sexy-as-hell man taught me that."

The steel coils of doubt and guilt that had been winding their way through him, squeezing and choking him, finally unraveled and allowed him to take a full breath as they shrank back into the shadows. Exhaling, he felt the pricking of moisture behind his eyes, and his throat tightened for a whole new reason.

Olivia settled back in and laid her head on his chest as Erik stared at the ceiling and ran her long hair through his fingertips. He thought she fell asleep until she spoke softly in the darkness. "Will you tell me about that day?"

She sounded unsure, like she wasn't sure she should ask or maybe she expected him to get upset. Normally, he'd shut down any talk about that mission, but he knew now that she was *it* for him, so regardless of what might happen tomorrow or the next day, he needed to lay himself bare and stop hiding all the shit he'd rather she not see. It was time to bite the bullet and open up.

"We were already two days into what was supposed to be a six-hour op. The boys and I were assigned a snatch-and-grab mission for a high-profile extremist near Basra. The bastard kept giving us the slip, but we lucked out and pulled some solid intel from a local source on his location, so we went with it. We reached the compound and I called in to signal our position, but our radios were down due to interference from the electrical equipment inside the compound.

"Normally, we wouldn't go ahead without being able to reach operations, but this would be our only chance to catch him, our only chance to end the chaos and horror he brought on the people of his country and mine.

"So I gave the green light, and we stormed the compound. One hard knock on the door and we found out real fucking quick what hurt was. They'd rigged the entry with explosives. Soon as it popped open, the breach team vanished in a shitstorm of smoke, fire, and steel. Hell, Smoke is lucky his night vision cut out when it did and he stalled to fix it just before the blast went off. If he hadn't, he'd have a lot worse than just burn scars to hide.

"But we're rangers, and rangers don't quit, so we didn't let the breach hang-up stall our violence of action. We poured into that shithole like a swarm of militant wasps, and you know what we found? Fuckall."

"What do you mean?" she asked carefully. "The guy wasn't there?"

Erik shook his head once, still in disbelief. "It was a bad tip. The intel was misguided, the source planted. I lost two men—two *brothers*—because of shitty intel and an even shittier decision that *I* made. It's my fault Smoke is who he is now, and it's my fault Harley and Jazz lost their lives that day and left behind families. I may not have detonated the bomb, but they died as a direct result of my command, and that's just as bad…if not worse.

"That's why I started questioning my judgment after that explosion at the power plant. It reminded me of how I failed my men as a lieutenant, their leader, and their friend. It was my call to make. I made it, and even though some of the guys had doubts about the situation, they followed me," he said. "My decision led to two of my men dying, others wounded, and Smoke—well, you saw firsthand what he has to see every day for the rest of his life. He won't even entertain the idea of dating because of what he looks like beneath his clothes. That's on me."

"Does he blame you, too?" she asked.

"Fuck no. Sometimes I think that's worse than if he did."

"If the roles would have been reversed, and you were the one who was injured in the line of duty while following your friend and lieutenant, would you blame him?"

"I know what you're doing, but it's not the same."

Olivia pushed up onto her elbow and looked down at him, her golden hair cascading over her shoulder and spilling over his. He waited for her to argue or say something, but all she did was stare at him. Not with judgment or disappointment or even frustration, but something that looked like acceptance and love…and still she didn't speak.

Aw hell, she was using his own technique on him. Then again, he supposed in a lot of ways shrinks were similar to interrogators. They both knew how to get people to say what they didn't want to say. And damn if she wasn't good at this shit.

Sighing heavily, he said, "It's the same. But it doesn't make it any easier to swallow."

"Maybe not yet. Give it time."

"It's already been years and I haven't gotten very far."

"You're only now starting to deal with any of it. It might as well have happened a few months ago for as much as you've dealt with your guilt since coming back." Olivia placed her soft hand on the side of his face and gazed deeply into his eyes. "You are a strong and honorable man. There is nothing you wouldn't do for your country, your city, and your brothers. Those are all things you know and have confidence in.

"Where you lack in confidence right now is your ability to lead. But you've been leading your company for years now without incident. That's literally thousands of calls where you brought yourself and your men back safely, or at least without any fatal injuries. That's amazing in itself, but let's look at it from another angle. Dozer, Smoke, Bowie, and Preacher: Do you think any of them are particularly dense or maybe have a death wish?"

"Not a chance. Those guys are sharp as hell. They might be adrenaline junkies, but we all are to some extent or we wouldn't have chosen the careers we did. That doesn't mean we have a death wish. Aside from Bowie, anyway." When her brow knitted together in concern, he used his thumb to smooth out the wrinkles marring her flawless features. Shaking his head, he said, "Leave it alone, sweetheart."

She gave him a wan smile. "Sorry, force of habit. Okay, so then you can agree that there's no way in hell your guys would've signed up to work under you if they had any doubts about your ability to lead them and make the right calls. They were all there that day, and as you pointed out, Smoke has lasting scars. If anyone had reason to doubt you, it would be them, and yet they follow you into burning buildings without hesitation, over and over again. You *will* heal, Lieutenant Erik Thomas Grady. I promise you that."

This woman was a miracle, a Godsend sent to rescue him. Maybe it was karma or the universe's way of repaying him for the people he'd managed to rescue over the years, both as a ranger and a firefighter, he didn't know, and frankly, he didn't care. All that fucking mattered was that she was *his*.

"Livvie, I—" *Love you.* Erik fought an internal battle. *Tell her… Don't tell her…* He wanted to, so fucking badly. The words were heavy in his soul, on his tongue, and he wanted nothing more than to set them free, to let her know just how much she meant to him. But he couldn't. Not yet. "Thank you."

She smiled. "You're welcome." Then she gave him a kiss that was at once sweet and sensual, just like her, and burrowed back into his side, falling asleep in mere seconds.

Resting his cheek on the top of her head, he held her tight, stroked the smooth skin of her arm, and tried to reassure himself that not saying it was the right thing to do. It's not that he didn't want to tell her exactly how much she meant to him, but he couldn't put that on her now. It wouldn't be fair to her. Once he got his head on straight, he could offer her love from the kind of man she deserved. Then he'd be free to prove his unconditional love for her every day for the rest of their lives.

Because despite the incredible gift she'd given him tonight—despite the fact she'd proven to him beyond the shadow of a doubt that she could handle it when the darkness consumed him—it still killed him to know he hurt her during his flashback, and he couldn't help but worry that it might happen again. His brain, his actions—it was all too unpredictable.

Erik planned to talk with Dr. Marion about it tomorrow. He had to know what the odds were of this happening again; if just by being with her, he was putting Olivia in danger.

*Danger…risk…* A chill raced through his veins as he realized something else. Something he'd thought of and then shoved into the back of his mind the day Livvie had told him about her husband's death. At the time, their relationship had barely gotten off the ground so he justified ignoring the one thing about himself that made him a terrible match for her.

He was a goddamn firefighter. A man whose survival odds have been a constant gamble, from the time he turned eighteen and entered the army to the time he entered the fire service at twenty-eight. Erik's job was a game of Russian Roulette. Slip in the bullet, spin the chamber, snap it in, cock the gun, pull the trigger. Odds were good that all he'd hear is a click and he'd make it through the end of his shift safe and sound. But there was always that chance. The chance that someday that bullet lines up just right and makes Livvie a widow…again.

Flashes of her crying at his grave had beads of sweat popping out on his forehead that he swiped away with the back of his hand. Taking a slow, deep breath, Erik closed his eyes and pushed the images of leaving Livvie behind from his mind. It was something else he'd have to think about, but not right now.

For now, he'd cherish holding her in his arms and feeling her soft breaths skate across his chest. There was a good chance he'd have to let her go until he could get his shit together. He just prayed it wouldn't be permanent, because living without her would be an entirely new kind of hell. One he wasn't sure he could survive.

...

Olivia woke from being jostled in the middle of the night. The bed was literally shaking. As her eyes adjusted in the darkness, she turned over to face Erik, concern gripping her heart with sharp talons, despite the fact that she'd suspected this might happen tonight.

He was in the middle of a nightmare. He lay on his back, the sheet twisted around his legs, his body covered in sweat as he jerked and writhed, fighting off some invisible attacker in his mind and mumbling unintelligibly.

Bracing herself on her elbow, she looked down at him, being careful not to hover. "Erik, wake up. It's only a dream," she said, her voice firm, hoping to penetrate through the thick fog of his nightmare. She tried calling his name a few more times, but to no avail. Desperate to get through to him, she propped herself up on one hand and placed the other on his chest.

Then all hell broke loose in the span of a heartbeat.

Gasping like an emerging drowning victim, Erik jackknifed in the bed, his eyes flying open. He stared straight through her, his mouth set in a snarl as he growled, seeing something other than what lived in the present. A bolt of lightning-quick panic streaked through Olivia as he swept her under him, pinning her to the mattress with his massive body and her wrists shackled on either side of her head.

"Erik!"

Olivia hadn't even finished shouting his name when she saw the moment he woke up. He stared at her, his eyes full of confusion, but finally grounded in the present. "Livvie?" His voice was gravelly and laced with fear and uncertainty. "What happened?"

"Nothing," she said, willing him to feel her strength, her confidence that everything was going to be okay. "You were having a nightmare, that's all. It's okay." His brow furrowed and he looked around—at the place he'd been lying next to her, the tangled sheet, their current positions with him still holding her wrists to the bed.

She felt him start to tremble as realization dawned on his face. "Oh my God, Livvie. In my dream, I was… And then… Oh fuck." Erik bolted from the bed and scrubbed his hands down his face. Then he crossed to where his clothes lay in a heap on the floor and started shoving his legs through his boxer briefs, his motions jerky and agitated.

Olivia turned on the bedside lamp, gathered the sheet around her, and scrambled over to him. "Where are you going?"

Yanking his cargo shorts onto his hips, he answered without looking at her. "I have to go. I'll send Preacher back to get you in the morning."

"I don't need a ride from Preacher. I need you to stay with me."

He finished securing his belt and finally met her gaze. "That's the last fucking thing you need."

His skin was pale and covered in a sheen of sweat. It killed her to see him so shaken, so unsure of himself. "You're wrong." She placed a comforting hand on his chest, but the thundering beat of his heart under her palm told her it wasn't helping. "Everyone has nightmares, Erik, and I knew there was a good chance you'd have one tonight after the flashback. This is perfectly normal."

"*Fuck* normal. Goddamn it, Livvie, *I hurt you*."

"No, you *didn't*," she shot back, clutching the sheet tighter around her as though it would help her hold him to her as well. "You rolled me beneath you—a move, I'd like to point out, you've done to me more times than I can count—and you woke up as soon as you had me on my back." Olivia stepped into him and cupped the side of his face. "I promise I won't knowingly put myself in danger, Erik. If at any time I feel like things have escalated, we'll just sleep separately until things calm down."

He shook his head and took a step back to escape her touch, a fact that she tried not to let affect her, even as she felt her heart crack open.

"So, what?" he asked, arms spread. "We just wait and hope I don't actually choke you out the next time? Fuck that." After shoving his feet into his shoes, he snatched up his T-shirt from the floor and pulled it on. "I'm obviously a hell of a lot less stable than I've been trying to convince myself of the last couple months. We can't be together until I'm sure I have my shit in order, bottom line."

Erik crossed the room, his long strides eating up the distance to the bedroom door. "Erik, stop," she said, following him, her throat constricting with the fear of losing him. "We can get through this; you just have to trust me."

Pulling open the door, he turned around and stared down at her, liquid fire swirling in his eyes as he visibly lost the battle of keeping himself in check. His voice got louder by the second, and she was helpless to stop the hot prick of tears as they started to well up.

"Christ, Livvie, what don't you get about this? I'm like a fucking land mine that's been stepped on. It's not a matter of *if* I'll go off but *when*, and I'll be damned if I'm letting you anywhere near the blast zone!"

She shook her head, the movement jostling her tears free

to roll unchecked down her face. "Please don't do this," she whispered. "I love you."

Erik's features softened, his whiskey eyes glistening with the moisture of their shared pain. He reached up to frame her face, the rough pads of his thumbs gently swiping away her tears. "I know," he rasped.

He lowered his head, took her lips in the sweetest, most heartbreaking good-bye kiss, then walked out of the house… and out of her life.

# Chapter Seventeen

"Hi, I'm Lieutenant Erik Grady."

The receptionist behind the front desk didn't bother to look up from her computer screen or pause the incessant typing on her keyboard. "Uh-huhhhh," she dragged out in a way that said, *And?*

"I have an appointment at fourteen hundred with a Sergeant Cody Adams."

"Okay, sir, last name, last four."

Apparently she hadn't paid attention when he announced himself the first time, and "last four" referred to the end digits of his SSN. Not even thirty seconds into the visit, and he already felt sprayed with the stench of indifference. "Grady," he bit out. "Eight-six-one-seven."

"Okay, Mr. Grady, have a seat in the lobby, and Sergeant Adams will be out to see you soon."

*It's* Lieutenant *Grady, not Mister.* He hadn't studied his ass off for more than a thousand hours, poring over textbooks and training guides to be called *Mister.* Then again, there was a small chance he was taking things harder than usual because he seriously didn't want to be here, but whatever.

Irritated with the entire situation, Erik mentally dismissed the distant receptionist. Instinct drew him to a chair on the far side of the room where he had a full view of the facility from his position. Lowering himself into the seat, he rubbed the sweat from his palms on his jeans and tried to steady his nerves with a deep breath.

He felt like complete shit. Staying away from Olivia was worse than he ever imagined. He couldn't sleep, forgot to eat half the time, and the other half he couldn't taste anything other than the smoky burn of the one glass of whiskey he allowed himself every night. If he didn't put a limit on it, he'd fast become a drunk, wallowing in his self-made misery.

It'd happened so fast, but she'd become his entire world, and now, without her, his world was…off. He missed her smile, her laugh, the way she teased him, the way she spoke so formally whenever she got worked up, the perfect way her body fit to his, and the way she sighed every time she stepped into his arms…he just plain fucking missed her.

He was a miserable bastard without her. And since his head was more fucked up than ever, he spent the majority of his time putting himself through punishing workouts while blasting death metal to kill any and all thoughts. Sometimes it worked well enough to make him think he was doing okay. But it only took a few moments of silence for the darkness to whisper through his mind, replanting the doubts and fears faster than he could crush them.

After bringing Olivia's Fourth of July party to a sudden and humiliating end, Erik had done his best to brush off the incident to everyone unlucky enough to witness it. Not that any of them believed his bullshit. He was either a really shitty actor or what they saw that night had been so profound that no one with two brain cells to rub together could ever believe that it wasn't a big fucking problem. Whatever the reason, the looks of pity he got—even from his own men—turned his stomach inside out and brewed violence in his veins.

If there was one thing he hated more than anything, it was weakness in himself. He'd been raised to be strong—physically, mentally, and emotionally—and then the army and special forces took those strengths and maxed them out. The worst feeling in the world was knowing the men he respected the most and the woman he cared for more than he'd ever thought possible had seen him mentally incapacitated. If having a hallucination wasn't weakness, he didn't know what was.

The session with Dr. Marion following his "episode" had been the most difficult so far. Erik spent the entire hour keyed up and did a fair amount of ranting, demanding to know why the hell he'd gotten *worse*—by graduating to a full-blown flashback—instead of better.

Marion spouted off various facts and statistics about the process and possible side effects when someone goes through behavioral cognitive therapy. Something about temporary regressions where the original symptoms can spike and even create new ones as the client—Christ, he hated that word—comes to terms with the root of his or her issues.

Translation: things'll get a lot fucking worse before they get better. Just what he wanted to hear.

But the real kicker of the hour came when the major asked him about how Erik handled things with Olivia afterward.

*Oh, you know, the usual. I told her we should stop seeing each other, she disagreed and countered that I should take my aggressions out on her during sex, and because I'm a selfish fucking prick, I fucked her within an inch of her life and reveled in every goddamn second of it.*

Yeah, not something he'd be sharing with anyone anytime soon, much less her uncle.

Instead, Erik stuck to the basics of the argument they'd

had both before and after the sex. About him not being good for her as messed up as he was, and that he thought it'd be best if he stayed away until he could be 100 percent sure he'd never again have another incident that put her at risk for being harmed.

That's when Dr. Marion prescribed him this visit to the Boston Vet Center. A place where disabled veterans came for things like group therapy, occupational therapy, and meditative yoga.

A place that made Erik's palms sweat and his muscles grip his bones so tight they might snap. He was nervous as hell to be there, and it made him feel like a complete asshole. Erik may not have served with any of these men, but they were all a part of the same brotherhood, and that meant he'd take a bullet for any one of them without hesitation. So then why did the thought of meeting them scare the ever-loving hell out of him?

*Because you're afraid you'll look in their eyes and see yourself. Just another broken soldier, used up and no good to anyone anymore.*

"Lieutenant Grady?"

Erik stood and shook the man's outstretched hand. "Sergeant Adams," he said in greeting.

"I'm good with dropping the formalities if you are. My mother insists I still answer to Cody on occasion," he said with a bright smile. "Says it's to keep me humble and remind me that beneath the badass is still her baby boy."

Erik felt some of the tension in his muscles ease as he returned the smile. "Does it work?"

"Hell yes, but if she knew that, she'd be making me couch pillows with my name in needlepoint, and then I can kiss my badass balls good-bye." Cody gave a dramatic shudder.

Chuckling, Erik said, "Then I'll go with Cody and hopefully it keeps your balls where they belong."

"I appreciate that, my friend. Now," Cody said as he clapped him on the shoulder, "what do you say we go meet up with the others hanging around today and make some new BFFs?"

Cody had a good sense of humor and a quick wit about him that Erik instantly liked. His easygoing personality helped Erik relax, at least a little. From the looks of him, Cody couldn't be a day over twenty-five, which pretty much made him a kid in Erik's book, and the fact that he could easily get a second job as an Abercrombie & Fitch model gave the impression he hadn't seen any time downrange. He was more "bright eyed and bushy tailed" than "sun's out, guns out," but Erik supposed combat experience wasn't a job requirement for working with those who had.

Erik took a deep breath and released it in a slow, steady stream. "Lead the way."

For the next couple of hours, Cody introduced Erik to almost a dozen men and women who'd all come back from deployments missing pieces of themselves—physically, metaphorically, or both. A few were amputees with one of them being a double, but most of them suffered with TBIs from IEDs (Traumatic Brain Injuries from Improvised Explosive Devices), and pretty much all of them had PTSD in some form or another.

If you asked, most would tell you they were there because they'd fucked up. They'd had a split second to make a decision but made the wrong one, and the second after that, shit went to hell in a handbasket and their entire world narrowed down to one ugly truth: they'd lost.

Lost the use of their legs or the ability to hold their children or even the capacity to withstand something as basic as a trip to the grocery store without having a damn panic attack. (Because what the fuck did it matter whether they chose Lucky Charms or Frosted Flakes when there were bad guys who needed killing?)

They'd gone from being elite warriors to struggling civilians in the blink of an eye. Their new reality was accepting—or, more accurately, *trying* to accept—that they'd never again be as good as they once were. Whereas they used to spend hours every day training in things like close-quarters combat and the shoot house, now their time was spent learning how to cope with the post-war mental shit and accomplish new ways of doing the physical shit.

It'd been a humbling experience for Erik to spend the afternoon with the brave veterans at the Center. They'd all been cut down while fighting in the pits of hell and then crawled and clawed their way back through it again as they relearned how to acclimate and live as different people with new disabilities. And there he was, standing in front of them with all his appendages and answering the "So how're you fucked up?" question with the pathetic story of how fireworks damn near made him piss himself before doing a solo reenactment of his last battle in Iraq. Made him feel like a pussy in comparison, and he wondered what the hell he was so worried about with Olivia.

Then he remembered how absurdly real that flashback was. How he'd had no idea he was crouched in the corner of his girlfriend's parents' kitchen with his only immediate threat a floor of shattered glass and wasted alcohol. How he could've twisted the situation even more, believing Livvie was an enemy sneaking up on him, and seriously hurt her… or worse.

Yeah, he was plenty fucked up, thanks.

"So what's it like being a fireman?" Cody asked as they walked down the hall to his office.

"Similar to the military, really," he said dismissively. "It's all about high-pressure situations. You're either in them, training for them, or waiting for them to happen."

Cody grinned. "So you're saying it's not all kittens in trees and calendar shoots."

Erik laughed. "I've been on a few kitten calls in my time, but it'll be a cold day in hell when I sign on for a calendar shoot."

"Careful, you could be forced into it by the mayor to boost the FD's image, like that guy in Chicago. You hear about that?"

"Luke Almeida? Yeah, bro, that story spread quick. The commish used it as an example of what could happen if we ever made BFD look bad. I heard his brother ate it up, but Luke hated every minute of it, the poor schmuck."

Cody stopped at the vending machines and dug a couple of singles from his wallet. "Yeah, well, the way I hear it, that *poor schmuck* ended up getting the girl of his dreams, proving that love really does conquer all."

The kid said it with a hint of humor, but glancing at his expression, Erik could tell he wasn't being the least bit sarcastic. When they each had a bottle of water in hand, they continued on. "Speaking from personal experience?"

"Absolutely," Cody said proudly. "Love is the only thing that can conquer the kind of battle-borne demons men like you and I live with. Well, that and regular visits to a shooting range, am I right?"

Erik stopped, stuck on the first thing Cody said. "You were downrange?"

Again, Erik took in the man's appearance. His blue Oxford shirt with rolled sleeves was tucked neatly into a pair of dark jeans that were distressed on the thighs by a machine, not from actual years of wear, and he wore a permanent grin. If he'd been deployed overseas, it was more likely he'd been a fobbit—a service member who never went outside the wire of the forward operating base. Not that Erik felt superior to non-infantrymen, but shit was a whole other world outside the security perimeter of the FOB.

"No offense, Cody, but you don't seem fucked up enough for that."

"Ah, that's because you haven't seen the hardware," he said, bending over to raise the legs of his pants. "They go all the way up to mid-thigh, or what used to be, anyway."

*Fucking hell.* Cody was missing both legs, replaced by metal prosthetics that disappeared into his boots. "What happened?"

"Afghanistan, 2011. We were on our way to Forward Operating Joyce in Kunar when our bird took an RPG and small arms fire. The Chinook zigged and I zagged, right out the fucking door. I fell three stories, but a Toyota full of hajis was nice enough to break my fall. Unfortunately, it also broke my legs and my back. I remember all of that, but not the grenade that fragged my shit as I was being pulled out of there. It took care of my broken leg problem, seeing as there wasn't much of them left after that."

Erik rubbed the back of his neck that burned with shame. "Jesus, man, I had no idea. What I said, about you not being fucked up enough, that was an asshole thing to say. I'm sorry."

Smiling, Cody opened the door behind him and allowed Erik to enter before closing it. "Don't give it a second thought; I don't anymore."

"How?" As soon as the question left his mouth, he wanted to reel it back in. Suddenly everything he said made him feel like more of a dick.

"Don't get me wrong, I wasn't always this well-adjusted and handsome." Cody took a seat in one of two guest chairs in front of the office desk. "Actually, that's not true. I've always been this handsome."

Erik chuckled, and he sat in the remaining chair, grateful for the man's good grace and humor. "I should introduce you to my buddy Smoke. You guys can bond over your obvious sense of modesty and compete for how many ladies' numbers you can bring home in a night."

"Sounds like my kind of guy, but my digit-collecting days are over."

He glanced at Cody's left hand. "No ring yet?"

"There will be soon." Cody flipped a framed picture around on his desk of what appeared to be an engagement photo of the happy couple with her ring hand on prominent display. "Wedding's in a couple of months."

"Congratulations, man, that's awesome."

"Thanks," he said, returning the picture to its original position. "What about you?"

"What about me?"

"A special someone. I mean, at your age, all your good years are behind you, so you probably shouldn't wait too long to lock something down, you know?"

Erik tried to hide his smile behind the hand that scratched over the beard growth on his jaw, but there was no point. The kid wasn't about to take him seriously even if he managed to appear offended.

"Yeah, okay, smart-ass. I deserved that one." They shared a quick laugh, but when it died out, Cody raised an expectant eyebrow. Fuck, thinking about Olivia killed him. Clearing his throat and adjusting in his seat, Erik said, "There is someone, but we can't be together right now, and I don't know if she'll still be waiting when—*if*—the time comes we can be."

"What's the holdup?"

Erik drew his brows together in disbelief. "I told you and the others out there about the incident I had. That happened at my *girlfriend's* parents' house, dude." Cody's expression remained unaffected. *Zero* hint of an "aha" moment on the horizon, and Erik felt his blood heating. "I fucking dragged her into the flashback with me. *Literally.* Then that night I had a nightmare and barely woke up before I attacked her."

"And?" Finally, understanding dawned in Cody's eyes. "Ah, shit. She left you."

"What? No, man, you don't get it," Erik ground out through clenched teeth as he shot to his feet and started to pace like a wild animal in a zoo exhibit. "She argued against the breakup, but I was out of my goddamned mind. It's not safe for us to be together until I get my head straight and I can guarantee I'm not a threat to her."

"Hold up, man," Cody said as he held up his hands in a placating gesture. Since the pacing wasn't doing him any damn good anyway, Erik stopped and faced the now standing man. Cody looked from his hands to the stock-still Erik with a hint of awe. "Cool, I feel like Chris Pratt in *Jurassic World*. How do you feel about the new call sign Raptor?" Erik narrowed his gaze in fair warning. "Okay, ix-nay on the allsign-cay."

Erik blew out a heavy breath and scrubbed his hands over his eyes a few times, dropping back into the chair. He was mentally exhausted and physically keyed up. Not a good combination. All he wanted to do was head to Olivia's and lose himself in her arms. Listen to her laugh at his bad jokes and feed her spoonfuls of ice cream while watching that cheesy superhero show where the main character trained shirtless like it was an Olympic sport.

But instead, he had yet another night alone in his apartment ahead of him. Wasn't *that* awesome?

Cody sat down again and leaned forward with his elbows on the arms of the chair. "Look, Erik," he said, his tone decidedly more serious, "all jokes aside, I know what you're talking about. I thought the same thing after the crash. You wanna talk about feeling like you're fucked up? Try waking up with leg pain so excruciating you practically vomit, only to realize that they aren't even there, and instead of waking up in your tent, you're in the CSH."

Cody's words sliced into Erik like .30-cal AP shells

through body armor. CSH, pronounced "cash," stood for Combat Surgical Hospital, and Erik could only imagine what it would have been like to regain consciousness in one of those. Two of Erik's men had lost their lives in that battle that went FUBAR faster than he could blink, and Smoke had ended up in the CSH with the burns he'd sustained, but unbelievably, Erik had lucked out in that he'd never been wounded serious enough to be laid up like that.

"Along with the obvious physical struggles, I had the usual psychological stuff, like anxiety, nightmares, all that shit. By the time I got stateside, I'd already made the decision for Jenna that we were over. I wasn't about to strap her to a less-than-whole man for the rest of her life. I loved her too much for that."

Hearing those words set Erik on edge. It pissed him off that a man who served his country and suffered from injuries made in the line of duty—a man Erik respected and liked immensely in just the few hours since they'd met—thought of himself as *less than*, simply because he lost his legs and gained a few legitimate head issues.

"That's bullshit, Adams. Look at you," Erik said, gesturing at the kid. "You're more put together than a lot of civilians I know."

Cody smiled. "That's because you're seeing all of Jenna's hard work. I never would have come as far as I have—at least not as *fast* as I have—without her love and support." Leaning back, he turned the picture around again and gazed at the 2D image of his fiancée with a reverence Erik rarely saw from battle-hardened soldiers. "She wouldn't leave me, bro. I was a miserable bastard, and when she wouldn't leave, I did my best to push her away. She just kept showing up at the hospital, helping me with my physical therapy. She told me she'd be marrying me whether I liked it or not, so I might as well quit my bitching."

"Sounds like you've got yourself one hell of a woman."

"Don't I know it," Cody said. "You'll get to meet her. She's here all the time, dropping in and acting as an emotional drill sergeant for anyone getting down on themselves. And if you don't get your head out of your ass, I'll sic her on you, too."

"My head's not in my ass." That was a lie. Cody had made it plain as day. Erik just wasn't ready to admit it yet.

"Look, it's cool, I get it. You need time to process and all that," the kid said as he stood. "Just don't take too long, man. Like you said, by the time you figure it out, she might not be there anymore. If she didn't take off after you pulled her into a game of *Call of Duty* in her kitchen, my guess is she's worth holding onto."

Cody held the door open and they agreed to meet again in a few days, then Erik shook his hand and walked into the hall. Just before turning down the passage that would take him to the lobby, Cody called out to him from his doorway with one last piece of advice. "I know you're afraid of making things worse for her, but believe me when I tell you, she's a hell of a lot stronger than you're giving her credit for."

Erik gave him a nod of thanks and turned the corner, wondering how a kid he'd just met had managed to figure out his life better than he could. Time to change that.

# Chapter Eighteen

"Hey, munchkin, who's been drinking all my Johnny Walker? Don't tell me you've acquired good taste since the last time I visited."

Olivia would have laughed at her brother's jab if the mention of the whiskey didn't make her think of the man who'd been the one to drink it. Then again, pretty much everything made her think of Erik. He was like a constant companion, riding shotgun in her mind, whether she was awake or asleep.

"God, no, I still abhor all things whiskey," she said from her place on the couch. "It was a friend."

After pouring himself two fingers, he brought his glass and joined her in the living room. "Well, make sure your friend buys you a bottle for Christmas if he's going to keep drinking that one."

That made her smile as she rolled her eyes at him, then took a healthy sip of her wine. Perhaps with her goofy brother here, her buzz would be a fun one for a change instead of the alcohol just amplifying her broken heart.

It'd been a little over four weeks since Erik insisted they couldn't be together, and she missed him like crazy. Missed his sarcasm, his teasing, his protectiveness, and his intensity.

Everything about Lieutenant Erik "Wolf" Grady—his appearance, his demeanor, his loyalty, and even his love—vibrated with an intensity that charged her from the inside out. Before meeting him, Olivia had considered her life to be absolutely fine, better than average, perfectly pleasant. Now she knew that those were all ways of saying dull, bland, inadequate, and a whole slew of other synonyms she would list if she had a thesaurus in front of her.

In the beginning, she'd tried talking to him out of the ridiculous notion that he needed to keep his distance until he got better. She called and texted multiple times a day, but after a week of no contact, she resigned herself to letting him go. It was the hardest decision she had ever made.

To make things easier on both of them, she worked from home on the afternoons he had sessions with her uncle. It took two weeks before she stopped angling for information on how Erik was doing, and after three weeks, she managed to fall asleep without crying. Hooray for progress.

"So what's his name?"

Olivia snapped her attention over to her brother. How long had she been in her own head? "Whose name?"

"The guy who finally got you to move on with your life. I want to know when I can intimidate him—I mean, meet him."

The image of Robbie—an illustrator for children's books—trying to intimidate Erik made her laugh. That'd be like Roger Rabbit trying to scare off Thor. Not possible. "I don't know who you're talking about. There's no guy."

He swirled the ice around in his glass as he arched a blond brow and said, "Come on, I know I'm not a super-smart shrink like you and Uncle Eddie, but give me some credit. Someone's been enjoying my whiskey, the pictures of you and Brett are gone, and Ben and Jerrys have a big-ass cat tree where their papasan chair used to be."

Avoiding his scrutinizing gaze, Olivia drank more of her wine and looked out the window at the orange-tinged sky as the sun began to set on the opposite side of the building.

"The only thing I can't figure out is, if you've moved on," her brother continued, his voice going soft and serious, "why do you look like you're in mourning all over again?"

Sadness pricked at the back of her throat and she was helpless to stop the hot tears from welling in her eyes. She tried to speak, to brush it off and tell him it wasn't what he thought, but she couldn't get the words out. It didn't matter, though. Spewing lies wouldn't work when the truth was streaming down her face.

"Oh, munchkin, I'm sorry, I didn't mean to make you cry. Come over here."

Knowing he wouldn't take no for an answer, Olivia set her wineglass down and scooted to his side of the couch. She curled into his side, taking comfort from him as he wrapped his arms around her in one of his famous big brother hugs. Resting his chin on the top of her head, he told her to "spill it."

She told him how they met at the liquor store, how they re-met at her office, how he doggedly pursued her, all the way through the night he eventually left her. She told him everything, the story tumbling out like an avalanche of craggy rocks, slicing her open again and again, until she was left raw and bleeding.

"So that's how I went from denial to bliss to heartache in less than three months," she said as she sniffled and rubbed her cheeks on his soft T-shirt to soak up the last set of tears she had in her. The well had finally dried up. For now, at least. "The cruel irony is that in the beginning, all I wanted was for him to leave me alone. And now, all I want is for him to never leave me. Guess that's karma for you."

"That's bullshit," he said, his voice lacking the usual rancor infused in that phrase. "Of everyone I know, Liv, you're the person least likely to ever have bad karma. You need to cut yourself some slack. Most people in their twenties don't have to deal with the death of a spouse, and from what it sounds like, you instinctively knew he was someone you could care about. After what you went through, that would be a pretty scary thing."

"I know, you're right. I just…wish it didn't have to end like it did. It kills me to know he's going through so much right now, and I can't be there for him. I feel so helpless."

"Hey, he's got Uncle Eddie, though, right? At least you know he's getting the help he needs."

Straightening, she pulled free of his embrace and offered him a wan smile. "Thank you, Robbie. For listening and letting me blubber all over you."

"That's what big brothers are for, munchkin," he said, rubbing the top of her head playfully.

She scolded him as she smacked his hand away and took her ponytail holder out to redo her now messy hair. He chuckled at her expense on his way into the kitchen to refill his drink while she pulled her hair up and herself together. If she was going to salvage Sibling Movie Night, she needed to switch tracks.

"So what movie do you want to watch? I'm thinking comedy, the dumber the better." Before he had a chance to offer his suggestions, Olivia's phone chimed on the counter. "Can you see who that is?"

"It's a text from Wolf." She froze mid-pony-pull as her stomach dropped out. "What the hell kind of a name is Wolf?"

"It's not a name," she said, finishing her hair in a trance. "It's a call sign." And what she'd entered for his contact info as a nostalgic nod to the man she'd first met.

Robbie caught on and crossed the room to hand her the phone. He nodded encouragingly. "See what he wants."

Taking the phone with shaking hands, she slid the notification over and opened up the message as she held her breath.

*You still owe me a third date, gorgeous.*

The air in her lungs expelled with a *whoosh*. Date? What the hell was he smoking? He'd walked out on her, never returned any of her calls, and now he wanted a date? Maybe he felt guilty about the way he ended things and wanted to move forward as friends. Maybe Uncle Eddie had him doing a twelve-step program and he needed to atone to anyone he'd wronged. Hell, knowing her uncle, he may have ordered Erik to make things right with his niece, considering Eddie had been grumbling his unhappiness to Ruth about Olivia not being her "usual sunshiny self."

When she still hadn't responded, the ellipses started waving, letting her know he was typing out another message.

*One last date. To state my case, remember? That's all I ask.*

How could she forget? She thought back to that morning in the courtyard next to the Pru when he'd asked her to give him the three dates. But now she had a sinking feeling that the case he wanted to make was no longer about them staying together. It was about why they had to be apart.

"You going to answer him soon or wait until you've completely gnawed your lower lip off?"

She raised her eyes to Robbie, releasing her abused lip as a mix of embarrassment and nerves washed over her. She hadn't even realized he'd sat next to her again and read the text over her shoulder. "I don't know what to say," she admitted.

"Don't make it so hard, Liv. Do you want to see him?"

"Yes, but…" Olivia sighed. Maybe she was overthinking things. She should just take things as they came. At the very least, being in his company for a few hours had to soothe some of the permanent ache that had taken root deep in her chest. But at the end of the night she'd be back to square one: missing him with a desperation that defied reason.

God, the pain would be fresh, like ripping off a barely healed scab. But it didn't matter. She didn't have the strength not to go to him if he wanted to see her.

The true test would be whether she had the strength to walk away if the time came. Because, for as desperately as she wanted to be with Erik, she couldn't be in a relationship if he wasn't willing to stay with her whenever he struggled with his PTSD. He could learn to manage it, but it would never truly go away. It's something he'd have to deal with his entire life, and she loved him too much to be able to survive losing him over and over again.

*Okay. When?*

*How about now.*

She was in the middle of typing "I can't tonight" when three strong knocks echoed through the small room. Olivia and Robbie looked at each other, one of them with a curious brow arched and the other with eyes as wide as silver dollars.

"Well, that's my cue," Robbie said, pushing to his feet and crossing to the kitchen to set his glass in the sink. "I'll call you tomorrow and you can catch me up. Unless you're otherwise engaged, then you can fill me in at Mom and Dad's over Sunday brunch."

Three more knocks. "Livvie?"

Shit, he heard a man's voice in her apartment, and the slight edge to Erik's tone said he didn't like it.

Olivia followed Robbie, suddenly feeling very anxious about seeing Erik and the whole unknown outcome thing. "You don't have to leave," she rushed out. "You can stay in the bedroom until we're done talking, and then we'll watch the movie when he's gone."

"Livvie." Robbie stepped in close and lowered his voice. "Do you have reason to be afraid of this guy? Does he have a temper? Because if that's the case then he can pound all he wants, but he's not stepping foot inside that door. I might not stand a chance against a former ranger, but that's what the cops are for."

"God, no, Robbie," she said quickly. "Erik would die before he ever hurt me. I'm just…nervous, I guess."

Her brother gave her a quick hug and kissed her on the forehead. "All you have to do is talk to him, munchkin. Can't be that hard; you do it for a living. If it makes it any easier, have him lie on the couch and charge him a few hundred bucks." A trembling laugh escaped despite the horde of butterflies threatening to choke off her airway. "Just breathe, and call me if you need me."

Olivia nodded then stared at the door in trepidation as Robbie opened it wide. Erik gave the man next to her a hard look, which Robbie returned (bless his big brother, beta heart), but just when she thought she'd have to step between the two men to prevent an ER trip (for the lean artist, not the buff ex-ranger), recognition registered in Erik's eyes.

Erik extended a welcoming hand as his posture sent a mild warning to not get involved. "You must be Robbie."

Her brother gave him a firm shake. "You must be Erik."

"Grab a drink sometime?"

Olivia's eyebrows shot up to her hairline. Of all the things she'd guessed Erik would say, that hadn't been on the list. On the other hand, Erik knew how close she was with her brother. It would make sense for Erik to offer an olive branch, which by Guy Standards would involve some kind of alcohol—by *their* standards, an expensive whiskey.

Robbie glanced at Olivia then looked back at Erik. "That all depends on you, man." He gave her one last reassuring nod, then left them alone.

Olivia swallowed, attempting to cure the dryness in her throat, as Erik stepped inside and closed the door behind him. In the span of mere seconds, he'd stolen her breath. He wore a thin, black Henley that hugged his powerful shoulders and broad chest before hanging loose around his trim waist and dark jeans over his black motorcycle boots. A dark shadow dusted his strong jaw and her fingertips tingled at the sight of his fresh buzz cut, itching to run over the soft prickles and watch as his lids lowered to half mast on a low groan.

His gaze raked down her body, slow and sensuous. She felt her cheeks heat with a blush that spread down her neck and chest. Wearing a pair of pink cotton shorts and baggy white shirt, she was the furthest thing from sexy, but he looked like he wanted to devour her where she stood. His alpha side showed tremendous restraint when he stopped a full two feet away from her and kept his hands fisted at his sides.

Damn it, her emotions were all over the place. Part of her wanted to retreat, to gain some perspective along with some breathing room. The other part of her wanted to lunge and close the last of the distance he'd wedged between them over a month ago.

"Olivia…" Her name sounded like it was being torn from his lips, tortured and rough, and it affected her in ways she couldn't begin to name. "Jesus, you're more beautiful than I remembered."

Her breath caught in her chest at the tension snapping between them like static electricity as he lifted a hand, presumably to touch her face or maybe tuck errant strands of hair behind her ear as he'd often done, but he stopped short and dropped it back at his side. She couldn't remember when she'd ever seen Erik hesitant and unsure. It looked as foreign to her as she suspected it felt to him.

Whatever the outcome, the faster they got this over with, the better. *Just rip off the Band-Aid so you can lick your wounds in peace.* Clearing her throat, she crossed her arms over her middle and did her best to put on her professional face. Maybe if she could detach herself from the situation, this wouldn't actually kill her.

"Okay, Lieutenant. Time to state your case."

...

It'd taken a level of control Erik wasn't aware he had not to pull Olivia into his arms the moment he saw her. To keep himself from burying his face in the crook of her neck and drag in deep lungfuls of her rose-petal scent. To claim her soft lips and kiss the hell out of her until their lungs screamed for air.

But he couldn't. He didn't have that right. Not yet.

*Maybe not ever again.*

*Fuck.*

Insecurity wasn't a feeling he was familiar with. Give him heavily armed insurgents or a burning building any day of the week, but just the thought of potentially getting shut down—for good—by the woman he couldn't live without was fraying his nerves faster than a flashover in a five-alarm box fire. And considering her eyes were red and glassy like she'd been crying even before he texted her coupled with her closed-off demeanor, he wouldn't bet on himself to come out of this "mission accomplished."

God, he hated this awkward tension between them, made worse by the fact that it was all his doing. He'd done a lot of soul-searching since leaving the VA Center that first time. Hearing Cody talk about his fiancée and the way she'd helped him to heal—and more importantly, that *he* hadn't had an adverse effect on *her*—made Erik realize there wasn't any reason he and Livvie couldn't do it, too.

*Then fucking talk, Grady, before she throws your sorry ass out.*

"I'm…goddamn it, I'm so fucking sorry, Livvie. I should have stayed, talked things out with you. Or at the very least waited to talk to the major before I jumped to conclusions."

Ever the sympathetic, caring woman, Olivia's hazel eyes softened. "You realize I'm just as qualified as my uncle to offer advice and guidance when it comes to PTSD, right?"

"Of course I do, but to my way of thinking, your logic was likely clouded by your feelings for me. But even if that hadn't been the case, I was *convinced* it was only a matter of time before I seriously hurt you." Her gaze dropped, suddenly taking a strong interest in the grout in the tile floor, but he pressed on, his voice low and raspy. "What I didn't take into consideration, is that hurting you emotionally could be just as damaging…if not more."

Glancing up at him beneath her lashes, she asked, "So what's changed?"

"Me," he said, taking a small step closer. "I knew I had to do a lot of soul-searching, do a lot of work on the way I process and react to things. I reacted poorly that night, and I can't tell you how fucking sorry I am, but I can't change the past. I can only try to do better in the future."

Tears welled in her eyes, but she blinked them away. His Livvie was so strong, and damn if he didn't admire that about her more than anything else.

"How do I know you're not going to do the same thing if you get triggered, Erik? It was hard enough losing Brett—a man I was with for almost a decade, yet didn't love nearly as much as I love you—but at least he didn't leave by choice. You willingly pushed me away, and it made losing you hurt so much worse. I can't be with you if you're going to pull away every time something goes wrong."

Jesus, could he have been more of an asshole? Erik grit his teeth and erased the last few inches between them that had felt more like miles. Then he held her hands, stared into those endless limpid pools, and stripped away the final barrier that the soldier in him had used as body armor for his heart. It no longer had a place in his life. Not if he wanted Olivia.

And he'd never wanted anything so desperately as he wanted her and her love.

"For years I've trained myself to only let others see my strength. To hide any weakness that could make me vulnerable, that could make my men doubt my abilities as their leader," he started. "But underestimating *your* strength, that was the biggest mistake I've ever made, and I swear to you that it's one I'll never make again.

"I know I have a long way to go to manage my PTSD, to get where I don't feel like I've lost all control anymore. But I'm going to continue to see the major and make regular visits to the Boston Vet Center. I'm a work in progress, but as your uncle says, I'm committed to the mission of good mental health as much as I am to making you happy."

She dragged her teeth over her bottom lip. "From now on we communicate? Full disclosure to our pasts, present, and concerns or plans for the future?"

"All of it. You will *always* come first. I need you in my life, and nothing is more important than that. *Nothing*." Her mouth turned up in a sweet smile that begged him to kiss her, to seal the deal right fucking now. But he had one more thing to get out. Drawing a steadying breath, Erik threw down his trump card. "Which is why I've decided to retire from active duty as a firefighter."

Olivia's eyes flashed wide. "What?" She shook her head, her flaxen ponytail swishing behind her shoulders. "Erik, no—"

He interrupted, his tone firm-as-hell. "Yes, Olivia. I'm moving to the political side of the department and taking a desk job." His mouth hitched up in one of his signature smirks.

"The worst injury I can sustain is a paper cut, but I promise to keep a box of Band-Aids around at all times."

"Erik, you can't give up being a firefighter," she said adamantly. "You love your job; it's what you're *good* at."

"So I'll love my new job and I'll be good at that one, too," he argued. "Either way, it doesn't matter because the job that means the most to me now is loving you and being good at *that*."

"No, you can't," she said. "The city needs you. Your team needs you—"

"Not half as much as I need *you*."

Again, she shook her head. "You'll be miserable as a desk jockey, Erik. You've told me so yourself a dozen times."

Well, fuck. This wasn't the reaction he'd expected. He thought for sure it was his ace in the hole, the final piece that would have her jumping into his arms. Regardless of what she said, he knew that the risk inherent in his job weighed heavily on her. She was just too selfless not to insist he remain a firefighter. But he had no intention of giving in, so she'd have to let it go eventually.

"As long as I can call you mine, I'll be the happiest desk jockey in New England. Let me worry about me, okay?"

Her eyes bounced between his and her teeth captured the corner of her lip as her wheels turned. He knew she was analyzing every possible detail, every possible outcome. His Livvie never did anything without careful consideration—a trait that probably was less in his favor than if she was the type of woman to get caught up in the moment—and every second that passed twisted the blade that he'd plunged into his own heart the night he walked out on her.

After an eternity, she finally said, "I'm only agreeing to table this conversation for later, once Eddie clears you for duty."

"I can agree to that." He'd take it and run, for now. He

could worry about wearing her down another day, maybe after he plied her with sex and a gallon of her Cherry Garcia. "So does this mean what I hope it means?"

A hint of a smile eased up one side of her sexy mouth. "What do *you* think, Lieutenant?"

"Honestly, I'm afraid to assume anything right now, baby. Take pity on me and give me the words. Please, Livvie," he said, stroking the side of her face with his thumb, "tell me I have one last chance. That's all I need. Tell me you'll trust me with your heart again."

Olivia turned her head and placed a kiss in the center of his palm. "Yes," she whispered. "I trust you with my heart."

Erik's relief rushed through him so fast it was a miracle his knees didn't buckle before he grabbed her face and finally—*fucking finally*—kissed the hell out of her. Opening to him immediately, their tongues met with the urgency of a long separation, ended at last. She tasted of sweet red wine and perfection, and the mewls of rapture she made in the back of her throat were sure to be his undoing.

Tearing himself away, he drank in the love shining in her eyes as he drew in labored breaths. "God, Livvie, I need you so fucking much."

Her gaze flitted all over his face like she was trying to take in every detail all at once, while her nails skimmed over his scalp, sending goosebumps firing off over his skin. "Take me to bed, Erik. Make love to me."

In a flash, he swept her up into his arms, and carried her into her bedroom where he laid her on the soft mattress. He kicked off his boots and yanked off his shirt before following her down, positioning himself between her open legs, the place on her body that was made perfectly for his.

"I don't know what I did to deserve you, but I intend on deserving you every day from here on out," he said, softly brushing wispy strands of hair off her face. "I love you, Livvie.

With everything that I have and everything that I am, I fucking love you."

Her eyes shimmered behind a pool of tears that began streaking down her temples from the outer corners as her mouth spread into a glorious smile. A few minutes ago, seeing her tears had shredded him into pieces. Now, they were putting him back together.

"I'm so in love with you, sometimes I can scarcely breathe," she whispered.

Erik's heart swelled near to bursting. "Then I'll breathe for the both of us."

Lowering his mouth to hers, he poured all the passion and love he had into the first kiss of the rest of their lives. Today was a new beginning for both of them. There was nothing they couldn't do, nothing they couldn't accomplish, as long as he had his woman.

*My Livvie.*

# Epilogue

"How is it possible Preacher got even worse at cooking while I was gone?"

The cook in question shoveled a spoon full of chili into his face while casually flipping Erik off with the other hand. "No one's forcing it down your throat, Wolf. Feel free to make your own chow."

"And miss out on the only reason I get to bust your balls?" Erik tore off a bite of French bread and spoke around it. "Not a chance."

The dozen or so guys sitting around the long table chimed in with their complaints and jibes at Preacher, which inevitably bled into giving one another shit about any and everything under the sun.

Damn, he'd missed this. The brotherhood, the esprit de corps he couldn't live without ever since joining the army and he learned what it felt like to have men at his side and at his back who he knew would lay down their lives for him just as quickly as he'd do it for them. A warm tingle hit the back of Erik's eyes, and it took several hard blinks to push it back as he stared into the bowl of brownish-red paste Preacher called chili. He wouldn't be going into active duty, but just knowing he was technically back to work did amazing things for his morale. Erik was making progress, slow but sure, and it felt good.

A week ago, Marion had finally signed off on the paperwork that allowed him back to active duty after being gone for sixteen long weeks. If it hadn't been for Olivia, he'd have gone crazy after only a month, if he even made it that long. She'd occupied most of his waking thoughts and kept him plenty busy when she wasn't in the office. She was the best distraction he could've asked for.

Preacher spoke up over the noise with a big-ass grin on his face. "Hey, ever consider that maybe I *do* know how to cook, but it's more fun watching all of you whine like a bunch of pussies?"

A few of the men looked like they actually believed him as they stared at their bowls and then back at the man with the light mocha skin and crystal blue eyes. Tyler's mother was a beautiful black-haired Irish woman and his dad was African American. It gave him the most exotic look Erik had ever seen on a man. He could have easily had a career—and had been approached several times—as a male model, but Preacher never considered it. As handsome as he was, he didn't have a vain bone in his body.

Dozer waved his spoon back and forth in the air. "No fuckin' way, man. I've seen your fridge and it ain't filled with nothin' but moldy takeout and TV dinners."

"Maybe we should all pitch in and send Connelly to a night school for some cooking classes," Smoke added. "It'd be worth the scratch if we didn't have to suffer through his kitchen rotation anymore."

Preacher snorted out a laugh. "Yeah, because between both of my full-time jobs I have so much free time on my hands to spend it learning how to make this miserable lot happy at chow time."

Everyone laughed and ribbed Preacher a bit more on his cooking before Bowie changed the subject. "So, Wolf, you sure about this playing-house gig with the doc?"

Erik looked across the table at Bowie, who was buttering his thick slice of bread with a six-inch serrated hunting knife. No one batted an eye at the man's ever-present lethal accessories. He had a passion for anything with a blade. Everyone knew the man had knives strapped to his person, whether visible or not.

"Meaning what exactly, Bowie?"

Bowie wiped the polished knife, spun it around in his hand, and stabbed it into the wooden table. "You know," he said with a mischievous grin while gesturing with his hunk of bread, "watching Lifetime movies, taking cold showers because she used all the hot water, swapping newspaper sections at the breakfast table, playing with her cats. All that exciting ball-and-chain shit you get when you set fire to your bachelor card."

Bowie and a few of the guys laughed, throwing in a few choice phrases like "pussy-whipped" and "ball-less bastard." Erik noted that the men with wives or serious girlfriends didn't chime in but merely shook their heads and chuckled at the imbeciles. Before, Erik would've assumed their silence meant they were just as pussy-whipped as the currently accused and had no room to talk about others. But now he knew differently. They didn't say anything because they had something that the perpetual bachelors didn't understand and never would until they found that person they loved more than themselves.

The whole crew was laughing, but half of them didn't realize the other half were laughing *at them* and not with them. Erik drank the rest of his iced tea to wash the chili paste down then smiled at Bowie. "We haven't moved in together, but I do spend more time at her place than mine. As for the ball-and-chain stuff, you don't quite have it right. See, we haven't watched more than the first five minutes of *any* show because she has an affinity for climbing into my lap—naked—anytime we're on the couch. We no longer need alarm clocks because our bodies got used to waking each other up with a nice, slow fuck when the sun hits her bed every morning."

More laughter, some *oh, damn*s, and other more colorful things came from the men. Erik kept his eyes on Bowie and took satisfaction in the way his cocky smirk weakened a little with each of his points. But he wasn't done making them yet, so he continued.

"As for the showers you mentioned, brother, I never have cold showers for three reasons." Erik lifted his hand from the table and used his fingers to count them out. "I never let her shower alone because there's no way I'm within fifty feet of her wet and soapy naked body and not getting in on that. Two, even if we've been in there so long that the water goes cold, we're too distracted with other things to notice or care. And here's the best one: I never have to choose between an ice-cold shower or jerking myself off when my dick gets harder than a Halligan, because I have a sexy-as-fuck woman who's more than eager for me to use it with her whenever the mood strikes." Erik smirked and turned his three outstretched fingers into just the one in the middle. "You can keep your bachelor card, buddy. I'll take my 'ball-and-chain shit' every fucking day of the week."

The room erupted with shouts, high-fives, and more laughter from the other members of the ball-and-chain club while the single guys argued their choice for carefree lives and random pussy. His true brothers, the ones from his squad, turned all their teasing onto Bowie, who enjoyed Erik's response just as much as the others. Offering his fist to his superior, Bowie smiled wide and said, "Happy for you, brother."

Erik bumped his knuckles to the man's and nodded his thanks just as Bill Marshall poked his head into the kitchen. "Grady, she's here."

"Shit, she's early. Stall her, Chief, will you?"

"What do I look like to you, your fucking mother?" the ornery old bastard griped.

A chorus of complaints that the chief wasn't playing nice made the man give in. "All right, all right, but hurry it up."

Earlier, they'd parked The Animal and Engine 42 outside in the sunshine after washing both rigs, then set up their rudimentary plan. Olivia was supposed to bring Angie and Cindi and meet him at the station at fifteen hundred hours, and he'd wanted everyone to be waiting with him when she walked up. Now they all looked like a band of suspicious dummies filing in around each apparatus, but it was too late to do anything about it now.

True to his word, Bill was chatting the girls up out front, not letting Olivia past him. Erik jogged over to her as Dozer, Bowie, Smoke, and Preacher took their positions by each of the doors on Rescue 2 and Engine 42, waiting for the signal.

"Hey, gorgeous," he said before kissing her on the cheek. Bill stepped back with the others, as did Angie and Cindi who were in on it too, giving him space to do his thing.

"Hey," she said, looking around cautiously. "What's going on? Why is everyone outside?"

Erik gave her a wide smile, hoping it disguised the knots his stomach was currently tying itself into. He couldn't believe how nervous he was for this. "Because they're nosy as hell, but they're family, so I suppose they have a right to be. Actually, the guys want to show you something." Then he moved off to the side and gestured to the trucks. It was now or never. "Okay, boys, open 'em up!"

• • •

Olivia watched in nervous fascination as one by one, the men from Erik's team opened the doors on the trucks, which had huge pieces of white poster board taped to them, each with a different word painted in bold black letters.

Will. You. Marry. Me.

Her jaw fell slack and her stomach bottomed out. *Oh my God, he's...he's...* She'd been so focused on the distraction, she didn't realize Erik had moved until she turned to look at him, only to find him dropped to one knee, holding up a princess-cut solitaire in a platinum band.

Her trembling hands flew up to cover her mouth and nose, and her eyes instantly welled with tears of... Oh God, she didn't even know. Fear? Excitement? Shock? Or maybe they were purely the happy tears of a woman who realized she found the man with whom she shared one soul, one heart, one love.

"Livvie," he said softly, reaching up to pull her hands down and hold them in his. "Just let me get through what I want to say before that beautiful brain of yours starts overthinking things, okay?"

She chewed on her bottom lip and gave him a slight nod, which he returned, and a calm sense of rightness flooded her.

"Livvie," he began again, louder this time, she supposed for everyone else's benefit, "I come from a good family whose parents are still together and very much in love, but I never really considered myself to be a forever kind of guy. My careers as a soldier and a firefighter always came first, no matter what, and I didn't think that would ever change.

"Then you walked into my life, and you turned my world upside down. I told you back then that I don't believe in coincidences, and I'd like to think that you don't believe in them anymore, either. You're my light in the darkness, baby, and I can't live without you. Marry me, Livvie."

She laughed from a combination of nerves and the fact that the alpha in him didn't allow his subconscious to pose it as a question—on the banner or verbally—and she could no longer hold back the torrent of overwhelming emotions. Tears flowed faster than she could wipe them away and her throat constricted until it hurt to swallow. Her heart swelled even more, if that were possible, but she needed to make sure he agreed to a few things before she gave him her answer. "I have three conditions that are nonnegotiable."

The brilliant smile on Erik's face reassured her he knew she was doing the same thing he did to her that first night at the liquor store before they drove to the hotel. "I'm all ears, gorgeous."

"Number one, where I go, my cats go. We're a package deal."

"No question. I'll treat Ben and Jerrys like they're my own."

She tried to hold it back, but a hint of her smile showed through. "Good. Number two, we keep the freezer stocked with at least five pints of assorted Ben and Jerry's ice cream."

"Sweetheart, I'll buy you an extra freezer for nothing but your ice cream. You'll never run out for as long as those knuckleheads are in business." His smile turned into his cocky grin. The same one that melted her the first time she saw him. The one that said *I got this*, whether *this* was a silly negotiation or a silent claiming. "Come on, Livvie, tell me your last condition so I can kiss you already."

Her smile faltered. The first two were easy and nonissues. She knew Erik loved her cats and thought her ice-cream addiction was quirky and adorable. It was the third one that might instigate a battle of wills. Something they'd have to get used to, since they were both so stubborn.

"Number three—and the most important one of all—you

have to keep your job as a firefighter."

Erik's dark eyebrows slashed into a *V* and set his jaw. "No, this job is dangerous. It was a Godsend when I retired from the army, but I don't need it anymore like I used to. What I *do* need is *you* and about eighty years to spend loving you. So my answer is no."

Hearing those words and the conviction they were spoken with did both amazing and terrible things to her heart. The man she loved was willing to throw away everything that meant the world to him just because he thought his life-or-death job would be too much for her handle someday.

But Brett had had a safe desk job, and it hadn't prevented the car accident that ultimately took his life. And yes, the job of any first responder was dangerous and put them at risk for injury or worse, every time they answered a call, but it wasn't like they weren't properly trained and prepared for any and every situation they could come up against.

She'd thought about this situation a lot over the last couple of months, knowing this conversation would have to happen, and no matter how she twisted things around, she always came out with the same answer.

"Erik, I can't tell you how touched I am that you would do this for me—it only makes me love you more, if such a thing is possible—but I love you for who and what you are. Brave, loyal, selfless, and a protector of innocents. So if I'm getting married, *that's* the guy I want to get married to. That's it, only him. You swear that you'll stay on as a firefighter and continue to lead your Rescue company, and you'll have your yes."

"Olivia—"

"It's nonnegotiable, Lieutenant. I'm not interested in marrying a desk jockey. So what's it gonna be?"

For what felt like minutes—*hours*—Erik looked positively shell-shocked. She started to worry she'd need to call Preacher over to check his vitals. But then he sprang to his feet and answered by grabbing her face and kissing the breath out of her. He paused only once to slip the ring on her finger before dragging her back in for another kiss that said all the things his heart wanted hers to hear...and it did.

While he was busy making her forget her own name, the firefighters of the Roxbury station cheered and handed out bottles of nonalcoholic beer—presumably to act as placeholders for when everyone was off-duty and could go out for proper celebratory drinks. She laughed and accepted hugs from Erik's coworkers—his brothers and sisters for all intents and purposes—and squealed over the ring with her girlfriends. They were one huge family now, forged by fire and the love of friendships.

She could hardly believe it, but she was well and truly engaged to the man she once knew only as Wolf. A man who'd known nothing about her other than what his instincts told him she needed that night. A man who doggedly pursued her, won a silly (and totally rigged) bet that awarded him three dates with her, showed her how to live with a little more spontaneity and a little less control, and all along made falling in love with him absolutely effortless.

A man who came to her for help to heal from his past and move on with his life, and ended up doing that very thing for her as well.

A man who was, and always would be...her hero.

# Acknowledgments

My husband, Brian, and growing-too-old teenagers, Alyssa and Austin. You are not only the greatest loves of my life, you're my full-time support system. Without your encouragement, patience, and understanding, I wouldn't be able to continue pursuing my dream job.

Liz Pelletier, my editor and friend, who has worked tirelessly on this book to help make it the absolute best it could be and is always there for me when I need her most.

Nicole Resciniti, my agent and friend, who has worked so hard for so long to help make this series happen. I will forever be grateful that you're in my corner.

Rebecca Yarros, for being an amazing friend who keeps me (mostly) sane and productive during our nightly "rock star hours" sprinting sessions. I'm so happy you share my vampire tendencies and love for all things Stephen Amell and *Arrow*. #Olicity4ever

Cindi Madsen, my great friend and "wifey" who's such a character in real life that I couldn't resist making her one in my book. Thank you, Cin, for all the sprints, chats, and virtual hugs.

MK Meredith, my BD and the sweetest, strongest woman I know, for all the random pick-me-ups that bring a huge smile to my face and touch my heart. You're so special to me.

Drew Panico, my helper elf in Boston who answered my never-ending questions about his great city. Without his incredible attention to detail and lengthy correspondence, the setting for this book wouldn't be nearly as vibrant (or very accurate). I'm so glad we've become friends, Drewbie.

Sergeant Cody Grannan of the U.S. Army for being my consultant on all things military. I can't thank him enough for answering all of my many, *many* questions. He more than deserves getting a character named after him. His patience and candid answers have been invaluable to my accurate portrayal of the military backgrounds and personas of the heroes in this series. Any inaccuracies or mistakes are not the fault of Sgt. Grannan, but are my own. (P.S. It doesn't matter that you're a total badass in real life, you'll always be Cody-Gnome to me. Suck it up, buttercup.)

Cecily White for answering my psychologist questions.

"TND" for our hilarious Twitter conversations while I'm working in the middle of the night, including the one that inspired the BOB = vibrator/designated driver bit.

"T" for being my official Firefighter Bracket Buster.

Jenna Behnken, my caffeine dealer at Capputan, my office away from office.

Bloggers! Your endless support, enthusiasm, beautiful graphic teasers and trailers, reviews, and awesome pimping in general…you are what connects us with readers. Your job is not always (if ever) easy, and you don't even get paid for your efforts but rather do it for the love of reading and sharing that love with others. I admire you. You are *essential*. And you are appreciated beyond words.

And last, but never least, to all of my readers, especially

the members of the Maxwell Mob. Your humor and constant support keep me going every day. I love each and every one of you. A thousand times, thank you.

# About the Author

Gina L. Maxwell is a full-time writer, wife, and mother living in the upper Midwest, despite her scathing hatred of snow and cold weather. An avid romance novel addict, she began writing as an alternate way of enjoying the romance stories she loves to read. Her debut novel, *Seducing Cinderella*, hit both the *USA Today* and *New York Times* bestseller lists in less than four weeks, and she's been living her newfound dream ever since.

When she's not reading or writing steamy romance novels, she spends her time losing at Scrabble (and every other game) to her high school sweetheart, doing her best to hang out with their teenagers before they fly the coop, and dreaming about her move to sunny Florida once they do.

Visit and chat with Gina on all her social media homes:

www.ginalmaxwell.com

*Also by Gina L. Maxwell…*

SEDUCING CINDERELLA

RULES OF ENTANGLEMENT

FIGHTING FOR IRISH

SWEET VICTORY

SHAMELESS

RUTHLESS

TEMPTING HER BEST FRIEND

*Discover more Entangled Select Contemporary titles...*

### GROUNDS FOR SEDUCTION
a *Seattle Steam* novel by Shelli Stevens

Madison Phillips is focused on making her new coffee shop a success. She also wouldn't mind if the sexiest cop in Seattle, Gabriel Martinez, would start seeing her as more than just his best friend's little sister. When her shop gets robbed and she's the only one who can identify the increasingly violent Espresso Bandit, Gabe's there to keep her safe. Having Gabe act as her personal bodyguard is certainly no hardship, and Maddy's ready to try anything to tempt him into providing some hands-on protection.

### HARD PLAY
a *Delta Force Brotherhood* novel by Sheryl Nantus

Jessie Lyon is a job, a rescue mission. A giant pain in my ass. She is sexy as hell and refuses to back down. She's saving her family name and will do whatever it takes. Might be what I like most about her. Problem is, she's going to get herself killed. It's my job to make sure that doesn't happen. She isn't making it easy.

### COMPROMISING POSITIONS
an *Invested in Love* novel by Jenna Bayley-Burke

When David Strong agrees to help teach a yoga class based on poses in The Kama Sutra, he's put in one compromising position after another. Especially since the instructor is his best friend's little sister-in-law, doesn't have a lot of experience with men, and is totally off-limits. Sophie DelFino has fantasized about David for over a decade, but he has a type, and she's far from it. He's also got all sorts of rules and reasons why they shouldn't be together. Good thing Sophie is all about bending the rules.